Girl on Fire

Tony Parsons left school at sixteen and his first job in journalism was at the *New Musical Express*. His first journalism after leaving the *NME* was when he was embedded with the Vice Squad at 27 Savile Row, West End Central. The roots of the DC Max Wolfe series started here.

Since then he has become an award-winning journalist and bestselling novelist whose books have been translated into more than forty languages. *The Murder Bag*, the first novel in the DC Max Wolfe series, went to number one on first publication in the UK. All of the DC Max Wolfe novels have been *Sunday Times* top five bestsellers.

Tony lives in London with his wife, his daughter and their dog, Stan.

Also by Tony Parsons

The Murder Bag
The Slaughter Man
The Hanging Club
Die Last

Digital Shorts
Dead Time
Fresh Blood
Tell Him He's Dead

Girl on Fire

TONY PARSONS

arrow books

5 7 9 10 8 6

Arrow Books
20 Vauxhall Bridge Road
London SW1V 2SA

Arrow Books is part of the Penguin Random House group of companies
whose addresses can be found at global.penguinrandomhouse.com.

Copyright © Tony Parsons 2018

First published by Century in 2018
First published in paperback by Arrow Books in 2019

www.penguin.co.uk

A CIP catalogue record for this book is available from the British Library.

ISBN 9781784755348
ISBN 9781784755355 (export)

Typeset in 14/17.75 pts Fournier MT by
Integra Software Services Pvt. Ltd. Pondhicherry

Printed and bound in Great Britain by Clays Ltd, Elcograf S.p.A.

For Tim Rostron of Tufnell Park and Toronto

1

I woke up and the world was gone.

All was silent, all was black, the darkness so complete that it was as if all light had been drained from the world.

The dust was everywhere. The air was thick with it – hot and filthy, the dust of a freshly dug grave. And a strange rain was falling – a rain made of rocks and stones, the fragments and remains of smashed and broken things that I could not name. The destruction was every-where, in my eyes, my mouth, my nose and the back of my throat.

I was flat on my back and suddenly the devastation was choking me.

I pushed myself up, coughing up the strange dust, feeling it on my hands and my face.

I stared into the pitch-black silence and felt a stab of pure terror because for the first time I was aware of the heat. There was a great fire nearby. I looked around and suddenly I saw it, blazing and flaring, the only light in the darkness. The heat increased. The fire was getting closer.

Move or die. These are your choices now.

Then I was on my hands and knees, scrambling away from the fire, gagging up the filth that filled the air. A wave of sickness was sweeping over me, and I was aware of a pain that was everywhere but seemed to radiate out from the inside of my right knee.

I fell on my side with a quiet curse and touched the slice of glass that was embedded in my leg. It was a small but thick chunk of a plate-glass window that was never meant to shatter. I felt it gingerly, my knee raging with pain, trying to make sense of it all.

Where had the old world gone?

What had happened?

I remembered that I had been in the Lake Meadows shopping centre in West London, buying a new backpack for my daughter, Scout. She wanted a plain and unadorned Kipling backpack now that, aged seven, she considered herself far too mature for the backpack she currently carried to school. It was only a year old but featured the female lead of last summer's big blockbuster movie, *The Angry Princess*, a beautiful cartoon princess who looked fierce and threw thunderbolts from her elegant fingernails. And Scout was done with all that little kids' stuff. She wanted me to buy her a big girl's backpack. And that's what I had been doing when it happened.

I remembered paying for the new grown-up rucksack and stepping out into the concourse wondering where I could get a decent triple espresso.

There had been people and lights and smiles, the smell of coffee and cinnamon rolls, the soft sounds of shopping centre music, some song from the last century. It was something other than a memory. It felt like a dream that I was forgetting upon waking.

And now the light ebbed and flowed because the darkness was broken up by the great fire but also by some weak grey light from the outside world creeping into the ruins through a shattered roof or wall.

Now I could see the bodies in what had been the shopping mall.

Some of them were unmoving. Some of them tried to sit up.

But this new world was silent.

Then I realised that the world was not silent. Not really. My hearing had gone the moment that everything went away.

There was a young security guard sitting on the ground nearby. His uniform was covered in the grey dust. He turned his face towards me and tried to speak.

No – he was speaking but I couldn't hear him.

I pulled the broken glass from my knee, cried out with pain and crawled to his side.

His mouth moved again but his words were indistinct.

I stared at him, my eyes streaming in the dust, shaking my head.

He repeated his words and this time, above the ringing in my ears, I heard him.

'A bomb,' he said.

'No,' I said. 'Too big for a bomb.'

'My arm,' he said.

He was holding his arm, staring at it with confusion.

His right arm was missing below the right elbow.

I put the bag containing Scout's new rucksack beneath his head.

Then I took off my leather jacket, pulled off my T-shirt and tore it into three pieces.

The security guard was trying to hold his injured arm in the air, using gravity to stem the flow. I nodded encouragement.

'That's good,' I said.

People were slowly walking past us. They were not running. They were too dumbfounded to run. They staggered out of the swirling clouds of dust, some of them still carrying their shopping, too numb to drop it, too shocked to let go of their bags, as if none of this was possible. I placed a strip of T-shirt in the security guard's wound and held it there.

The blood seeped through almost immediately.

I left the scrap of bloody T-shirt plugged into the wound and placed a second piece of the T-shirt on top. This bled through more slowly.

As gently as I could, I removed the guard's tie, measured approximately four inches above the wound and tied a tourniquet on what remained of his right arm. Then I placed the final piece of T-shirt on the wound.

And this time no blood came through.

My hearing was back now and I could hear the screams and the sirens. I could see bodies scattered in the ruins. I could feel the great fire. The horror flooded over me and made it difficult to breathe.

I thought of my daughter and I didn't want to die.

Objects began to rain harder from the sky. And now some of them were as small as pebbles while some of them were chunks of matter big enough to break your neck. The security guard and I flinched and cowered and tried to protect our eyes.

The sky was falling down on the living and the dead — great clumps of concrete bringing with it more clouds of dust, as if the sky itself had been made from these things, and now it was smashed for ever.

A piece of something struck me on the shoulder. I felt nothing, but the pain in my right knee made me clench my teeth until my jawbone ached.

I took the security guard's left hand and guided it to the scraps of T-shirt stuffed into his wound. He was still attempting to hold his arm in the air. He was doing good.

'You're going to make it,' I told him. 'I'll get help.'

Then I was on my feet, and I began to walk towards the sound of the sirens. But my right knee no longer worked the way it should.

I felt it buckle beneath me and suddenly I was down on my hands and knees again.

I slowly got up and walked on, favouring my left leg now, trying not to put too much weight on the right side.

I could feel the heat of the fire and I could smell the stink of the fire.

Kerosene?

But an ocean of the stuff, all of it ablaze, and that made no sense. Where would that much kerosene come from?

A man in a business suit walked by carrying a bag from the Apple store, every inch of him coated in the grey dust that filled the hot, fetid atmosphere. I spat out some filth and took a deep breath, inhaling the burning air. It seared my lungs.

The fire was getting closer.

Move or die.

A life-size puppet was hanging from what had once been the basement roof of the shopping mall. There were long thick straps of webbing attached to the puppet's chair and they held him from the ceiling, as if waiting for some giant hand to move him. The puppet was close enough for me to see the expression on his unmarked face.

And I saw that this had been a man. The man had been a pilot. And some freak accident had prevented him from being smashed to a billion pieces after falling from the sky.

I had heard of this happening but I had never believed it.

But now I believed.

And now, finally, I began to understand.

That reeking, sickening smell was Jet A-1.

Aviation fuel.

Move or die!

'Excuse me,' an elderly woman said, her politeness heartbreaking in this new world. 'Please stay with us.'

She was sitting on the floor, cradling the head of a man her own age who looked close to death. I knelt beside them, gasping as the pain in my knee surged through the rest of my body, and as I took her hand I saw what had brought this new world into being.

'A bomb,' the lady said.

'No,' I said. 'It's too big for a bomb. A helicopter came down.'

And through the smoke and the dust and the twilight ruins I saw a smashed and crumpled Air Ambulance, its cockpit a ruined pulp of red aluminium and steel and glass, the four rotor blades twisted and bent yet somehow not broken.

It looked like a giant insect that had been swatted by some enraged god.

Behind it was a wake of wreckage that seemed to stretch on forever, twisted and burning and broken, a tangled mess of steel and glass and concrete, flesh and blood and bone, human beings and buildings. Everything smashed.

But there were new lights now, the red and blue lights of the first responders.

'I'll bring help,' I promised.

And I left the old man and woman and started off towards the red and blue lights, but my knee went again and I fell flat on my face in what remained of that shopping centre.

So I got up and tried one more time, treading very carefully so as not to step on the bodies that were scattered all around, moving very slowly to protect my busted knee, as if everything that I thought I knew would have to be learned again.

And as the tears cleared the dust from my eyes, I saw this new world clearly.

I saw the men and women who came with the red and blue lights of the emergency services.

I saw the trail of total ruin that had been left in the wake of the fallen helicopter.

And the rage choked my throat when I saw the injured – that gentle little euphemism for those who now carried terrible wounds that would never heal, not in this lifetime.

Then I wiped my eyes with the back of my hands, sucked in some air and began to stumble towards the reds and blues of our lights.

2

I stood by the side of the low stage, sweating inside the stab-proof Kevlar jacket despite the chill of the hour before dawn, my right knee still pulsing with pain seven days after the Air Ambulance helicopter came down on Lake Meadows shopping centre, killing dozens of innocent people.

The current fatality list stood at forty-four, but the number crept higher every day as the emergency services continued the painstaking work of sifting through the crash site. Nobody knew for sure exactly how many had died and I suspected that we would never know with total certainty.

I was in the briefing room of Leman Street Police Station, Whitechapel, feeling the weight of history. Murder detectives hunted Jack the Ripper from this station. Today it is the base of SC&O19, the specialist firearms unit of the Metropolitan Police.

The briefing room was packed.

Rows of Specialist Firearms Officers in grey body armour worn over short-sleeve blue shirts were listening intently to the young female sergeant on stage. There was a lectern up there but she stood to one side, tall and athletic and affable, and I thought that she was young to be a sergeant in any part of the Met, let alone the firearms unit.

Specialist Firearms Officer DS Alice Stone.

She sounded far more relaxed than she had any right to be.

Behind her a large screen showed a photograph of a three-storey house.

It was a small, neat Victorian terrace on Borodino Street, London E1, its bay windows covered with net curtains. Only a postcode away. We believed it contained the men who had brought down the Air Ambulance helicopter.

The young sergeant touched the iPad she was holding and architectural plans appeared on screen. She began talking about the morning's MOE – method of entry – and I felt the sweat trickle down my back.

It had nothing to do with the weight of the Kevlar jacket.

Someone always has to go in, I thought. *After all the hours of surveillance and analysis of intelligence and briefings, somebody still has to go through a locked door and into the unknown.*

'The entry team for Operation Tolstoy will be breaching the front door of the target with Hatton rounds fired from a shotgun,' DS Stone said, her voice calm and classless, just the hint of some affluent corner of the Home Counties in her accent. 'Distraction stun grenades will be deployed immediately prior to entering the premises.' She paused. 'We have every reason to believe that the men inside are armed fanatics who would actively welcome a martyr's death. So it's CQC when we are inside.'

CQC is Close Quarter Combat, moving through a series of rooms and corridors until the inhabitants are subdued and dominated. Many SFOs either have military training or they have grown up around guns – shooting game with their family in some muddy field.

I wondered which one it was with young DS Stone.

Then she smiled. She had a good smile. It was wide, white and genuine. The trouble with most smiles is that they are not the real thing. This was the real thing.

'And then we're all going for breakfast,' she said. 'On me.'

The room full of SFOs in grey body armour all grinned with her.

Still smiling, she turned to the side of the stage.

'DC Wolfe?' she said. 'We're ready for you now.'

I climbed the few steps up to the stage, shook her hand and took my place at the lectern where my laptop was waiting.

'Our colleague DC Wolfe from West End Central is going to give you the background on today's target,' DS Stone told them.

She took a step back, giving me the floor.

'As you know, we initially believed the Air Ambulance helicopter was brought down by some kind of surface-to-air missile,' I began. 'But overnight intelligence confirms that it was brought down by a UAV – an Unmanned Aerial Vehicle.' I paused to make it clear. 'A drone,' I said, and for just a moment I could taste the dust of that murderous day in the back of my throat. 'Drones are legally allowed to fly up to four hundred feet,' I said. 'This one was at just under five thousand feet when it hit the helicopter. One mile high. Above the clouds and directly above Lake Meadows shopping centre.' I paused, remembering exactly why we were here today. 'Forty-four dead so far,' I said, 'including a crew who dedicated their lives to helping strangers. And you know the worst of it? *The men who did this would consider Lake Meadows to be their lucky day*. That Air Ambulance could have come down in some field. It came down on a shopping centre in the heart of West London.' I took a breath and let it out. 'Owners of UAVs do not need to register on any database but intelligence from Counter Terrorism Command has revealed it belonged to one of these men.'

I touched my laptop and two faces appeared on the screen behind me. They were the passport photographs of two young men so close in age and appearance that they could have been twins.

'Asad and Adnan Khan,' I said. 'Twenty-six and twenty-eight years old. Returnees from Syria. Military

trained. Battle-hardened. They came back to this country eighteen months ago. They were under surveillance
for the first year but resources were diverted elsewhere
because the brothers were keeping their noses clean.
And now we believe we know why.'

I hit another button and a dozen receipts for Unmanned
Aerial Vehicles appeared. They were all from different
drone websites. They all had either Asad or Adnan
Khan's name and address on them.

'There have been a number of near misses at
Heathrow over the last year,' I said. 'Drones almost
missing planes and helicopters that were landing or
taking off. The assumption was always that it was
just a few knobheads failing to control their new toy.
Until now.'

The light from the screen had lit up the faces of the
SFOs. As they studied the images of the Khan brothers,
I realised with a shock of recognition that I knew one
of the SFOs. I had grown up with him.

It was Jackson Rose.

Jackson was the nearest thing I ever had to a brother
but, like a lot of childhood friends, there was now an
unknowable distance between us. I had no idea that he
had even joined the Metropolitan Police. The last I heard
he had ended up where so many ex-servicemen find
themselves – sleeping on the streets. He had lived with
me for a while but it had not worked out. He did not

look at me now but stared straight ahead at the faces of the Khan brothers behind me.

I hit the laptop again.

A man's face appeared, the blank-eyed image taken from his driving licence.

'Ahmed – known as Arnold – is the father of Asad and Adnan Khan. Mr Khan is the long-term tenant at the Borodino Street address. He raised his family there. Fifty-nine years old. Looks older. All our surveillance and intelligence suggests that Mr Khan is not a person of interest.' I turned and looked at his image. 'He's been a bus driver for more than thirty years. Also in the property are his wife, Mrs Azza Khan, sixty, and Layla, the sixteen-year-old daughter of a third brother, Aakil, who was the eldest and died fighting in Aleppo.' Two more faces appeared next to the image of the old man – a stout, unsmiling woman in a hijab headscarf and a grinning teenage girl in a school portrait. 'Like Mr Khan, Mrs Khan and Layla Khan are not persons of interest. They have had what the security services call innocent contact with our targets. Layla's mother – Aakil's wife – died of cancer ten years ago. We understand that Layla has been brought up by her grandparents.'

The room stirred uneasily. Our job is always more complicated when the guilty are under the same roof as the innocent.

DS Stone stepped to my side.

15

'Questions?' she said.

A few hands went up. Stone nodded at one of them.

'If there are more civilians than villains in there,' one of the SFOs said, 'then why are we going in so hard, boss?'

'It's the call of the DSO,' DS Stone said. 'And in my opinion, it's the only call she can make.'

The DSO was the Designated Senior Officer, the senior police officer taking ultimate responsibility for today's operational decisions. This morning it was DCS Elizabeth Swire, who would be in contact from the main control room of New Scotland Yard.

'Asad and Adnan Khan are unlikely to leave room for negotiations,' Stone said.

She looked at me.

'Now for the bad news,' she said, not smiling now.

I hit the laptop and two hand grenades appeared on screen.

They looked like death – black, lattice-faced spheres with a gold-coloured handle and ring pull, identical to a key ring. You could clearly read the name of the manufacturer on the side. Cetinka, it said.

'This make of Croatian hand grenade was believed to have been decommissioned twenty years ago at the end of the Balkans wars,' I said. 'But these were photographed in the evidence room of West End Central two days ago.'

I let that sink in for a moment.

'Because an unknown number of these hand grenades — as is frequently the case with decommissioned ordnance — were never destroyed but stolen, stashed and sold. Some of them have found their way across from the Balkans to our streets. Three days ago a Criminal Informant told detectives from Homicide and Serious Crime Command at West End Central that a known weapons dealer had sold two of these grenades to two brothers in East London. And from the description of the men and CCTV images, we believe they were Asad and Adnan Khan.'

The room was totally silent now.

'So we go in hard,' DS Stone said. 'And we dig them out. We subdue and control before they know what's hit them. And then we go for the most important meal of the day. And the only thing you need to worry about is your cholesterol level.'

They grinned at her again.

Jackson Rose was grinning, too, and I saw that gap between his two front teeth that I knew so well. And now he looked at me and nodded.

'If there are no more questions, then we will get cracking,' DS Stone said. 'I will be leading the entry team. We shall be making just one pass,' she said, meaning that the lead vehicle would drive past the target address once before entry. 'DC Wolfe will be riding with us for TI,' she said, meaning target

17

identification. 'Let's take care of each other out there,' she said.

They applauded her. They loved her.

Jackson approached me as I came off the stage.

'What's wrong with your leg?' he said. 'You're walking all funny.'

'I banged it,' I said. 'You join the Met and forget to tell me?'

I was aware that we sounded like an old married couple.

'I was planning to,' he said. 'We'll talk at breakfast.'

He briefly hugged me, Kevlar banging against Kevlar, and then followed his fellow SFOs to the weapons' room where they signed out their firearms, scribbling their names on receipts as their kit was passed to them from the massive steel-mesh cage that enclosed the armoury.

They all had Glock 17 handguns, Sig Sauer MCX assault rifles – the Black Mamba, short and superlight, perfect for close quarter ops – and M26 Tasers.

And one of them signed out a shotgun – the Benelli M3 Super 90 that would be our front-door key. The SFO who checked it out was attempting to grow a wispy beard to cover the traces of acne that still clung to his youthful face. He stared at me without smiling.

'Let's go, Jesse,' Jackson told him.

DS Stone signed out her weapons and we walked down to the basement car park where a convoy of Armed

Response Vehicles and unmarked vans were all waiting with their engines running.

'This is us,' she said, indicating a white florist's van. Jackson Rose and the young man with the attempted beard and the shotgun were among those climbing into the back. There was a faded slogan on the side of the van.

'BEAUTIFUL' BLOOMS OF BARKING

DS Stone laughed. She really was unnaturally calm.

She held two PASGT helmets in one hand. She handed one to me. I strapped it on.

'I love those inverted commas around "beautiful", don't you?' she said. 'Why do they *do* that?'

Then she saw that I was not laughing.

'What's the problem, Detective?' she said.

I nodded as I put on the PASGT, tightening the strap of the combat helmet.

'We're using a florist's delivery van for the entry team?' I shook my head. 'As I understand it, Borodino Street is in a very devout and poor neighbourhood. I wonder how many fancy bouquets of flowers get delivered to this neck of the woods.' I indicated the van. 'From Beautiful Blooms of Barking or anyone else.'

The car park was in the basement of Leman Street Police Station but you could see the first light of a beautiful summer's day creeping into the entrance.

DS Stone was not laughing now. I watched her put on her PASGT helmet. She shrugged her shoulders, getting comfortable in the body armour as she held her assault rifle at a 45-degree angle, the business end pointing at the floor. The car park was filling with the fumes of all those engines. Then she smiled at me and it made me think that maybe I would like to sit next to her at breakfast.

'We will be in and out before anyone gets a chance to wonder where the roses are,' she said. 'OK, Max?'

But it didn't go down like that.

3

The back of the florist's van smelled of old sweat and fresh gun oil.

The SFOs crammed inside were at home inside the restricted space. We call them a Tactical Support Team. They call themselves *shots*. I suspected that this wasn't the first time these shots had used this van.

DS Alice Stone stood at the back doors, deftly shifting her weight to remain standing as we sped through the empty streets. The other nine SFOs in her team sat opposite each other on low benches, most of them giving their kit and weapons one final check. Jackson Rose sat there almost meditative, staring at nothing. The boy with the wispy beard – *Jesse Tibbs*, it said on his name tag – adjusted the position of the shotgun between his legs. He glared when he saw me watching him. In the front of the van were a driver and a radio dispatcher in the passenger's seat, both in plain clothes.

'Five minutes,' the driver called over his shoulder.

DS Stone spoke into the radio attached to her left lapel.

'All calls, this is Red One – ETA for entry team is five minutes,' she said, raising her voice above the engine, but still professionally calm.

It was two miles from Leman Street Police Station to the target address on Borodino Street, a quiet residential road not far from Victoria Park.

Close to the back doors I crouched by a monitor relaying live images from the camera hidden in the roof of the van. The screen was black-and-white and split into the nine live CCTV images giving a 360-degree view of the outside. There were also two spyholes drilled into either side of the van.

It was not quite 5 a.m. Still one hour to sunrise. The city still washed in that half-light that precedes true dawn.

The streets looked empty. But the constant radio traffic coming from the front of the van told a different story.

These streets were teeming with our people.

The radio dispatcher in the passenger seat kept up a constant stream of communication. On the monitor I saw a line of Armed Response Vehicles parked just beyond Leman Street and as we got closer to the target address I saw vans of uniformed officers in riot gear, their stacks of ballistic shields by the vehicle making them look like a medieval army, parked up next to smaller vans of dog handlers with firearms and explosives search dogs.

And ambulances. We passed an entire convoy of ambulances in a derelict petrol station, waiting for disaster.

As we got closer to Borodino Street, there were undercover surveillance officers in observation posts, scattered across the neighbourhood – I saw a British Gas tent and two Thames Water vans that had nothing to do with gas and water.

There was a second response team on standby, a back-up Tactical Support Team of shots parked up a block away from the target address. Just one street away, an armoured Land Rover was double-parked, its big diesel engine idling. A helicopter whirred in the milky sky of early morning.

On Borodino Street itself, there were dark shadows on the rooftops – the snipers in their elevated close containment positions, the Heckler & Koch G36 carbines black matchsticks against the slowly shifting sky.

'It's like Piccadilly Circus out there this morning!' Stone smiled, and her team laughed with wild relief.

We were an army.

But someone has to go in.

'You OK, Raymond?' DS Stone said.

She was addressing the shot who was sitting between Jackson Rose and Jesse Tibbs with his shotgun. This Raymond nodded, too quickly, his face shining with sweat as he again checked his weapon. He looked supremely fit but older than the other shots, as though he had lived some other life before this one. Maybe another ex-serviceman, I thought.

'One pass,' DS Stone called to the driver.

'Copy that, ma'am,' he called back.

We turned into Borodino Street.

DS Stone crouched by my side, steadying herself with a hand on my shoulder as she stared at the monitor.

The florist's van passed the house without slowing down.

One screen out of nine showed the front of the house.

There was no sign of movement.

I could feel Stone's wound-tight anticipation as she stood up and leaned against the back doors. She quickly checked the spyhole.

A female voice came from the radio on her lapel. It was DCS Elizabeth Swire, the Designated Senior Officer running the show from New Scotland Yard. All other radio chatter was suddenly silenced.

'Red One, can we have your sit-rep, please?' DCS Swire said.

'No movement at the target address, ma'am,' replied Stone. 'Red One requesting permission for attack run.'

A pause. We waited. All of the shots stared at their leader.

'Red One awaiting instructions,' DS Stone said calmly.

'Permission granted,' came the response. 'Proceed with attack run.'

Stone gave her team the nod.

'We're going in,' she said calmly. 'Standby.'

The van had turned right at the end of the street, and now it made another right and then turned right again.

No one was checking their kit now. They all waited, their eyes on their team leader as Stone picked up her Sig Sauer MCX assault rifle. I stared at the monitor, aware that I had stopped blinking. The monitor told me nothing.

'All calls, entry team is in final assault position,' DS Stone said above me.

All eyes were on her. The van slowed but did not quite stop.

'Remember your training, look after each other and watch out for those grenades,' she said.

She hefted her assault rifle.

'On my command,' she said.

There was a moment when we did not breathe.

'Go!' Stone said. 'Go! Go! Go!'

'*Wait*,' I said.

The front door was opening.

It was happening very slowly.

Whoever was leaving the house was taking their time.

DS Stone was kneeling by my side.

'Someone's coming out,' she said into her radio.

A beat.

Our van was crawling now.

'Establish ID and hold,' said DCS Swire.

A large woman in a black niqab was shuffling from the house. She adjusted her headscarf as she turned to the street, only her eyes showing above the veil.

'Is that Mrs Khan?' DS Stone said.

I stared hard at the monitor. The photographs I had seen of Mrs Azza Khan revealed a sturdy, fierce-faced woman. I could not see the face of the person leaving the house but they had feet like landing craft. And those feet were wearing Doctor Martens boots.

'That's a man,' I said.

Then DS Stone kicked the back doors open and she was jumping out the back of the van.

'*Stop! Armed police! Stand still! Show me your hands!*'

The figure in the niqab brought his hands out from inside the billowing niqab. He was holding some kind of assault rifle.

And he shot DS Alice Stone in the head.

The SFOs were all screaming the same thing as they piled from the van.

'*Shots fired! Officer down!*'

'*Shots fired! Officer down!*'

'*Shots fired! Officer down!*'

The burst of automatic gunfire seemed to crack the day wide open.

All of the firearms used by the Metropolitan Police are configured to not fire on semi-automatic, meaning every single trigger pull fires only one single shot and later that shot has to be justified to people who never heard a shot fired in anger in their life, except possibly on the grouse moor.

So that unbroken burst of automatic gunfire from the figure wearing the niqab was not merely deafening.

It froze the blood and scrambled the senses.

Because police gunfire never sounds like that.

Only enemy gunfire sounds like that.

Then the last of the shots were barging past me as I climbed from the back of the van.

'*Stop! Armed police! Stand still!*'

'*Stop! Armed—*'

One of the shots banged into me so hard that I tumbled from the pavement to the gutter and almost fell. Then I looked up. The veil had fallen away and I was staring at the bearded face of Asad Khan, the older of the two brothers.

I watched him raise his assault rifle, a fifty-year-old Heckler & Koch G3. He pointed it at the nearest SFO and pulled the trigger. Nothing happened. He stared at his elderly weapon. People were screaming. I looked down and saw the lifeless body of DS Alice Stone crumpled half on the pavement and half in the road. A halo of blood was growing around her PASGT helmet.

Khan fired again.

And this time the sound split the sky, made your ears ring, and promised death. The burst of gunfire made a ferocious tattoo on the side of our van. I looked at it and saw the holes punched in the metal all along the legend *'Beautiful' Blooms of Barking.*

'Armed police!' Jackson was shouting. 'Drop the weapon and show me your hands!'

I looked up and watched Jackson Rose aim his Heckler & Koch at Asad Khan.

The gunman's rifle was held almost casually at his side, as if he had injured his arm or was in a state of disbelief at what was happening.

He started to raise his G3 and Jackson shot him.

SFOs are trained to aim at the centre of mass – the largest part of the body, the torso, the centre of the chest, the largest target. They are not trained to kill. They are trained to hit the target. Jackson's single shot threw its target backwards, the muzzle blast flashing yellow.

The old assault rifle clattered in the gutter next to Asad Khan.

'Suspect down!' somebody screamed.

Two SFOs were on their knees by the side of DS Stone. Her blood soaked the grey leggings of their body armour.

Jackson took two paces forward and leaned over Asad Khan.

I called his name. 'Jackson!'

And then Jackson shot him again.

Another muzzle flare.

He looked at me calmly.

The front door was open and SFOs were pouring inside.

'Armed police!'

'Armed police!'

'Armed police!'

Then Jackson barged past me, his mouth twisted with rage.

'Let them stick that in their report,' he said.

An ambulance was already hurtling down the street, blue lights blazing and siren howling.

A female SFO was crouched by the body of Asad Khan, attempting to stop the blood pouring from his chest. They try to kill and then we shoot them, but after that we try to save their lives. This is what we do, I thought.

This is who we are.

I looked at the face of DS Alice Stone and I felt my throat close tight.

The two SFOs with DS Stone were talking to her but I realised with a jolt of shock that they were administering to the dead.

And then I went inside the house.

The light immediately went out in the narrow hallway and I could hear SFOs screaming in the dark. I banged my bad knee against a box and winced with pain. I realised the hallway had one of those lights that go out automatically, the kind they have in cheap property where someone who doesn't live there is worried about the energy bills. I fumbled on the wall, found the round switch and hit it. The musty yellow light came back on and I could not understand what I was looking at.

There were boxes all the way down the dingy hallway.

Drones.

Dozens of them. Some of them unopened. Some of them scuffed with dirt and grass, the metal scarred from repeated crash landings.

The SFOs seemed to be above me now, on the first and second floors.

I walked to the end of the corridor and opened the kitchen door.

A child screamed.

Shrill, high-pitched, full of terror.

No, not quite a child. But not yet fully grown. A teenage girl of about sixteen was cowering on the floor by the oven with a woman and a man around sixty. The woman and girl were in their pyjamas. The man, his hair grey and thinning, was in a London Transport uniform.

They were, I realised, Ahmed 'Arnold' and Azza Khan, the parents of the brothers, and Layla, their granddaughter, the daughter of their third son who had died in Aleppo.

'*Papa-Papa!*' Layla cried, and at first I fought she was calling for her dead father. '*Papa-Papa! Papa-Papa!*'

But she turned her terrified face to her grandfather and I saw that she was talking to him.

'Don't kill us!' Mrs Khan begged me as she clung to her granddaughter and they both closed their eyes.

At their feet there was a pink and purple rucksack with *The Angry Princess* on the side. It was exactly the same as the one I had been sent to the shopping centre to replace.

'Listen to me,' I said. 'You're safe now. But you must go – go immediately.' I helped them to their feet. 'And when you come out of the front door – this is very important – hold your hands above your head with the palms showing.' I demonstrated. 'Like this. It's very important that they can see the palms of your hands, OK? Then nobody will hurt you.'

They copied me. The woman snatched up her grand-daughter's *Angry Princess* rucksack and threw it over her shoulder.

And then they ran, their hands in the air before they were out of the kitchen, palms forward as I had shown them.

I walked from the kitchen, my balance off from what the gunfire had done to my inner ear, and I noticed for the first time that there was a basement door facing the entrance to the kitchen. From the bottom of the stairs, a dim light was shining.

I went down the stairs, shouting my name and rank.

In the basement there was an SFO with his assault rifle at his shoulder. It was the shot who DS Stone had addressed in the back of the van.

You OK, Raymond?

And before him there was a man on his knees.

It was the other brother, the youngest one. Adnan Khan, with his hands in the air. I looked at his palms expecting to see hand grenades but his hands were empty. The SFO glanced at me and then back at the brother on his knees. Adnan Khan was surrendering.

Nobody moved.

We all waited.

'Raymond?' I said. 'Ray? You prefer Ray or Raymond?'

He did not look at me. But I saw something inside him react as I said his name.

'What's your full name and rank, Officer?' I said, my voice harder now.

'Vann,' he said. 'SFO DC Raymond Vann, sir.'

The shots had been a blur of grey body armour, PASGT helmets and firepower. In my mind, they had been an inseparable, indivisible group. Even Jackson Rose, my oldest friend, had looked like just one part of a band of brothers and sisters. It was only now that I saw DS Stone had sought out this one man to make sure he was ready for what was coming.

You OK, Raymond?

But now DC Raymond Vann aimed his assault rifle at the man before him and he seemed totally on his own.

'Please,' I said. 'DC Vann. Raymond. Ray. *Don't do it.*'

But he did it.

One single shot.

So loud in the small subterranean room it felt like the last sound I would ever hear. The muzzle blast dazzling in the twilight of the basement as Adnan Khan was thrown backwards, the death wound in his chest already blooming.

Then I was stumbling back up the basement's short flight of rickety steps and down the corridor piled high with boxes of drones and towards the front door. I bounced off the walls, keeping going, wanting to be far away from that basement. It was light outside now. The day had begun while we were inside the house.

The pain in my ears was so intense that I touched them and looked at my fingertips, expecting blood. But there was nothing there. It felt like there should be blood.

I staggered out of the house and into the dazzling light of the new day. Police tape was already going up at both ends of the street. The helicopter seemed much lower and louder. The second response team was piling out of the back of their van and pouring into the house where everyone was either dead or gone.

And paramedics were putting DS Alice Stone into a Human Remains Pouch. We don't call them body bags and they are not black, like the movies. This one was white with a long black zip. They had cleaned up her face and it looked like her. The young always look like themselves when they die fifty years too soon. Two paramedics were easing her inside with the tenderness of parents putting a sleeping child to their rest.

I could hear radio chatter and someone sobbing.

Jackson sat dry-eyed in the open doors of the florist van, still holding his weapon. An exhibits officer was meant to take it from him, but it was still too soon and too chaotic for formal procedures to kick in. Right now there was only the numb disbelieving shock that follows action. I sat by his side. He pulled off his PASGT helmet and wiped his face with the back of his hand. Then he gently patted my back. We did not speak.

The Specialist Search Team had arrived and was waiting for the nod to tear the place apart. No grenades, I thought. Not yet. At the far end of the street I could see the CSIs getting into their white Tyvek suits and blue nitrile gloves. The gang's all here, I thought.

Then a senior uniformed officer stood before Jackson and me, shouting and waving his arms. Jackson looked away and yawned. The officer was silver-haired, fifty-something and his shoulder badge showed the red-and-silver crown of a superintendent.

I stared at his lips. My hearing was still off but I could make out his question. I could understand what he was asking us. And he was asking it again and again and again.

'*What the hell happened here?*'

I blinked at him and said nothing.

The image of the muzzle blast in the basement was burned black on the back of my eyes.

And now it would be there for ever.

4

By the time I got to West End Central an hour later, a crowd was gathering in Savile Row.

Under the big blue lamp outside number 27, a young uniformed officer was keeping a watchful eye. There was a sky-blue ribbon on his jacket pinned just above the patch that said METROPOLITAN POLICE. You were seeing these ribbons everywhere, in memory of those who had died when the helicopter came down. In normal times, any adornment to a Met uniform was strictly against all SOP regulations.

But these were not normal times.

The young copper nodded in recognition and stood aside to let me pass.

I turned back to look at the crowd. They were builders from construction sites and office workers passing by. In hard hats or sharp suits, they were mostly young men. The mood was subdued as they talked quietly among themselves, but their number seemed to be growing by the second.

'What's this lot want?' I said to the young uniform.

He nodded to the glass doors of West End Central.

'They've got one of the drone bastards locked up inside, sir.'

I stared at him.

'But I just watched them die.'

He shrugged. 'That's what I heard, sir.' He hesitated, and then indicated the crowd. 'And I think they want to remember the forty-five dead,' he said. 'They want to mourn, they want to grieve, but they don't know where to go. Lake Meadows is still a crime scene.'

'There are forty-four dead,' I said.

He shook his head. 'They found another one.' His eyes flooded with tears and I watched him fight to regain control. 'A little kid. So it's forty-five now.'

I lightly touched his arm.

'Are you all right out here on your lonesome?'

He grinned. 'As long as they stay like this, sir.'

I rode the lift up to the top floor.

Edie Wren was alone in Major Incident Room One.

'Hey,' she said, and handed me a triple espresso from Bar Italia before turning back to the big HDTV.

They were showing Borodino Street, filmed from a news channel helicopter. The street was taped off at either end and the lights of the CSIs surrounded the house, brighter than daylight. The white-suited teams were everywhere.

In the left-hand corner of the screen there was another helicopter shot, a view of Lake Meadows that had become horribly familiar over the last seven days, the shopping centre a charred and blackened scar on the face of the shining city, closed to the public but crowded with bulldozers and cranes and white tents, at once a crime scene and a mass grave.

And in the bottom right-hand corner of the screen, there was a blacked-out head and shoulders silhouette.

Edie turned to me. 'They haven't told her next of kin yet,' she said. 'That's why they're not showing her face. They must be trying to reach her husband.' Edie pushed back her tangled mop of red hair and shook her head with disbelief. 'I met her once. Alice. DS Alice Stone. When I was in uniform. She was a team leader even then. And she shone, Max. She was like the cool kid at school that everyone wants to be friends with. And she was *nice*. A decent human being and a real high-flyer.' Edie looked back at the screen. 'I think her team were all in love with her.'

'Yes,' I said. 'That's her.'

I removed the lid from the Bar Italia carton and bolted down a triple espresso. 'Thanks.'

'Must be a bit cold by now but it's the thought that counts,' Edie said, holding out her arms. 'Come here.'

She hugged me awkwardly. I hugged her back, equally awkwardly as she accidentally gave me a gentle headbutt, the embrace of colleagues who liked each other but were working out exactly what that might mean. As far as I knew, she was still seeing her married man. As far as I knew, the creep was still promising to leave his wife.

But it still felt good to hold her.

And I was suddenly bone-tired. I closed my eyes and I could have slept in her arms for somewhere between fifteen minutes and a lifetime. Then I felt her let go of me and step back. When I opened my eyes, Edie was watching me and waiting.

'What happened on Borodino Street?' she said.

'It went wrong from the go,' I said. 'From the moment the jump-off van pulled up outside.'

I told her almost everything. I told her about the figure in the niqab coming out of the house and Asad Khan opening fire before we had even got started. I told her what happened on the street. I told her about Alice Stone and Asad Khan dying within seconds of each other. I told her about telling Mr and Mrs Khan and their granddaughter Layla to raise their hands and run.

But I did not tell her about the basement and Adnan Khan on his knees and DC Ray Vann looking at him through the sights of his assault rifle. I didn't tell her about the single shot in the basement that was still ringing in my ears, or the muzzle blast that was still burned on the back of my retina.

The sounds of the crowd down in Savile Row drifted up through the open windows. I looked at Edie, still not understanding what they were doing here.

'It's probably because we've got the Khan family, or what's left of them,' Edie said. 'They were brought here after the op. The father and the mother and the girl, Layla, the daughter of the brother who got slotted in Syria. Mrs Khan and the girl are on the second floor with the FLO.'

Family Liaison Officer.

'And what about Mr Khan?' I asked.

'He's down in the custody suite.'

'Why have they got him locked up?' I said.

'Waiting for CTC,' Edie said. 'Then they're shipping him over to Paddington. That's why there's a bit of a mob outside – because we have the old man. It is all very civilised so far, but I think they would quite like to see him hanging from a lamppost. He had three sons and all of them were terrorists. It's not a good look, is it?'

CTC is Counter Terrorism Command and Paddington is Paddington Green Police Station where almost all terrorists are interrogated. When the news reports that a terrorist suspect is in 'a central London location' it means that they are inside Paddington Green. IRA head-bangers, failed suicide bombers and graduates from Guantanamo Bay have all graced the cells and interview rooms of Paddington Green. It looks like a budget hotel, if you can imagine a budget hotel with two-inch-thick steel doors.

I thought of the Khans cowering with terror on the floor of the kitchen. I remembered the old man, the old woman and the teenage girl fleeing with their hands in the air. It had not crossed my mind that the old man, Ahmed Khan, was ready to die for jihad.

'They looked like victims to me, Edie,' I said. 'They looked like they'd had innocent contact. They didn't look like terrorists.'

She shrugged.

'But the old man must have known, right? Maybe the old lady and the kid had innocent contact. But the father? I mean – he *must* have known about his sons, Max. I hear the place on Borodino Street was full of drones. Not even hidden. What did he *think* they were doing with them? Innocent contact means he knew nothing. And how could he have known nothing, Max?'

Maybe she was right. I rubbed my eyes as we rode the lift down to the second floor.

We heard Mrs Khan before we saw her. She was shouting in Urdu and crying her eyes out.

'Translator?' I said.

'On his way,' said the FLO. 'Stuck in traffic.'

The FLO was struggling to calm Mrs Khan while the girl, Layla, sat hunched at a desk letting her long black hair fall over her face. Uniformed officers watched the woman and the girl with wary reserve. It is never easy to deal with the relatives of the wicked. They are always tainted by the sins of their family. They are always suspected.

But Edie Wren sat down next to Layla Khan and gently took her hands. The teenage girl gasped with shock at her touch and tried to pull her hands away.

But Edie smiled gently and would not let go.

'I like your nails,' Edie said. 'Layla, is it? I'm Edie. I work here.' She studied the girl's nails, which were a garish shade of green. 'So where did you get them done? They're really pretty.'

The girl swept her mane of long black hair from her face.

'I did them myself, didn't I?' Layla Khan said, and even as her grandmother continued to shout in Urdu, there was nothing in her voice but the streets of London.

She blinked at Edie with huge brown eyes, as if amazed that small acts of human kindness still existed in the world.

5

I took the lift down to the custody suite.

The custody sergeant on the desk signed me in.

'You were in Borodino Street?' he said.

I nodded.

'I heard about that young shot they killed,' he said, his eyes shining with emotion. 'That's all anybody is talking in here. It's so senseless. Forty-four dead in that shopping centre and now this bloody mess.'

'Forty-five,' I said. 'Apparently they just found a child's body.'

'Forty-five? Those animals.' He shook his head. 'And that young DS. Alice Stone. Where does it end, sir?'

'I don't know if it does,' I said. 'Not in our lifetime.'

'Are you going to have a word with this scumbag?'

'Yes,' I said. I waited until the sergeant gave me eye contact. 'But we got them,' I said. 'Both of them. As far as we know, this man is just a relative.'

The custody sergeant did not look convinced. I followed him into the observation room and we looked in at Ahmed Khan. He sat unmoving in his cell, perched on the edge of a bed that had not been disturbed, a gaunt, hollow-cheeked man, as thin as his wife was stout. They were built like one of those married couples in an old seaside postcard, I thought, the husband a slight, unassuming figure who wouldn't hurt a fly and his wife a loud, big-boned creature who would swat anything that got in her way. For the first time I noticed that he too was wearing a sky-blue ribbon on his London Transport uniform. And I wondered if I was kidding myself. I wondered if I was being played.

'You want an audio feed on this?' the custody sergeant asked me.

I shook my head. 'It's not a formal interview. I just need to talk to him before the heavy mob get here.'

The custody sergeant nodded but I could see he didn't like it. Too bad. I had earned the right to talk to Ahmed Khan. The sergeant unlocked the door of the custody suite. I went inside and heard the door slam shut and lock behind me.

Ahmed Khan did not look up at me from where he sat on the edge of the custody suite's low single bed. The events of the last few hours had left him catatonic with shock.

'Remember me?' I said.

His eyes slid towards me.

His head jerked sideways. That was a negative.

44

I held up my hands, palms facing outwards.

'How about now?' I said.

Then there was recognition on that skull-like face.

'You told us to run. You were very kind. And we ran. And we held up our hands but I was still afraid they would shoot us. I saw my dead son. In the street. My Asad. And I saw the dead policewoman. Everyone was shouting ... '

He hung his head at the memory.

I sat down next to him on that miserable little bed.

And I stared at him hard with that inbred, hard-earned cop hunger for guilt. I wanted to see it for myself. I needed to see if I was kidding myself that this man was a victim. I remembered Alice Stone, her body half in the street and half on the pavement, and I felt my heart harden. Maybe Edie Wren was right.

He must have known!

Except I could not believe it. The first time I saw him he looked like a victim. And, whatever his bastard sons had done, Ahmed Khan looked like a victim to me.

But if he had not known about his sons in the past, then he sure as hell knew now.

'Why am I here?'

I felt pity for the man. But it was a stupid question.

'One of your sons killed one of my colleagues. He would have killed all of us if he had the chance. Your house is full of drones just like the one that brought

45

down that Air Ambulance helicopter over Lake Meadows shopping centre in West London.' I leaned closer to him and almost whispered in his ear. 'Do you really need to ask me why you are here?'

He closed his eyes and rocked.

'My sons,' he said. 'They said things – but they were the things that all the young men say.'

'Like what?'

'They said – *We destroy their buildings but they destroy our countries, Papa.* Just talk. Just the talk of all the young men. But I told them – *This* is your country. And I never dreamed that they would be the ones ... that helicopter ... all those people ... children ... '

He squeezed his eyes tight to make the world go away.

I watched him fight for some control and then the shock was subsiding and the grief was kicking in. I stood up and looked down at him.

'So exactly how much did you know, Mr Khan?'

He shook his head. His eyes were still closed.

'Did you know your sons brought that helicopter down?'

'No!'

'Your house was full of drones. What did you think they were doing with them?'

'A business, they said. *To make a business, Papa. Booming drone industry. Next big thing, Papa. Many opportunities, Papa.*'

'And you believed them?'

'Yes.'

'And did they have anyone helping them with this new business? Anyone providing the cash? Anyone advising them? Anyone else you saw associated with what they were doing?'

'No.'

He was too certain.

'Your son – Asad – left the house dressed in a woman's robes. What did you think, Mr Khan – that he was off for another day at the office?'

He looked up at me now.

'Asad knew they were watching him. Your people. The police. The intelligence services. Whoever does the watching for you. They had stopped watching my sons some months after they came back from Syria but recently they had started again. And Asad *knew*. He knew they were watching and he said it made it difficult for doing business. So he was hiding from the ones who were watching.'

'The intelligence services had started monitoring your sons again because they were suspected of planning fresh terrorist atrocities. They should never have stopped watching them after they had returned from Syria.'

'But they were just aid workers!'

I couldn't work out if he believed this crap or not.

'Your sons were not aid workers in Syria. They were fighters for jihad.'

Now he looked at me and his dark eyes were full of pain.

'They were good boys. They were helping the poor. The victims of war. The children.'

I banged my fist against the wall and watched him flinch.

'Every murdering bastard I ever met was a good boy who was nice to his dear old mum and wanted world peace. Every gang member. Every thug. And certainly every terrorist. You see the truth at last, don't you?'

'I saw my son's body in the street,' he said, and his eyes closed at the memory.

The son that had killed DS Stone. The son that Jackson had slotted.

Whatever human sympathy I felt for the old man did not extend to any of his sons.

'Did you know he had that firearm?'

'No.'

'Did your sons have other weapons?'

'No. I don't know. No.'

I leaned towards him and lowered my voice. Because there was something that worried me more than anything else.

'What about the grenades?' I said. 'Your sons bought two grenades. Two Croatian grenades. Where are they now?'

He shook his head. 'I have seen no grenades. No weapons. Are my wife and granddaughter safe? Is my other son safe?'

I realised he meant Adnan. He had not seen Adnan dead in the basement. And nobody had told him.

I could still see Ray Vann raising his Sig Sauer. I could still hear the single shot from a semi-automatic assault rifle fired in a confined space. I could see Adnan Khan being put down.

'Both your sons died at the scene. Adnan died inside the house after you left with your wife and granddaughter.'

'Did you see him die?'

I stared at him.

'No,' I said.

His shoulders shook as he wept and I wondered at his naivety.

But I looked at the sky-blue ribbon on his London transport uniform, the sky-blue ribbon that so many Londoners felt the need to wear, and I had no doubt about his innocence.

'Where will they take me?' he said, rubbing his eyes with the palms of his hands.

'They're going to take you to Paddington Green Police Station.' A pause. 'It's where the Metropolitan Police interrogate terrorist suspects.'

He looked as though he had been kicked in the stomach.

Then he was silent for a long while.

I could hear voices outside the cell. The heavy mob had arrived.

And then he spoke, and his words came out in a torrent.

'I tried hard to be accepted in this country,' he said. 'When I came here in 1976 to marry my wife, my colleagues didn't like me at first. *Pakis out*, they told me. But then they liked me. Or at least they accepted me. *Because I would work on Sundays*. And I would work at Christmas. I would work on all the days they wanted to be with their families. And then they accepted me. And they called me Arnold.'

'The other bus drivers called you Arnold?'

'English joke. Because I do not look like an Arnold. And because my name sounded strange to them. But it was hard and it took many years. I tried to explain all of this to my sons. But they did not listen to me. This is your country now, I said. *But, Papa, they said, a man's faith is more important than a man's country. Because all countries belong to God*. When can I go home? Can I go home after Paddington Green?'

'They are going to take your house apart,' I said. 'The floors, the ceiling, the walls. They are going to rip it to pieces.'

'To punish us?'

'To search for evidence and weapons. To find those grenades I asked you about. To find out who else they knew and what else they were planning. Not to punish you, Mr Khan. But they're doing it now. You will not be going home for a while.'

And if someone decides to tie you to the sins of your sons, I thought, you might never be going home.

There were voices outside and then the sound of the key in the lock.

The door opened and a huge man with a mop of white-blond hair filled the doorway. I had first known him as DCI Flashman, a Homicide detective at New Scotland Yard. Now he had to be at Counter Terrorism.

He gave an elaborate sigh at the sight of me.

'Step outside, Wolfe,' he said.

Khan seemed to have slipped back into his trance. The custody sergeant stared at him with distaste as he locked the door behind me.

Flashman's bulk dominated the corridor.

There were three people with him. Two uniformed sergeants to do the heavy lifting and a woman – older, bookish, John Lennon specs – who looked like some kind of lecturer or academic. She had the air of the campus about her.

Except I knew she wasn't an academic.

Flashman made no attempt to introduce her and I didn't ask. Because I knew exactly where the woman was from.

And I couldn't keep my mouth shut. If DS Alice Stone was still alive, I would have kept my mouth shut. But she was in a mortuary and they still hadn't been able to reach her next of kin. Her family still didn't know she was dead. Her husband still didn't know she was never coming home again.

I looked at the woman who needed no introduction.

'Why the hell weren't you watching them?' I said.

Flashman's face clouded.

'*Wolfe.*'

'You watched the Khan brothers when they came back from Syria,' I said. 'But then you stopped.' I shook my head. 'And you only started again when West End Central told you they'd been shopping for hand grenades.'

Flashman moved his large bulk towards me, a big man who was accustomed to getting his way.

The woman from MI5 held up a hand to stop him.

'Because we can't watch all of them, DC Wolfe,' she said in a voice full of reason. 'Because there are too many of them, especially now that so many are coming home. Because our resources are not limitless. There are a few thousand of them and there are a few thousand of us. These men were on our radar but not under the microscope. Surveillance is highly labour-intensive and we simply do not have the manpower or the resources to put every returnee under twenty-four-hour surveillance for the rest of their lives.' She looked at Flashman. 'What is it now?'

'Thirty officers per subject for twenty-four-hour surveillance,' he said. 'Plus multiple vehicles, including at least a couple of motorbikes.' He watched me under his belligerent, hooded eyes. 'And that's only if they never have a day off for weekends and Christmas.'

'I know that's no consolation after what happened today,' she said. 'And I am truly sorry for the loss of your colleague.'

I nodded.

And now it was Flashman who couldn't keep his mouth shut.

'You're right out of order, Wolfe. You shouldn't be talking to a CTC suspect. And you shouldn't be opening your disrespectful cakehole to *us* as if you're running this show.'

'We *gave* them to you,' I told him. 'Information from my CI about the weapons dealer handed you the Khan brothers after they bought two grenades from him.'

He sneered at me.

'That was a false lead.'

'What?'

I was genuinely shocked.

'The grenades. They didn't buy any grenades. We have had a Specialist Search Team in Borodino Street tearing that house apart. And guess what, Wolfe? *No grenades.*

TONY PARSONS

All we found in the way of weapons was that old assault rifle that killed DS Stone. Your information was wrong. And the Khans were edging back on our radar anyway, before we got the nod from you. So don't pat yourself on the back too hard.'

Flashman nodded to the custody sergeant and he unlocked the door. The two big coppers stood in the open doorway for a moment, considering Ahmed 'Arnold' Khan with real loathing. Then they went inside, roughly cuffed his hands behind his back and brought him out. Flashman narrowed his eyes at the sky-blue ribbon on Ahmed Khan's London Transport uniform, then nodded briefly and they took Khan away.

Flashman turned to me.

'Now why don't you go back up to the top floor and get to work on some domestic that went a bit too far?'

'And why don't you catch some real terrorists?' I took a step towards him. 'Where were you when we were on Borodino Street, Flashman? Washing your hair?'

He made a move towards me but the custody sergeant stepped between us.

I shook my head at Flashman, nodded to the woman from MI5 and walked to the lift.

Edie was already back in MIR-1.

'The gang's all here,' she said. 'A social worker and a translator. The social worker is for the girl – that

54

Layla, she's such a sweet kid — and the translator is for the old lady, Mrs Khan, who apparently only speaks Urdu.'

'But her husband told me they've been here since the Seventies.'

And hadn't she spoken to me in English in the kitchen, if only to ask me not to kill her?

Edie grinned. 'Early days then. Give her time. She'll get the hang of it yet. Maybe she only speaks English when it suits her. What's the drill now?'

'They will eventually cut Mrs Khan loose but the local authority will almost certainly take the girl into temporary care,' I said. 'Which could last forever, or at least until she's eighteen.'

Edie's smile fell away.

'The poor little cow. Where does Mrs Khan go?'

'Anywhere she likes.' I nodded at the TV. 'But not home.'

The Specialist Search Team looked as though they had begun to dismantle the property in Borodino Street. Floorboards and piles of bricks were stacking up in the front garden. And I saw that Flashman was right. If those two grenades had been inside, our people would surely have found them by now.

'Excuse me?'

A tall young black woman hovered uncertainly in the doorway of MIR-1.

'I'm looking for DCI Whitestone,' she said. 'I'm TDC Joy Adams.'

Edie and I looked at each other. Our team had been undermanned since the death of our colleague Billy Greene. This must be Billy's replacement.

'DCI Whitestone's on leave,' I said.

'Leave? What – like a holiday?'

Her accent was South London mixed with a distant touch of Jamaica.

'Yes, exactly like a holiday. Even Homicide cops get some leave every once in a while.'

Trainee Detective Constable Joy Adams nodded and looked around the deserted MIR-1. She was wearing a black trouser suit and her hair was in tight cornrow braids that were pulled into a short ponytail at the back. I could tell she had thought carefully about how she should look on her first day in Homicide and Serious Crime Command.

And I could also tell this large empty office was not what she had dreamed about during her training at Hendon.

'It's usually a lot livelier than this,' Edie said.

TDC Adams nodded, her eyes drifting across the empty workstations to the scene in Borodino Street on the TV screen. The blacked-out silhouette was still in the bottom right-hand corner.

'That isn't our investigation?' she asked.

'No,' Edie said. 'It's somebody else's job. But don't worry – there's always another murder along soon.'

But TDC Adams was ready to go to work now. The noise drifting up from the street was getting louder. The crowd was growing.

'Come here,' I said, and she followed me to the window. 'You see all those people out there?' I said. 'They're too close to our front door. And there are too many of them. And they could get angry. And that would be bad news for everyone.'

Adams' bright eyes were waiting.

'So you get as many uniformed officers as you can find and go out there,' I told her. 'You're in charge, not the uniforms. But you stick with them. Don't get separated, OK? Be polite but firm with the people, but you move them back to the end of the street.'

'Burlington Gardens?'

'No, the other end. Conduit Street. I don't want them milling around in Piccadilly, wandering around the Ritz. Then you set up a perimeter so that nobody enters Savile Row who doesn't need to be here. Can you do all that?'

'Yes, sir.'

She headed for the door.

I stayed at the window and a few minutes later TDC Joy Adams appeared down on the street accompanied by half a dozen uniforms. I watched as – gently but firmly – she ushered the crowd to the far end of the street. She was going to do all right.

'Max,' Edie said. 'Look.'

She was staring at the TV where the blacked-out silhouette had finally been replaced by the face of DS Alice Stone.

It was some kind of official portrait but Alice Stone still was smiling that big, good smile that she had.

I felt something choke up inside me.

'Looks like they reached her next of kin,' Edie said.

6

It was the end of the long day and Fred's gym was almost empty now.

Down on a yoga mat, a woman in her fifties who looked maybe thirty silently moved and breathed her way through Surya Namaskara, the Sun Salutation, bending and unfolding and stretching her body so that the series of graceful asanas looked like just one long fluid movement. One of Fred's shaven-headed regulars in a frayed London Marathon T-shirt wearily banged the heavy bag with eighteen-ounce Lonsdale gloves. Someone turned off the treadmill, caught their breath and headed for the showers. And Fred stood before me, his long silver hair pulled up in a topknot, looking like a pirate who was about to go for a serious run.

Toots and the Maytals were on the sound system singing of young Trenchtown rude boys fifty years in the grave and up on the giant TV screen the first fight between Micky Ward and Arturo Gatti was playing with the sound turned off.

Fred counted out the reps of ten as I rose from a bench on one leg, held it, and sat down again still using the same leg. We did it until my quad muscles were burning.

With my knee still healing, my exercise regime at Fred's was all about my quads – squats, lunges, step-ups and, most of all, the torture of standing up and sitting down using just one leg. Whenever I felt like I couldn't go on, when my leg muscles were stiff with lactic acid, when my quads were alive with pain, I looked up at Micky Ward and Arturo Gatti knocking lumps out of each other.

And I carried on.

And then Jackson Rose walked into the gym.

He nodded at us as Fred strapped some ankle weights on me and counted out five reps of ten as I forced out fifty burpies.

The regular in the London Marathon T-shirt walked off to the lockers and Jackson stood before the heavy bag, contemplating it for a moment before stepping back, bending his body so that his torso was at right angles to the ground and then kicking it where the head of a very tall man would be.

He did it gently at first, finding his range, and then he did it much harder. And then he did it harder still, twice, the kicks coming so close together that the sound of his instep repeatedly striking the bag seemed to become one unbroken sound, like hailstones. Then he stood back, bouncing up and down on the soles of his feet, his hands loose at his side, a thin film of sweat on his face.

Fred and I were grinning at him.

'Oy, Conor McGregor,' Fred said. 'You training or dancing?'

Jackson showed us his gap-tooth grin.

'Got some spare kit?' he said.

So Jackson and I trained together on one of Fred's famous circuits. A dozen three-minute rounds on the speed ball, the uppercut bag, the heavy bag and the super heavyweight bag, that long two-metre slab of hard leather that drained every ounce of energy out of you, a one-minute break between rounds filled with ten burpies and ten press-ups. Forty-eight minutes with no breaks. Recover while you work.

'You'll sleep well tonight,' Fred said as the final buzzer went after the last press-up, when we were on our hands and knees and the tank was empty for both of us. Jackson smiled at me and I saw that he was full of that exhausted happiness that only comes on the far side of hard exercise.

After we were showered and dressed, Jackson said we should get a beer in one of the many pubs around Smithfield that cater to all manner of night owls, including the club kids at Fabric on Charterhouse Street and the night shifters from the meat market that has stood on this spot for a thousand years.

He could tell I was not keen.

'I know you want to get back to Scout. But have just one beer, Max. It's been a long day for all of us.'

I waited for the real reason.

'We need to get our story straight,' he said.

We sat at a corner table of one of those legendary Smith-field boozers that roar while the city sleeps, and we were the only men in there who were not wearing white coats, the only men in there who were not splattered with blood. I watched Jackson sip his San Pellegrino. It took some nerve ordering a sparkling mineral water in here, but Jackson Rose had never lacked nerve.

'Are you in trouble, Jackson?'

'Me? Trouble? No. I'm suspended, of course. Auto-matic suspension pending the Standard Operating Procedures enquiry because I fired two rounds from my weapon. And because I killed Asad Khan. But I'm not going to be in trouble. I followed SOP to the letter. I shouted a warning at the armed man who had just murdered DS Stone and who would have murdered again if he had the chance. I did what I'm trained to do. I even did my best to avoid over-penetration.'

He smiled at me, happy to be beyond the reach of those who would prosecute policemen for murder.

'Over-penetration is when a bullet goes into someone and straight out the other side,' he explained. 'Best way to avoid over-penetration is to shoot the target when they're flat on the ground. And that's what I did with my second shot. And that's what I told them. And that's what everyone saw – including you, right?'

I nodded. 'That's what I saw,' I confirmed. 'I'm glad you're in the clear, Jackson.'

'I fired two shots – a double tap – and then I stopped,' he said. 'SFOs need to know two things – when to start firing and when to stop. So I'm not in trouble, Max. You don't have to worry about me. I'm all right. It's the other part of the story we have to get straight.'

I looked around the pub.

Many of the men had plastic bags at their feet, full of pork chops, beef ribs, legs of lamb. And I saw now that though the men all wore white coats, and they were all smeared with blood, they were all smeared with different measures of blood.

Some of their coats were almost pristine white, flecked with a few discreet little Jackson Pollock flourishes. These were the wholesalers. And some of the men had been cutting up pigs, which are carved while hanging up, reducing the blood splatter. These had only modest amounts of blood on their coats. And then there were the men whose white coats were stained deep red with blood. They had been cutting lamb – meaning they had been cutting towards themselves, as lambs are cut on blocks. So they were all marked with different kinds of blood.

But every one of them wore a sky-blue ribbon on his white coat, as they remembered the forty-five innocent souls who had died when that helicopter came down.

I looked back at Jackson. He had not stopped staring at me.

'They will ask you about when DS Stone was murdered, but we don't have to worry about that,' he said. 'What we have to work out is what you tell them about what happened in the basement.'

'We don't have to work it out, Jackson. There's nothing to work out.' I leaned closer to him. 'You talk to your friend DC Vann?'

'I wouldn't call him a friend, Max. But he doesn't need to be my friend. Ray Vann's part of our mob. And this mob, Max, they remind me of the mob I was with in Afghanistan. You know what we fought for in Afghanistan? It wasn't freedom. It wasn't democracy. It wasn't Queen and country. *It was each other.* And it's the same here. We fight for each other.'

'Did Vann ask you to come and see me?'

'He didn't have to.'

'Why did Stone speak to him?'

'When?'

'In the jump-off van on our way to Borodino Street. Vann was the only member of the team that Alice Stone spoke to. "*You OK, Raymond?*" As if she was worried about him. As if she was concerned about – I don't know – his mental state, his stability. She didn't speak to anyone else. Why did she speak to Vann?'

Jackson sipped his sparkling mineral water, looking away.

'I didn't clock it. Must have been checking my kit. Getting in the zone.'

'What's Vann's background?'

'Shots tend to come from two places, as you know. You've got the country boys – and girls – who grew up with guns, shooting clay pigeons, pheasants and peasants. All those rural pursuits. And then you've got the ex-servicemen. The ones who got their training in the military. In a different sort of field from the ones they shoot pheasants in. And that was Ray Vann. He was in Iraq. Did well under fire, apparently.'

'So he was highly trained and he knew what he was doing?'

'Yeah.' His eyes slipped away from mine again. 'But to be honest, you never know.'

'What does that mean, Jackson?'

'The ones that grew up with guns – like Alice Stone, for starters – have not had the same life experiences as the ones who served. Ex-servicemen – we're like rescue dogs, Max. You never know exactly what we have been through. And what it did to us.'

We were silent for a while.

'What happened in that basement, Max?'

'What does Ray Vann say happened?'

'The target went for his weapon.'

'Is that Vann's story?'

'That's what he told us at the hot debriefing in the imme-diate aftermath. And that's what he is going to tell the IPCC.'

The IPCC is the Independent Police Complaints Commission. They have the authority to decide if a firearms officer who discharges his weapon should get a medal or be prosecuted for murder.

And now Jackson looked at me.

'What are you going to tell them, Max?'

'Did the Search Team find a weapon in that basement?'

'No. There were no weapons found on the premises in Borodino Road beyond the assault rifle used for the murder of DS Stone.'

'Then how did Adnan Khan reach for a weapon if there was no weapon found in the basement?'

'Vann thought that a known terrorist was reaching for his weapon, OK? You know – one of the bastards who murdered – what is it now? Forty-five? – innocent men, women and children. Don't forget the children, Max. Vann had to make that judgement in a fraction of a split second to save his own life and the lives of many more.'

'CTU say that the only weapon on the premise was the AK47 that killed Alice Stone. No grenades. No other weapons.'

I watched my friend's spine stiffen as something flared up inside him.

'Can we please all stop saying that Alice was *killed*? Or that she *died*? She was *murdered*, OK?' he said, as if I had disputed the fact. He took a breath. 'Down in the basement the last of the Khan brothers went for what DC Vann *thought* was a weapon, OK? Khan made a sudden, violent movement and so Vann shot him. That's what he is going to tell the IPCC when he talks to them first thing tomorrow.'

I sipped my beer and said nothing.

'They will talk to you, too, Max. You know they will! There were only three men in that basement. One of them is dead. The IPCC will have a chat with you and Vann. And you have the power to corroborate his version or tell a different story.'

He raised his mineral water in salute.

I stared at him and said nothing. I drank my beer. The pub was very loud.

'I know you're solid, Max.'

I held up a hand for silence.

'You don't have to worry about me,' I said.

'I know that, Max. Do you think I don't know that?'

'I'm not going to rat him out.'

I looked at my beer. I wanted to get home. I wanted to see my daughter sleeping. I wanted this long hard day to be behind me.

'But I'm not going to lie for him,' I said.

Jackson's face hardened.

'What's that, Max? Like some kind of personal code of honour or something?'

I shrugged.

'Call it what you like. I'm not going to rat him out, but I'm not going to lie for him.'

'They finally reached Alice Stone's husband,' Jackson said, the anger mounting.

'I know.'

'Her husband's a copper. New Scotland Yard. Got two little kids under the age of five. A boy and a girl. When they grow up, they're not even going to remember her, are they? They're not even going to remember their mum, Max! Because they were too little when their mother was *murdered*.'

'I'm not going to rat him out, but I'm not going to lie for him,' I repeated for the third and final time, just making sure we were clear here.

I bolted the remains of my beer and stood up.

'Come back soon, Jackson. Train with me at Fred's. Come and see Scout. Cook for us again. Walk Stan. I miss you. I do. You're the only brother I ever had.'

He was waiting for the rest of it.

'But don't you ever lean on me again,' I told him.

7

The next day was Saturday and I breathed out.

I woke up to sunlight pouring through the bedroom skylight and the best sound in the world.

Stan was snoring on the pillow next to me, his left ear a silky curtain falling across his eyes. As I sat up he stirred in his sleep, smacked his lips, but did not wake. I stared at his face, noting how the black smudge under his nose extended across his mouth to his chin before giving way to the smudge of white on his chest, like a tiny tuxedo shirt. Everything else about his fur was a shade of red, from the strawberry blond feathers of his tail and legs to the deep russet of his coat and ears and head.

I once looked at a sleeping woman in this much adoring detail.

But now it was a Cavalier King Charles Spaniel.

It had been a long march for Stan to reach that pillow. At first he had been kept in his cage at night. Then he was allowed to roam the loft after lights out. And now he had made it all the way to my bed.

TONY PARSONS

He shrugged with irritation in his sleep as I threw back the duvet, got down on the floor and pumped out a brisk twenty-five press-ups. When I stood up to flex my leg, feeling how time and Fred were slowly but surely healing it, Stan opened his large round eyes and considered me impassively.

He did not move as he watched me stretch and then do another twenty-five press-ups – slower this time, thinking about form now, the pain in my knee a steady but distant throb. Then I stretched again, and as I did the third set of twenty-five press-ups Stan closed his eyes, sighing contently as he slipped back into deep sleep.

By the time I did the final set of twenty-five press-ups – the hard set, the one where the lactic acid burns in shoulders and arms, the set that actually does you some real good – the dog was snoring loudly once more.

I went into the main room and turned on the TV to see what was happening in Borodino Street.

And there was the by-now familiar vantage point of the street viewed from a news helicopter, but where the road should have been there was nothing but flowers. It was early Saturday morning, and the crowds, kept on the pavement by two long lines of uniformed officers were already out in force.

The picture cut to a close-up of the crowd. A small child, a girl, was being led by the hand as she laid her

70

bouquet with all the rest. The camera pulled in tighter on one of the photographs placed among the flowers.

DS Alice Stone was smiling for all eternity. The image had become one of the favourite shots of Alice, taken on holiday in Italy just after the birth of her first child. She looked giddy with happiness. And now the crowds came to mourn her.

I understood their grief because I felt it too. But the outpouring of emotion for Alice Stone was still bewildering. This was one woman who was being mourned by people who had never met her in a way that the forty-five victims of Lake Meadows were not mourned by total strangers. Perhaps the loss of all those people was simply too much to comprehend, I thought. All those lives stolen in a moment. All those lost fathers and mothers, sons and daughters, husbands and wives. All those families torn apart, all that grief that would echo through generations. It was too terrible to grasp.

But we all understood what had been lost in Alice Stone. The death of this one police officer who had lost her life because she sought justice for what happened at Lake Meadows – this tough, smart and beautiful woman, a wife, a mother and a daughter – had come to represent all the innocent victims of the summer. The loss of Alice Stone was like an ache in the heart of the nation.

When the camera cut back to the helicopter's eye to take it all in – the sea of flowers, the grim-faced crowds, the house hidden behind huge white screens where the CSIs and search teams were finishing their work – I saw him for the first time.

He was at the end of the street, just beyond the police perimeter, a lean, long-limbed young man in a suit and a bow tie who appeared to be standing on some kind of small box. He was addressing a section of the crowd and I noticed them because they had their backs turned to the flowers, and the house and the spectacle of Borodino Street.

The young man on his box was not the only speaker. Further back, at the very edge of the crowds, a black priest was addressing a small makeshift congregation of perhaps a dozen people. Even from this distance, you could make out his dark clerical robes, the white dog collar. But when he knelt to pray, half of his flock turned away, and wandered towards the young man on the box.

It was impossible to know what he was saying and why he had them rapt. It looked like he was giving his own kind of sermon. And the priest could not compete.

I called Edie Wren, not taking my eyes from the TV screen.

'Edie, are you watching this on TV?'

'Max?'

I had woken her.

I felt bad about that but I needed to understand what I was looking at in Borodino Street. Who was this guy?

'Turn on your TV,' I said. 'There's some guy talking to the crowd outside the Khan house. It looks like — I don't know — it looks like he's *preaching* to them.'

'Max.' She was awake now.

'Are you watching it?'

'Max — forget about it all for a while, OK? I know you were in the middle of it when that Air Ambulance came down. I know you saw Alice Stone die. I know you will never forget any of it. Of course I bloody do. *But none of it is our investigation.* Let it go, Max.'

'You haven't turned on your TV?'

I couldn't pretend I was not disappointed.

'Enjoy your weekend, Max,' Edie said, fully awake now. 'You and Scout and Stan. Try to put Lake Meadows out of your head. Forget about Borodino Street for a while. I know it's hard. But you've done your bit, Max. Now let someone else deal with it.'

And then I heard the man in her bed, his voice thick with sleep, stirring next to her.

'*Who is it?*'

I felt embarrassed, humiliated and stupid.

Mr Big. Edie's married man.

I wondered how he swung this at home, what smooth lie he had told to be given an overnight pass on the night before the weekend. Friday night, Saturday morning. A business trip, I thought. It had to be a business trip.

'Work,' Edie said, and somewhere in my thick head I could see it all.

Her face turned away from the phone. The man in her bed.

'Max?'

'It doesn't matter,' I said. 'Sorry. See you Monday.'

I sat down in front of the TV.

It was hypnotic. The sight of a nation in mourning. We mourned the victims of the latest atrocity at Lake Meadows, and we mourned all those who had died in previous attacks, and we mourned all those who would die in the future. And we mourned Alice Stone.

Everyone knew her now. Everyone knew about her copper husband, her two small children, her idyllic childhood in the Lincolnshire countryside. Everyone knew her smile. The country was haunted by that smile.

I watched TV until Scout wandered out of her bedroom. Then I turned it off and I followed her into the kitchen even though I knew that she could make breakfast for herself now – using a step stool to remove the loaf from the cupboard and butter and orange juice from the fridge, growing up faster than scheduled, the way that the children of divorced parents always will.

'You want me to make some breakfast for us, Scout?'

A sly smile. 'Today I'm making breakfast for *you*.'

So I went downstairs to get the mail.

There were the two magazines I subscribed to, *Boxing Monthly* and *Your Dog*, and an assortment of bills, junk mail about PPI and flyers offering pizza and Phad Thai delivered to your door. A smiling Gennady Golovkin was on the cover of *Boxing Monthly* and a grinning Labrador Retriever was on the cover of *Your Dog*. It was only when I was back in the loft that I realised there was also a card from my ex-wife.

You know handwriting. Even when years have gone by.

Even in this age when nobody writes letters or postcards any more. You still know someone's handwriting, if they have been close enough. You never forget it.

Anne's handwriting was neat, small but thick somehow, as if she pressed too hard, as if she was trying to make her point on a world that was not paying her enough attention.

But the card was not addressed to me.

It was for Scout. I didn't open it. I didn't tell her about it. I left it between *Your Dog* and *Boxing Monthly* and sat down to eat the toast Scout had made for me. It was a bit burned but slathered in lots of glorious New Zealand butter, just the way I liked it.

'It's good toast, Scout.'

She was staring down sternly at the dog.

Stan was bug-eyed with longing.

'Carbs are *bad* for you, Stan,' she said. 'We have to watch your weight or you'll get sick and die.'

He licked his lips, ready to take his chances.

A light summer rain pattered against the giant windows of the loft.

'We're going to have to walk between the raindrops,' Scout said, and I laughed out loud.

Nobody could make me laugh like my daughter.

'Scout,' I said, as casually as I could manage. 'Your mum has written to you.'

I picked up the card and handed it to her, making her transfer her jam-smeared toast from right hand to left. I didn't know what else to say. There was nothing else to say.

Scout's mother had left us before Scout started school, walking out because she was in love with someone else and expecting his child and planning to build a new life. It was as simple and brutal as that. So that was all pretty final. There had been some patchy contact between Anne and Scout at first but it had spluttered out as the new life crowded in.

It might have been a bit different if Anne had not been pregnant when she left – and then quickly got pregnant again – but Scout did not fit easily into this new life. My ex-wife tried to fit her in, but she did not try hard enough. And so she drifted away and Scout and I were left to get on with it. Which we did.

It happens all the time. And when people talk to me as if they have never heard anything like it happening before – a father being left to bring up his kid alone, a mother too wrapped up in her new life to think much about the beautiful child from the old life – I always truly envy them their sheltered, civilised, cosy, middle-class lives.

Adults carry on, I thought, watching Scout hold the card, and children pay the price. And for a mad moment I thought that the card contained an apology to Scout and all the sons and daughters of all the divorced mothers and fathers. Only divorced adults get new lives, I thought. Divorced children are stuck with their old lives – and with their dumb-ass divorced parents – for ever.

Her fingers sticky with butter and strawberry jam and toast crumbs, Scout tore open the envelope.

'It's a party invitation,' she said.

She showed me the card. There were laughing cartoon animals juggling balloons and cake while driving toy cars. Inside was an invitation to a fourth birthday party.

I couldn't bring myself to think of the birthday boy as Scout's brother. Even half-brother was beyond me.

'Mummy's little boy,' Scout said. 'It's his birthday.'

'That's very nice,' I said.

'Is he four already?'

'I guess he must be.'

Scout frowned.

'But he's *young*.'

I had to smile at that. 'And what are you? An old lady? You're only seven, Scout. You're not getting your free bus pass just yet.'

I took the card from her.

And I saw that she was angry.

If this contact after so many years of silence was strange for me, then how must it be for Scout?

'You know your mother never stopped loving you,' I said, and I believed it, despite all the evidence. Or maybe I just could not bear the thought of my daughter not being loved exactly as she deserved to be loved.

'She's very busy,' Scout said.

It was always the default excuse for my ex-wife's disappearing act. Now, at seven, Scout spat it out with a bit of an edge.

Some absent parents think they can pick it up again when the time is right, when it suits them, and I have no doubt this is true. But abandoned children will not wait for ever for the absent parent to make things right. The clock is ticking.

'Look,' I said. 'You can go to this party if you want or you can skip it if you want. It's true the other kids will be smaller than you, but I'm sure you will have a good time. But it's up to you, Scout.'

'I don't *have* to go?'

'Of course not!'

'Then I'm not going,' she said.

'Fine,' I said, wanting our Saturday to begin again. 'Where we taking Stan today?'

'The big walk on Hampstead Heath. The two-hour walk. Down The Avenue, cut across Parliament Hill, then down to the bathing ponds.'

'Lunch in the Coffee Cup on Hampstead High Street?'

She gave me the double thumbs-up. We smiled at each other then both stole a quick glance at the party invitation, as if it had strange powers that we could not imagine.

By the time we came back from our two-hour walk on Hampstead Heath and Saturday lunch at the Coffee Cup on Hampstead High Street, I had forgotten about it. I was surprised to see it still lying on the breakfast table. But it had lost its power to hurt us.

We were left to get on with it, I thought.

And we did.

So please excuse us if we don't give a damn any more.

But on Sunday night I was in Scout's room laying out her school clothes for Monday morning when, half-poking out of a paint-smeared cardboard folder, I saw a painting that she had done in her first year at school.

MY FAMILY was the title.

At five, they were just starting to make sense of the world and their place in it. All the other children had drawings that seemed to be teeming with life. Stick-figure daddies with their important briefcases, and stick-figure mummies who either had a briefcase or a baby, and lots of stick-figure siblings, larger and smaller. But Scout had only her stick-figure daddy with no briefcase and a four-legged red daub with bulging black eyes.

That was the extent of Scout's family.

Me and Stan.

The first time I had seen the painting it had torn at my heart. There was too much white space, there was too little life, and there were not enough people in Scout's world.

And now that old painting tore at my heart again.

Because on one side of the painting Scout had added an extra figure.

A pretty lady with dark hair, hovering on the edge of the little family, the drawing rendered far more expertly two years on. As if drawing something could make it so, as if just wishing something could turn back time to when things were simple and our family was unbroken.

I tucked the drawing neatly into her file, so that she would never know I had seen it.

I had moved on. But it was too much to expect my daughter to do the same.

Scout was lounging on the sofa with Stan, playing a game on her phone.

'Maybe you should go to that birthday party after all,' I said, as lightly as I could.

'OK,' she said, very quickly, not looking up from the exploding fruit.

So when Scout was tucked up in bed and I was certain she was sleeping, I wrote the RSVP, sickened to my soul at the way the world turns the children of divorced parents into pocket diplomats, negotiating their way between a man and a woman whose love brought them into the world and who later decide to hate each other's guts.

Then without even thinking about it I turned on the TV and watched the latest news from Borodino Street. As far as I could tell, the young man in the suit and bow tie who was addressing the crowd on Saturday morning had gone. But the flowers were still there, and Alice Stone was still smiling in all her photographs and the sombre crowds were still there, waiting for something to happen.

Moonlight streamed in through the big windows of our loft, thrown open to let in fresh air on a muggy summer night.

The great bell chimed midnight at St Paul's Cathedral.

Sunday night slipped into Monday morning.

And I breathed in.

8

'Who *is* that guy?' Edie said.

When I walked into MIR-1 first thing Monday morning, she was watching the latest images from Borodino Street.

As they cut to the view from the helicopter, you could clearly see the same young man addressing the crowd at the end of the street. His audience was bigger today. Their faces were turned away from the house, the flowers, the mourners and the epic makeshift shrine to Alice Stone.

'He has to be harmless,' Edie said. 'Doesn't he?'

'There are enough cops on that street to pick him up if he's a crank,' I said.

We watched the scene in silence. The tiny back garden was stacked high with torn-out floorboards. A skip was piled with plaster and bricks from the walls and ceilings.

'The search teams have hollowed it out,' I said.

'And still no grenades,' Edie said. 'What happened to them, Max?'

TDC Adams answered the phone.

'IPCC waiting for you,' she told me.

I had clocked the IPCC investigators as soon as I had walked into West End Central and I know that they had clocked me. They were an odd couple – an overweight man in his fifties, looking crumpled in a stained cheap suit and worn out before the day had got started, and a well-groomed, gym-fit young woman with long blond hair, her eyes sharp behind large black glasses. I had made no attempt to introduce myself.

The Independent Police Complaints Commission is the police watchdog with the power to decide if a serving cop who makes a split-second decision is a hero or a criminal.

They were only doing their job. But they were not my friends.

My Police Federation rep was waiting for me outside the interview room. He was one of those teak-hard old Londoners they don't seem to make any more, a tough, scrupulously neat little man who had been some kind of Mod in his youth – there was a care taken in his clothes, his hair, the way he carried himself.

'DC Wolfe? Andy Vine from the PFEW.'

The Police Federation of England and Wales.

We shook hands.

'Don't lose your rag in there,' Vine advised me.

The two IPCC investigators were already inside. The rumpled old boy looked as though he was ready for a nap. The young blonde took brisk charge.

'For the tape, can you identify yourself?' she said.

'DC Max Wolfe of Homicide and Serious Crime Command, West End Central.'

'I'm Marilyn Flynn of the Independent Police Complaints Commission,' she said. 'Also present is Gordon Hunt of the IPCC.' The old boy stirred at the mention of his name. 'DC Wolfe has the appropriate Police Federation representation,' Flynn noted.

Then she opened her file.

'This is an investigation into the two firing officers on Operation Tolstoy,' she said. 'What was your role in the raid on Borodino Street, DC Wolfe?'

'I was there for background briefing and to ID the targets. My department had interviewed a CI who had sold two grenades to the Khan brothers.'

'Allegedly,' said Flynn.

I looked at her.

I may have raised an eyebrow.

'*Allegedly* sold two Cetinka hand grenades,' she said, nodding her head for emphasis. 'But they didn't exist, did they? These grenades. They turned out to be a figment of your CI's imagination.'

'A cache of Cetinka hand grenades certainly existed because after the initial conversation with our CI we recovered two of them buried in a flower bed in a park in South London. Those were the two grenades that we photographed in West End Central. We had been informed that there were more grenades out there and that two of them had found their way to Asad and Adnan Khan. But it's true that the Search Team have so far been unable to find them at the address in Borodino Street.' I gave her a smile. 'That hardly means that they do not exist.'

'You don't think your CI may have lied to increase his value to you?'

'That is always a possibility with a Criminal Informant,' I said. 'But the Khan brothers were known returnees. These men were battle-hardened jihadists.' I took a deep breath. And then another. My rep was right – losing my rag would be bad news for everyone. 'We now believe that it was Asad and Adnan Khan who brought down that Air Ambulance helicopter on Lake Meadows shopping centre. They wanted to take as many innocent lives as possible. So it wasn't any kind of stretch to believe they were in the market for a couple of Croatian hand grenades.'

'But that has never been proved in a court of law, has it, DC Wolfe?' Flynn said. 'Their involvement in the Lake Meadows attack?'

'The house on Borodino Street was packed with drones. It was a drone that brought down that helicopter.'

I felt my blood rising. 'The Khan brothers boasted on social media about their exploits in Syria. Torturing non-believers, burning prisoners to death, beheading aid workers – the usual heroics.'

I felt my Federation rep stir nervously by my side.

I smiled again at Marilyn Flynn, letting some of the anger seep out of me.

'But you're right,' I agreed. 'They died before they could be brought to any kind of justice. So – never proven in a court of law. That's correct.'

She nodded, opened her laptop and hit a key.

Photographs of Jackson Rose and Raymond Vann appeared on the flat TV screen beside her. They were standard Met ID photos. But today they looked like police mugshots of guilty men. Even their call signs – Jackson was C7 and Vann was C3 – looked like jail numbers.

'For the tape, can you identify the two firing officers, DC Wolfe?'

'C7 is DC Jackson Rose and C3 is DC Raymond Vann.'

'Had you met either of the two firing officers before Operation Tolstoy?'

'I had never seen DC Vann before. But I grew up with Jackson – DC Rose. He's my oldest friend.'

She stared at me, letting it sink in, exchanging a look with the old boy, Gordon Hunt, before proceeding.

'You were on board the jump-off van with the entry team, correct?

'Yes.'

'What happened when you arrived in Borodino Street?'

'DS Alice Stone was murdered.'

A flicker of irritation on Flynn's face.

'Before the death of DS Stone.'

'The entry team were about to leave the van when the front door opened and someone wearing a niqab came out. One of those long black robes with a face veil.'

'We know what a niqab is, DC Wolfe.'

'I identified the figure as Asad Khan.'

'How long did the ID take you?' Flynn said.

'I don't know. A second? Five seconds? I really don't know.'

Time moves differently when you are in the presence of violent death, I think. *It stretches. A moment can feel like a thousand years.*

But sharing this thought seems pointless.

'Carry on,' Flynn said briskly.

'I made a positive identification of the target. DS Stone left the jump-off van and attempted to detain Adnan Khan. He was in possession of an assault rifle. He fired multiple shots at DS Stone. They proved fatal.'

'Is this the weapon?'

A profile of a fifty-year-old Heckler & Koch G3 appeared on the screen with the strapline EVIDENCE and a serial number.

'Yes.'

'Then C7 – DC Rose – shot Mr Khan,' Flynn said.

'No,' I said. 'The SFOs left the jump-off van. C7 – DC Rose – issued the appropriate verbal warning to Mr Khan. "*Armed police! Drop the weapon and show me your hands!*" DC Rose – C7 – followed procedure to the letter. And then I saw C7 fire two shots at Mr Khan. They both struck the target.'

A small smile on Flynn's glossy lips. 'You can remember his exact words? In all that confusion and gunfire? You have a remarkable memory.'

'Thank you very much.'

I felt my rep moving in his seat.

'Why did you enter the house?' Flynn said.

'I was there to ID the two targets. That was my role. We had only identified one target. I believed that the other brother, Adnan Khan, was in the house. And there was the possibility of other armed KAs being on the premises. We had no idea how big the cell was.'

'KAs?'

'Known associates. As you are aware, there is an ongoing investigation by CTU to see if the Khan brothers were part of a wider network of murdering nutjobs.'

'What happened inside the house?'

'I saw drones. Boxes of drones everywhere. That's when I knew these gentlemen had been responsible for bringing down that Air Ambulance helicopter.'

Flynn shook her elegant head.

'Let's forgo the speculation and stick to the facts, shall we, DC Wolfe?'

'Then these are the facts. I entered the house on Borodino Street and in the kitchen I discovered Ahmed Khan, the father of the Khan brothers, Azza Khan, their mother, and their teenage granddaughter Layla, whose father died fighting for Islamic State in Syria. They were all clearly terrified. I instructed them to leave the house as quickly as possible with their hands in the air.'

I raised my hands to demonstrate. Palms facing outwards, showing they held nothing.

Gordon Hunt stirred.

'Was that because you were afraid that some trigger-happy SFO might take a potshot at them when they came out,' he said, smiling.

It was not a question.

'No,' I said. 'I was afraid they could die in crossfire. My colleagues from SC&O19 conducted themselves with total professionalism throughout Operation Tolstoy.' I paused at a memory. 'Seconds after Asad Khan had shot and killed DS Stone, SFOs who loved her were giving Asad Khan first aid in an attempt to save his life.' I shook my head with genuine wonder. 'I never questioned their professionalism. I was simply trying to ensure there was no unnecessary loss of life.'

Gordon Hunt seemed wide-awake now.

'And after Mr and Mrs Khan had fled the building with their granddaughter you went down to the basement and witnessed C3 – DC Vann – discharge his weapon into Adnan Khan.'

Again, it is not a question.

'No,' I said. 'That's not what happened.'

I am not going to rat him out.

But I am not going to lie for him.

I felt the sweat trickle down my back for the first time today.

Because I suddenly understood that I was attempting to do the impossible.

How far can you bend the truth until it stops being the truth?

'I heard a single shot in the basement,' I said slowly. 'I then left the kitchen and went down into the basement. C3 had already discharged his weapon. I assumed that Khan had made some move for a weapon or that C3 – DC Vann – believed he had made such a move. I identified the target, Adnan Khan. He was dead.'

They let that sit there for a while. They made a point of not looking at each other. The perspiration slid further down my spine.

My Federation rep was perfectly still.

'Just to be clear,' Hunt said. 'You were not in the basement when Khan was killed?'

'No.'

Hunt consulted his notes.

'Because C3's testimony puts you down there.' He paused. 'In the basement, DC Wolfe, when the fatal shot was fired, DC Vann insists you were there and you witnessed Adnan Khan on his feet and making a sudden movement, as if to retrieve a weapon – although no weapons were found in that basement. You can't corroborate his version of events?'

'No.'

'Is he lying?'

I felt my mouth tighten.

'Our colleagues in SCO19 are under enormous – unimaginable – pressure,' I said. 'C3 is not lying – he is mistaken. Did you ever hear a shot fired in anger?' I said. 'Sir?'

'Are you trying to insult me, DC Wolfe?'

'I'm trying to see if you understand what sustained automatic gunfire does to *everything* – your hearing, your blood pressure, your balance, your heart rate, your perception of time. All of it. Gunfire is strange – it just seems to crowd out the rest of the world. It takes over. It dominates everything. So I don't think DC Vann is lying to you, sir,' I repeated for the tape. 'I think that he is mistaken.'

'Maybe you're the one who is mistaken, DC Wolfe. Is that also a possibility?'

'I am quite certain that I was not in that basement until after Mr Khan died.'

'Did Mr Khan get what was coming to him, DC Wolfe?' Hunt said.

'I don't think terrorists can reasonably expect to die of old age in their beds, sir.'

'Did you and C3 speak to each other?' Flynn said. 'When you finally arrived in the basement?'

'I believe I said his name. His first name. Raymond. I do not recall C3 – DC Vann – speaking to me.'

'But you said that you had never met before,' Hunt said. 'So how did you know his name?'

I told them the truth without thinking about it.

'Because DS Stone spoke to him when we were on our way to Borodino Street. She said, "*You OK, Raymond?*" So I knew his name was Raymond.'

'C3 says that Khan was on his feet and making a sudden move for what he assumed to be a weapon,' Hunt said. 'And *this* is why we are struggling to believe his version of events.'

Flynn touched her keyboard and two line-drawings of a little generic man appeared on the screen, face on and sideways. The sideways drawing has a line entering the drawn man around the middle of his chest and leaving around the bottom of his back.

'That's the post-mortem trajectory of the gunshot that killed Mr Khan,' Hunt said. 'Ballistics inform us that a single shot entered Mr Khan's heart and exited from the base of his spine. And as you can see, the autopsy agrees with this theory.'

'How do you explain it?' Flynn said. 'If Mr Khan was standing and making an abrupt movement for a weapon? Why did the gunshot enter his chest on entry and exit just above his buttocks? If he was standing, it doesn't make sense, does it?'

'I am not attempting to explain it,' I said.

The IPCC investigators took a moment.

'Mr Khan was on his knees when he was shot, wasn't he, DC Wolfe?' Hunt said. 'DC Vann was pumped up, understandably terrified, full of anger about what had just happened to his team leader on the street. He had an unarmed man on his knees and he executed him. Isn't that what happened, DC Wolfe?'

'I wouldn't know, Mr Hunt.'

'Because you were not in the basement when it happened,' he said.

And it wasn't a question.

Because they had no more questions for me.

I rode down to the ground floor with my Federation rep.

'Heroes before breakfast,' he said. 'Murderers before mid-morning tea. Who'd be a shot, eh?'

We shook hands.

'Not me,' I said.

Back in MIR-1, TDC Adams had a message for me.

'Paddington Green called,' she said. 'You should call DCI Flashman.'

I returned Flashman's call.

'You want Ahmed Khan, Wolfe?' he said. 'You can have him.'

'You're not charging him?'

'You were right,' Flashman said. 'He's as simple as he looks. As far as we can make out, all his known associates are other bus drivers. And get this, Wolfe: the old man says he wants to go home.' Flashman was chuckling with amusement. 'To the house on Borodino Street!'

I looked up at the TV screen. I saw the crowds, the flowers for Alice Stone, the house that had been torn apart. I could not imagine anyone ever living in that place again.

'So Ahmed Khan's not running an al-Qaeda cell from the number 73 bus, Flashman? That's a turn-up for the book.'

I heard his hot breath.

'The man had three sons,' Flashman said. 'Every one of them was a murdering jihadist bastard. He's bloody lucky to be getting out so soon. *Accept nothing, believe no one, check everything*. How did you miss that lecture at Hendon, Wolfe? Were you walking that little dog of yours?'

'If you smell guilt on him, then why are you slinging him out, Flashman?'

The police can hold someone for twenty-four hours before we either have to charge them with a crime or set them free. The only exception is if someone is suspected of terrorism. Then we can hold them for fourteen days.

'We need the cell,' Flashman said. 'This old bus driver is a cell-blocker for the really bad boys. We will let him sweat for a few more days – that should be long enough for the generous British state to find him and his family a safe house – and then we will chuck him out. Dig out the welcome mat, Wolfe.'

Edie Wren and Joy Adams were staring at me as I hung up.

'They're releasing Ahmed Khan without charge,' I said.

'And what are we meant to do with him?' Edie said.

I looked again at the crowds and the flowers and the cops on Borodino Street.

'Keep him alive,' I said.

9

At the end of a week when the death toll at the Lake Meadows shopping centre crept up to forty-six, and the crowds kept coming to Borodino Street, and the sea of flowers just kept getting bigger, I drove one hour west of the city and I parked the old BMW X5 in a spot where all I could see were green rolling hills with the river running through them, the Thames — and it was still the Thames out here — molten gold in the sunshine of early summer.

I let Stan off the leash and he busied himself nibbling the grass, delicately careful as a rabbit, while I sat on a bench by the towpath and stared upriver. The track leading to Henley-on-Thames had a scattering of joggers, dog walkers and tourists who had strolled out of town. As Stan munched grass — he found it aided his digestion — I watched the river with its sightseeing boats and the sculls of rowers.

After a while I saw them coming down the towpath.

A small woman with fair hair and dark glasses, maybe forty, and a teenage boy, no older than sixteen but a full head and shoulders taller than the woman. But they still looked like mother and son. The boy also wore dark glasses and there was an assistance dog loping at his side, a Labrador-Retriever mix with fur the colour of melted butter.

The woman was Detective Chief Inspector Pat White-stone, my senior officer and the most experienced homicide cop in West End Central. The boy was her son Justin, who had lost his sight in one of those mind-less eruptions of violence that can come out of nowhere in the teenage years.

And the dog was Dasher.

Stan's nose perked up at the familiar scent of Dasher and he ran off to greet the party and his old friend. Whitestone and Justin greeted him warmly but Dasher, who had been trained to never be distracted from his role, merely gave Stan a quick butt-sniff for form's sake and then looked up at his master.

'How's the holiday?' I asked them.

Whitestone and Justin were walking the full length of the Thames Path, the national trail that runs for almost two hundred miles from the river's source deep in the heart of the Cotswolds to the Thames Barrier in the East End.

'Cool,' Justin said.

'You should do it with Scout,' Whitestone said. 'Best walk in the country.'

Justin walked down to the riverbank with the two dogs, Stan capering with mad glee by the side of the calm, solemn Dasher.

'Not too close to the water,' Whitestone called.

'I can *hear* it,' Justin replied, frowning with irritation.

Whitestone and I sat on the bench. We watched her son and our dogs.

'You can do it in fifteen days but we're taking three weeks,' Whitestone said. 'We had a rest day in Oxford, we're taking another one here and then one more in Windsor.'

'Legoland,' I said. 'I've been to Windsor with Scout.'

'Justin's Legoland days are over,' Whitestone said. 'How are you, Max?'

We had only briefly spoken on the phone after Lake Meadows, my boss checking in with me from her holiday to let me know – without ever actually saying the words – that she was glad I was alive.

'The knee's healing well,' I said.

Whitestone waited for more.

'I think about the people I saw after the helicopter came down,' I said, watching the river. 'There was a security guard who lost an arm. There was an old lady and her husband lying on the ground. And there was a man – a man in a suit and tie, some kind of executive – carrying a bag from the Apple store and he was covered in this grey dust. I wake up in the middle of the night thinking about them and I wonder if they made it out alive. And I wonder if they are awake in the middle of the night, too.'

She nodded with understanding. But there was nothing she could tell me.

'And was it a bigger network than just the brothers?'

'It doesn't look like it. Counter Terrorism haven't arrested anyone else and they are not charging Ahmed Khan.'

'The father?'

I nodded. 'Flashman's got him banged up in Paddington Green but they're going to release him in a few days. They're waiting for a safe house. Apparently there's a long waiting list for safe houses. And they're handing him to West End Central.'

'To us? Why??'

'To make sure nobody tops him.'

'You want me to come back early?'

I shook my head.

'Enjoy your holiday. Finish your walk. I can handle it. But Ahmed Khan doesn't want to go to a safe house. He wants to go home to Borodino Street.'

'And Borodino Street is still a crime scene.'

'But not for much longer. I don't know how long we can keep him in a safe house if he doesn't want to be there. The search teams and the CSIs have torn that house apart and there's still no sign of those two Croatian hand grenades that were meant to be on the premises. There's nothing left to bag, dust or photograph. There's nowhere left to search. And there's nobody standing trial for the murder of Alice Stone because the man who killed her is dead.'

Whitestone thought about it.

'The old man knew nothing about his sons? Really?'

Like Edie, she was struggling to believe it was a case of innocent contact.

'He's a bus driver,' I said. 'I know it sounds unlikely that someone could have a terrorist cell on the other side of the breakfast table and know nothing about it. But I believe that's what happened.'

'And the old man wants to go back to normal life,' Whitestone said, shaking her head. She took off her shades. They were prescription sunglasses, and her blue myopic eyes had a vulnerable look as she squinted in the dazzling early morning sunshine. 'He might find that normal life isn't there any more,' she said. 'Who's going to be in the safe house with him?'

'His wife and their granddaughter, if social services haven't got their claws into the kid. And I need to know what the drill is for the Khan family going home when their house is no longer a crime scene.'

Whitestone shook her head.

'There is no drill,' she said. 'It's always different with former crime scenes. People die in one place and it gets razed to the ground. Someone gets their head bashed in at some other place and life carries on as if nothing much happened. It all depends if someone wants to live there. Dennis Nilsen's flat is still in Muswell Hill but Fred and Rose West's house was bought by the local council and demolished. John Christie's house at 10 Rillington Place is a garden now but the house where Lord Lucan allegedly topped the nanny is still there in Belgravia. Property value has a lot to do with it. And the body count. Borodino Street in the East End? I don't know.'

'Three people died there.'

'Two of them don't count. Terrorists – even alleged terrorists – don't count. But Alice Stone died there, and she has struck a nerve in this country because she gave her life fighting the bastards who were responsible for Lake Meadows.' Whitestone shrugged. 'I can't honestly see how the Khans can go home. Their house is a memorial now. But if Ahmed Khan is not going to be charged with anything, and if the property is in his name, then I don't see how we can stop him.'

'Should we give him an Osman warning?'

An Osman warning is a notice issued by a police force to officially warn someone that their life is in danger but that we do not have sufficient evidence to arrest a possible offender.

'Has anyone made a threat on Khan's life?'

'Not that I am aware of, no.'

'Then the Osman warning can wait until someone threatens to kill the old boy.'

'I don't think we'll have to wait long,' I said. 'You've seen the crowds on Borodino Street. You've seen the strength of feeling about the death of Alice Stone.'

Whitestone nodded.

'And I share those feelings. When we're back in town, the first thing I am going to do is take some flowers to Borodino Street.' She paused, as if trying to understand her need to place some flowers with all those other flowers. 'Alice was the best of us,' she said.

We watched the dogs and the boy sitting down at the river's edge. Another rowing scull went past, seeming to glide on the surface of the river, the tiny coxswain in the stern urging the crew on. Justin raised his head at the sound of their calls.

'We heard from Scout's mother,' I said.

'What does *she* want?' Whitestone said. 'Don't tell me. She wants Scout back in her life.'

'How did you guess?'

'Guilt,' Whitestone said. 'I had the same with Justin's dad. It hits them every now and again. The absent parent. Terrible guilt. But they get over it remarkably well.'

'Is that all it is?' I said. 'Guilt?'

'What else would it be?' Whitestone said.

We stared at the river in silence, two single parents reflecting on the fecklessness of the absent parent and in that moment the fact that we were a man and a woman mattered a lot less than the fact that we were both single parents.

'Who's the kid preaching to the crowds in Borodino Street?' Whitestone said.

So she had seen him too. 'I don't know,' I admitted.

'Then you better find out,' my boss said. 'And keep looking for those grenades.'

'We've been doing nothing else, boss,' I said.

Knocking on for midnight on Friday in Camden Town, and the creatures of the night were coming out to play.

Some of them were coming out to play for the very first time – the wide-eyed rich kids from the big houses who were just the other side of their exams – and others had been coming out to play in these loud, dark places for ten, twenty or forty years. The man I sought was one of the forty-year men.

Nils looked like a diseased crow.

Thin, beaky, with a spiked-up hairdo that was a tribute to the young Keith Richards. That elaborate hair had stood in proud homage to Keith for four decades, thinned only slightly by time, it was now kept jet black with bottles of After Midnight dye from Boots the Chemist.

Nils strolled on to the stage of a semi-legendary club by the canal and turned his back to the audience, revealing several inches of butt crack as he bent over the electric guitars that waited in their stands.

A few of the audience – that motley Camden Town crew of hungry fresh young faces and drug-raddled party people – smirked and giggled at the bottom reveal as Nils fussed with the tuning of a battered Fender Telecaster.

They stopped laughing when he effortlessly slashed the main riff from 'Jumpin' Jack Flash'. His crow face impassive, Nils put the Fender back in its stand and turned his attention to the bass guitar.

Same routine. Bend, butt crack reveal, tune and then play a riff that was so good it was identical to the record. This time it was the bass line to 'Going to a Go-Go' by Smokey Robinson and the Miracles.

After tuning the guitars, Nils stood at the side with someone young enough to be his granddaughter. She was wearing a cowboy hat, mini-skirt and cowboy boots. The band slouched on stage to whoops from the crowd. They were around thirty years younger than Nils, closer to the age of the youngest members of the audience, and he watched over them with a slightly bored, paternal air as they picked up their instruments and began their first song.

Then he headed backstage with the girl. I followed them.

The changing room was a windowless cube that was stained with the inane graffiti of half a century. Nils and the girl in the cowboy hat were sitting on a couple of boxes as he chopped out lines of white powder on a cracked CD.

'Police,' I told the girl, showing her my warrant card. 'Time for bed.'

She was gone in a moment, getting out of there so fast she almost lost her cowboy hat.

I stared hard at Nils.

'How old was she?' I said.

'Come on,' he said, his voice coarsened by half a century of cigarettes, spliffs and goodness knows what. 'She's on a gap year, Max. Consenting adults and all that.' He stared wistfully at the door. 'Great veins,' he sighed. 'The plump blue veins of extreme youth.'

'You're not still shooting up, are you?'

'I stopped,' he said emphatically. 'No more needles.'

But I saw that he missed it. They always missed it.

'Just this now,' he said, indicating the white lines on the CD. 'And strictly up the hooter.'

'And you're still a roadie,' I said.

'Guitar technician. Roadie sounds so derogatory.'

'We're looking for that weapons dealer, Nils. Ozymandias.'

'I thought you might be. Ozymandias is not in his flat on the Elphinstone Estate. Hasn't been seen for weeks.'

The Elphinstone Estate is the closest my city has to a no-go zone for the law. A semi-derelict collection of flats that were built in the Sixties, property developers had been trying to pull it down for years but some of the residents steadfastly refuse to move out. So do all of the gangs that run their small businesses from the Elphinstone Estate. Nils had been a regular at the Elphinstone's shooting galleries for decades. He still scored his white powders and puff there, and knew all of the dealers and their clients, which was what made him one of my most valuable Criminal Informants.

'Yes, Nils. We know Ozymandias is not home. We looked.'

'Of course you did. Sorry.'

'And we know his real name. It's not Ozymandias, is it?'

'Probably not.' He indicated the white lines. There was a rolled-up fiver in his hands. He licked his lips. 'Do you mind if I ... ?'

I nodded.

'I mind,' I said, picking up the CD case, being careful not to spill the white lines. 'But we don't know where he's gone. And we don't know if he really sold two Cetinka hand grenades to the Khan brothers. And if he did, we don't know what happened to them. So we urgently need him to help with our enquiries, Nils. Where the hell is he?'

'Who knows? He could be fermenting civil war in the Crimea or he could be doing Spice in Ibiza. Ozymandias comes and goes. A free spirit.'

'That's not good enough.'

'Look – I told you what I heard. One of the little boys on the estate – some pound store gangster who wants to go out in a blaze of glory, just like a rap song – was talking about buying a couple of hand grenades from Ozymandias. Grenades up the ante, right? Better than a gun. Big status in the gangs. He bought a couple – they were the two you dug up from that park. Lucky it was you that found them and not some little kiddy who just wanted a ride on the swings and roundabouts, right? *What does this do, Mummy?* And someone asked the little pound store gangster who else was serious enough to be in the market for grenades and he said he heard they were bound for a couple of brothers just back from their jihad holiday in Syria. And my hot tip led you to the Khans, didn't it?'

'But not to the grenades, Nils.'

'That's not my fault! Look, in the past Ozymandias has gone out east when it got too hot at home.'

'Essex?'

'Bangkok. Pattaya. Manila. Saigon. But he'll be back when he runs out of money. Probably. And I'm sure those grenades are going to turn up, Max.'

I gave him back his drugs.

'Yes,' I said. 'That's what I'm afraid of.'

Saturday afternoon was party time.

I had been careful with my driving, making sure that I arrived on the wide, tree-lined street exactly five minutes after the assigned pick-up time, just late enough to not have to wait around outside.

It was one of those rich suburbs that make the city seem light years away, a neighbourhood where it was impossible to believe that anything bad could ever happen.

There were balloons on the door of the house where my ex-wife lived with her new family. Not so new now, I reminded myself.

I left Stan in the passenger seat, whimpering in protest at the outrage of being abandoned alone in the car in this weird-smelling place with its mown lawns and clean pavements.

But my ex-wife really hates dogs.

I took a breath and rang the bell, steeling myself for the sight of Scout unhappy and isolated and tearful sur-rounded by children half her size, ready to scoop her up and run for home.

But the door was opened by the new guy – how many decades would have to go by before I stopped thinking of him as the new guy? – and I immediately saw that Scout was having a good time.

She sat cross-legged on the floor, laughing and happy, a slightly torn paper party hat on her head, while four-year-old boys and girls milled around her in all their jelly-smeared, sugar-crazed anarchy, waiting to be taught some complicated hand-clapping game that only this big girl knew.

At seven Scout was a few years older than the birthday boy – I realised I should try to remember his name – and his little pals, but just one look told me that all my fears had been unfounded. Scout had enjoyed the party. More than this, thanks to her sweet nature and kind heart, she had been the star.

Anne stepped away from a group of parents drinking something bubbly and approached me. She was still a stunning woman – tall, dark, with an understated exotic look that made you think she could come from any-where in the world. She had once been a model but it had not worked out. It's a hard old game, looking good for a living.

'Max,' she said.

How many nights had we slept side by side? More than a thousand. And now we did not know each other at all. Now she had this other life and I had my own life too. Once she had been closer to me than anyone in the world and now she was this beautiful stranger. I would never get used to the distance between us. It would never seem normal to me.

'Scout's been so great with the little ones,' she said. 'It's been hilarious.'

So great, I thought. It's not enough being simply great. It has to be *so great*. And why was it *hilarious*?

Who was this woman?

We exchanged pleasantries and platitudes and I forgot what they were the moment they were out of my mouth. A group of adoring sprogs trailed Scout to the door.

My daughter was smiling – a broad, open beautiful smile.

Stan was still having a moan in the car.

But then nothing upset him like the thought of our pack falling apart.

10

On Monday morning, TDC Joy Adams and I drove to Borodino Street. She had brought flowers.

'Is it all right?' she asked me, nervously cradling the bouquet in the passenger seat of the X5.

I nodded. 'It's fine. But better get your warrant card out.'

The flowers for Alice Stone now filled the road. From one end of Borodino Street to the other, every centimetre of tarmac had been covered. The public had also been leaving their flowers around the Lake Meadows shopping centre but the affected area was so vast, a huge ruined swathe of the city that was still sealed off from the public, and the sprawling crime scene was surrounded by countless small pop-up shrines around street signs and lampposts.

Borodino Street, in contrast, was one unbroken sea of flowers.

We had taped off the pavements on either side of the road so that the public could pay their respects, say a prayer, leave their bouquets, take a photo on their phones or simply stand and stare at the outpouring of emotion, but there was a cordon of uniformed police officers at either end of the street to restrict the numbers allowed in at any one time.

'I'll wait for you,' I told Adams.

Adams approached a female uniformed officer at the cordon – we don't have WPCs in the Met any more – and when the young Trainee Detective showed her warrant card, she was allowed to jump the queue waiting to be allowed on Borodino Street. But Adams was not the only person to be allowed special access.

There was a priest staring thoughtfully at the flowers, and I wondered if he was the same priest that I had seen on TV, praying to a dwindling congregation.

. I could not see his face, but he was clearly a large black man, built more like a retired middleweight boxer than a man of God. Adams exchanged a few words with him and then they stood silently side by side at the edge of that great tide of flowers.

I realised they were praying and I looked away.

When Adams returned I nodded to the far end of the street where perhaps two hundred people were listening to a young man speak.

'The guy we want is over there,' I said.

The young man who addressed the crowd was tall and long-limbed, his face somewhere between hungry and starved, a boy made of bones. You could see him clearly because the soapbox he stood on raised him head and shoulders above his audience. He looked as though he had stepped out of a photograph from between the wars. He was perhaps twenty-one and his hair was shaved at the back and sides and cropped short on top. I could not tell if the hair was a fashion statement or just poverty.

We stood at the back of the crowd. They were all ages, and most watched him without expression, as if he was part of the great spectacle of Borodino Street. Closer to the front, there were cheers and applause and shouts of agreement.

'You fought their wars and you paid your taxes and you worked in their factories,' he said. 'You – and your parents and your grandparents – did everything they asked you to do. And your reward is their contempt. Your reward is changes to your country that you never asked for, changes that you were never consulted about and changes that you never wanted. You – and those who came before you – have given everything for this country. And your reward is a country that you no longer recognise. Your reward is leaders who despise you. Your reward is the murder of the brightest and the best of us.' He paused to scrape his fingers through his Depression-era haircut. 'Your reward is Borodino Street.'

He had one of those very old London accents, the kind that sounds almost Australian, untouched by affectation or higher education or moving out to the suburbs. He was not trying to be anything other than what he had always been, and what his family had been for generations. You no longer heard many accents like that.

He jabbed a finger towards the house on Borodino Street.

'You know, there is a part of me that admires the Khan family,' he said.

Murmurs of dissent in the crowd. Someone shouted an obscenity.

'And I will tell you why,' he said. 'Because they have a strong culture, a proud culture, a culture that does not apologise for existing. I don't blame them for settling in the weak, tired, overfed west where we are too feeble, too unsure of ourselves, to say – this country and all its values are worth preserving. And if we lack the courage to state that fact, my friends, then tomorrow belongs to them.'

When he was finished there was a smattering of wild applause among those closest to him but most of the crowd simply turned away, as if they would think it all over, or possibly forget about it immediately, as they were drawn back to the street full of flowers and the house that was still illuminated by police lights, even in broad daylight. As the crowd drifted away Adams and I pushed our way towards the young man.

I thought that someone who drew this kind of audience might have some kind of entourage. But he was alone apart from one short, broad-shouldered helper with exactly the same Buddy-can-you-spare-a-dime? haircut, a younger man with the aspect of a weightlifter or a baby bull. He was carefully placing the speaker's soapbox on to the passenger seat of one of those rickshaws that ferry around foreign tourists and local drunks – three skinny wheels, the back two set wide apart to ferry the fatties and the worse for wear, a plastic canopy over the plastic seat as protection against the English summer. And I saw that it was not a soapbox at all. It was a crate for Indian beer.

Kingfisher, it said on the side, the King of Beers.

I showed my warrant card to the one who had spoken. Adams hovered at my shoulder, doing the same, still getting the hang of showing someone her warrant card.

'I'm DC Wolfe. This is TDC Adams. Who are you?'

He smiled pleasantly.

'George Halfpenny,' he said. 'Have I done something wrong? The other officers told me that as long as I didn't obstruct their crowd control, then I was free to talk to the people.'

'You're free to talk until the mad cows come home,' I said. 'As long as you don't whip up any trouble. As long as you stay on the right side of the law. As long as

115

you don't incite violence. As long as you keep the party polite. Understood?'

'Understood. I have no intention of inspiring hatred or breaking the law. I just want to talk.' There was the glitter of passion in his eyes. 'I just have some things that have to be said.'

I nodded. 'But why are you here, George? Why are you here night after night after night?'

'We came down here – my brother Richard and I' – he indicated the fridge-shaped young man with him, and now I saw they were brothers, that they shared more than the brutal jarhead haircut – 'to pay our respects to Alice.'

Something inside me flinched at the unearned intimacy of using only her first name. But then I knew the entire country felt the same way. DS Stone was *Alice* to everyone now.

'Three people died at the same address,' Halfpenny said, staring at the house. 'One was a police officer – dedicated, selfless, brave. The other two were fanatics, murderers, men who believed they pleased their god with slaughter. I think we have a *duty* to remember Alice, don't you? We all have a duty to keep coming back.'

'Tell him,' his brother Richard said.

'It's OK,' George said quietly, soothing him.

The baby bull pushed himself forward.

'We are the Sons of Saxons,' he said.

I heard TDC Adams chuckle behind me.

'What's that?' I said. 'A band?'

'The Sons of Saxons are a cultural preservation society,' George Halfpenny said, untroubled by the possibility of mockery. 'We believe that the cultural identity of this country is worth preserving. We believe that one thousand years without being invaded has produced a country that is unique in the world.'

'You've got a lot of rabbit,' Adams observed.

She meant that he talked a lot. And it was true.

But George Halfpenny ignored her.

'The Sons of Saxons are not a band, Detective,' he told me. 'It's an idea. The jihadists taught us that, didn't they?' He indicated the floodlit house. 'Men like the Khan brothers. An idea is the most powerful thing in the world. But I promise you, there is nothing sinister about our motives.' His eyes were shining but his expression remained pleasant, his words reasonable. 'Honest, tolerant patriots have been sneered at for too long. We have been despised for loving our country, for believing that our traditions and culture are worthy of love and worthy of protecting. It's not about hating anyone. We're not *sieg-heiling* skinheads, Detective. It's about love. Love for our country, love for ourselves. But they sneer at the likes of us.'

'But who are *they*, George?' I asked.

He smiled gently. 'We both know who they are. The big shots. The elite. The educated, the rich, the ones in the big houses. You know who they are, DC Wolfe. They hate the people who built everything in these islands. We get called bigots, racists and simpletons for daring to love our country, for believing it is worth preserving, for feeling pride in the past, for not quietly slipping into the mists of history. The Sons of Saxons believe it is time to stop apologising for who we are and who we have been for a thousand years. May I go home now?'

'Where's home, George?'

'Camden Town.'

'Is this your rickshaw?' I said.

'It would be kind of stupid to steal someone else's rickshaw in front of two detectives from the Metropolitan Police,' he said.

'Don't get smart,' Adams snapped, and I saw the steel in her.

George Halfpenny laughed.

'I'm a rickshaw driver,' he said. 'That's what I do for a living.' He grinned at me, and I saw that nobody in his life had ever given a thought to his teeth. 'We are coolies in our own land now, Detective,' he said. 'This is the gig economy. We are men who work with our hands in a land where nothing gets made any more. We are men with strong backs with nothing to carry, a warrior race with brave hearts and nobody to fight. We are factory workers after all the factories have closed down.'

Adams was right.

He really did love to hear the sound of his own voice.

'Save the speech for the next performance,' I said. 'Listen, son, as long as you don't break the law you can do what you like. But I'll be watching you.'

'Thank you.'

'He called you *son*,' said his brother, shocked.

'It's all right, Richard,' George Halfpenny murmured.

He looked at the tide of flowers on the street.

'It's fitting we are here,' he said. 'It feels fated. *Borodino Street*. I wonder how many people know this street is named after a great battlefield.'

I felt a schoolboy memory stir.

'*War and Peace*,' I said. 'Tolstoy. Borodino was the battle in *War and Peace*.' I remembered that the raid when we lost Alice Stone was codenamed Operation Tolstoy. 'I knew it rang a bell.'

'That was *one* of the battles at Borodino,' George Halfpenny said. 'The Russians against the French in the Napoleonic Wars in 1812, seventy thousand casualties, the bloodiest day of the Napoleonic Wars. The Battle of Borodino. And then there was the Battle of Borodino Field in 1941, the Russians against Nazi Germany on the same fields, fighting to keep the invaders from the gates of Moscow. Borodino was a sacred site of patriotic wars, the killing fields where invaders were repelled. That's why it is so fitting for us to be here.'

'You know your history,' I said, only trying to be friendly as he climbed on to his rickshaw, his brother Richard sitting in the passenger seat like a stumpy potentate on a plastic throne, a protective arm around the Indian beer box.

And finally I had offended him.

'I'm uneducated, Detective,' George Halfpenny said, and for the first time I glimpsed the righteous fury in him. 'But that doesn't mean I'm stupid.'

11

In any normal broken family it would have been different.

In any normal broken family we would have built on the success of that birthday party.

In any normal broken family there would have been stilted texts, awkward emails, sufficient contact to arrange for Scout to return to the house on the street where it looked as though nothing bad had ever happened, and spend some time with her mother and her mother's new family.

But we were not a normal broken family and as the days drifted by after the birthday party, there was only silence.

I went downstairs for the mail and flicked through the bills, the restaurant flyers and the charity appeals. But there was nothing from Anne, and as time went by I suspected that there was going to be nothing.

This is what we dealt with, my daughter and I, and we dealt with it every day of our lives.

This is what happens. The absent parent has the very best intentions to put things right. They truly do. But then life gets in the way. There are distractions – other demands, far more urgent – and the child who was left behind is – at best – parked in abeyance and – at worst – forgotten.

Absent fathers do it. But absent mothers do it too.

And the feeling that pierced me as I stood with the takeaway flyers in my hand was sadness stained with anger.

Single mothers know this feeling.

And single fathers know it too.

I wanted more – what? Not love, because you can't demand love, you can't force love, you can't summon it up when it is not there, or it's buried deep beneath some new life.

I wanted more *kindness*.

That's what I wanted from my ex-wife for Scout.

I wanted more kindness for our beautiful daughter.

As I walked back up to our loft, my knee throbbing with a dull rhythm, I noticed that there was one mystery piece of mail, my name and address in elaborate script written with a fountain pen – and I noticed in a moment that it was not written by my ex-wife. Stiff to the touch, but harder than a child's birthday invite. It was an invitation of a different kind.

✝

The Gane Family
Are sad to announce the passing of
Mrs Elizabeth Mildred Precious Gane
On 3 July
A service conducted by Fr Marvin Gane will
be held at St Anthony's
Church, Brixton on 17 July at two o'clock
Light refreshments will be served afterwards
At the Muhammad Ali Youth & Leisure Centre

Mrs Gane was the mother of a dead colleague. I remembered her as a tiny, soft-spoken lady who wore hats like the Queen and who had not lost her Jamaican accent after half a century in South London.

Her son, Curtis, had been a Detective Inspector when I first came to Savile Row. On the night that we raided a paedophile ring operating out of an abandoned mansion on The Bishop's Avenue, Curtis Gane had stepped back on a derelict staircase to avoid a man holding a black carbon lock knife with a four-inch blade and had fallen two storeys, landing on his back and breaking the vertebrae connecting his head to his spine. Curtis never walked again and he never came out of hospital. If he had lived longer, we would have become friends. But there was not enough time for friendship.

The last time I had seen Mrs Gane was on the rooftop of West End Central on the day that one hundred police officers watched in silence as she scattered her son's ashes to the wind. I felt a stab of sorrow at her passing as I looked at the invitation again. Father Marvin Gane was her other son. I should call him, I thought, as I walked into the loft with the black-edge funeral invitation in one hand and the junk mail in the other.

But then I stared at the TV and forgot all about calling him.

Because something was happening on Borodino Street.

A man with two small children – one in his arms, one holding his hand – was looking at the flowers that filled the street. And I knew immediately that what was left of DS Alice Stone's family were visiting Borodino Street for the first time.

I had seen the man and the children in images that the media and the well-wishers had harvested from social media. Holiday pictures, wedding photographs, all those stolen moments of happiness that seemed so distant now. The man was older and the children were bigger but it was unmistakably the same family, dumbstruck with grief in a world with a lost wife and mother.

The crowd did not take their eyes from the man as he murmured to the children. The oldest child reached out for a balloon. His tiny sibling smiled in the sunshine. The view cut to the helicopter that seemed to hover permanently above Borodino Street and I saw, at the end of the street, George Halfpenny's empty rickshaw.

And then the TV image of silent mourning was replaced by scenes of chaos. A red strapline was running across the bottom of the screen:

BBC BREAKING NEWS: FATHER OF TERRORIST BROTHERS RELEASED WITHOUT CHARGE

Outside the blue-etched concrete block of Paddington Green Police Station, an excited pack of photographers and reporters hemmed in the diffident figure of Ahmed 'Arnold' Khan, and were leaning across a pair of beefy uniformed officers to bark questions in his face. Khan was still in the London Transport uniform he had been wearing in the holding cell of West End Central and he looked even thinner after his time in custody.

'This is coming to you from Paddington Green Police Station,' the presenter murmured as the screen filled with a ruck of bodies and noise, cameramen and reporters cursing each other as they jostled for position. 'We apologise for some of the industrial language but this is coming to you live,' said the presenter, as if that explained everything. He added a warning that 'this report does contain flashing lights'.

When a semblance of order had been restored, I saw that DC Edie Wren and TDC Joy Adams were standing just behind the officers protecting Ahmed Khan.

In front of him was a dapper-looking man in his fifties with a great mane of swept-back silver hair. I recognised him immediately as Sir Ludo Mount – Queen's Counsel, media star, the Elvis of human rights lawyers.

Sir Ludo began to speak in his booming upper-class tones, a voice that was accustomed to being heard and obeyed, and the baying mob of hacks and paps fell into a disgruntled silence.

'My client, Mr Khan, has suffered a travesty of justice,' Sir Ludo intoned. 'You do not lose your human rights because your children have allegedly committed a crime. You do not forsake your human dignity because of innocent contact.'

The reporters burst into voice.

'Are you claiming that the Khan brothers *didn't*—'

Sir Ludo silenced them like a schoolmaster from another age with a blaze of fire in his eyes and steel in his voice and the hint of a damn good thrashing in his study after double games.

'My client has been grotesquely mistreated by the Metropolitan Police, the right-wing gutter press and – indeed – this country. Mr Khan is an innocent man and today the Metropolitan Police have at last conceded his innocence.' Mount paused dramatically. 'But this is not the end of his fight for justice. It is only the beginning. I want a total reappraisal of the way firearms are used in this country. I want a formal apology from

126

the Metropolitan Police. And pending the verdict of the IPCC, I wish to bring a civil case against Detective Constable Raymond Vann. Good day.'

As if he were the king of London, Sir Ludo Mount gave an imperceptible nod to one of the uniformed policemen and the sweating coppers used their bulk to create a path through the pack of reporters.

Sir Ludo followed them and everyone else followed him in single file, Ahmed Khan, Edie and Joy Adams, a terrified-looking young woman who I saw was the same Family Liaison Officer who had been with Mrs Khan and Layla, and finally some more big uniformed officers bringing up the rear.

And all the while Sir Ludo had been addressing the media with Ahmed Khan blinking nervously at his side, there were two panels in the corner of the TV screen, one of them showing the scene in Borodino Street where a bereaved husband and two small children who had lost their mother were looking at the flowers, and the other, shot from a news helicopter, showing the great black scar of Lake Meadows blighting a large area of West London. It did not look like a crime scene today. It looked like a mass grave.

Jackson Rose called me.

'Are you seeing all this?' he said. 'Ahmed Khan? Alice Stone's family? Lake Meadows? And this tank-chasing lawyer?'

TONY PARSONS

'I see it.'

'Your mob are going to be looking after the old man while this slick brief keeps shouting about human rights and compensation and the flowers for the dead keep piling up.' A pause. 'You're going to be the most hated man in the country, Max.'

'What do you reckon, Jackson? Should I transfer to traffic duty?'

'No,' he said. 'But you should learn how to shoot.'

12

The safe house was on one of those streets where they were moving out the students and the working class and moving in the trust fund managers and the bankers. It was south of the river, Elephant and Castle way, but in eighteen months it would look like the future.

Building work was everywhere – scaffolding and skips, the constant buzz of drills, the calls of the men in a dozen languages. Already it hardly looked like South London.

I thought Flashman and CTU would have assigned a couple of plain-clothes officers to watch over the safe house, an age-appropriate man and woman pretending to be lovers, but there was only a detective I knew from New Scotland Yard, a large man tucking into a meat pasty in an unmarked squad car. He gave me the nod as I parked the BMW X5 and crossed the street to the nondescript door of a shabby terraced house that seemed untouched by the booming property market.

Edie Wren opened the door. I could hear a woman screaming, poised somewhere between hysterical grief and righteous fury. And I could hear placating voices, telephones ringing and Mrs Azza Khan raving in Urdu.

'Welcome to the nut house,' Edie smiled.

We went into the living room where Sir Ludo Mount was chairing a meeting at the dining table, his bright-eyed juniors sifting through files and tapping laptops and phones as Ahmed Khan sat quietly across from the lawyer. His wife was on the sofa screaming at a translator and the FLO and Layla sat miserably by her side, her long black hair falling across her face as she hid herself from the world.

'So they got Layla back from social services?' I asked.

'I got Layla back from social services,' Edie said. She glanced across at the teenager, her face softening. 'I made a few calls. The last thing she needs right now is being locked up in some care home. She's a really good kid, Max. And the only one I feel sorry for.'

'But the parents didn't do anything, Edie.'

'Apart from bringing those bastards into the world. Layla's the only truly innocent one among them.'

I looked at her.

'Don't worry,' she said. 'We'll keep the entire family safe from harm.'

TDC Adams was in a corner of the room hunched over her laptop.

'Curtis Gane's mother died,' I told Edie.

She nodded, trying to give the news the emotion and respect it deserved. I knew how much she had liked Mrs Gane. But there had been so much death recently. From Lake Meadows to Borodino Street, life in our city had increasingly resembled life in wartime. There was hardly time to process one loss before the next loss and then the next.

'Any death threats?' I said.

'You kidding?' Edie said. 'I've lost count of the people threatening to top the Khans. The BBC showed Mr Khan leaving custody just as Alice Stone's orphaned children were looking at all those flowers.' She paused to stare at the bus driver and lowered her voice, although no one could hear her with Mrs Khan at full volume. 'There's a lot of real anger out there, Max. Some of it is just the usual social media barking, but some of it is serious enough to be a cause for concern.' She pulled out her phone and called up Twitter. 'Bad Moses has been trending.'

'Bad Moses?'

She handed me her phone. 'Try to keep up, Max. Bad Moses just posted another message. Look.'

The Twitter account @BadMoses displayed a small colour photograph of a righteously enraged man with long flowing white hair and a flowing white beard holding a stone tablet above his head.

'Father Christmas?' I said.

'Close,' Edie said. 'It's Charlton Heston as Moses in Cecil B. DeMille's *The Ten Commandments*,' she said. 'Academy Award for Best Picture in 1956. I Googled it. There are reams of the stuff but this gives you a taste. Additional dialogue from the Bible.'

I read the message.

Do not avenge yourselves, beloved, but leave room for God's wrath. For it is written – VENGEANCE IS MINE; I WILL REPAY, SAYS THE LORD. #LakeMeadows #BorodinoStreet #AliceStoneRIP #BadMoses

The message was accompanied by an attached snatched image of Ahmed Khan leaving Paddington Green. It had an alarming number of likes and re-Tweets.

I gave Edie back her phone.

'You run this down?' I said.

I thought of what the woman from MI5 had told me.

We can't watch all of them, DC Wolfe. Because there are too many.

'Colin is trying to dig out the IP address of Bad Moses,' Edie said.

Colin was Colin Cho of PCeU – the Police Central e-crime Unit, tasked with responding to the most serious crimes on the Internet.

'But Bad Moses is running his posts through some kind of anonymiser like Tor or 12P, like they have in the Deep Web, the state-of-the-art anonymisers they use for distributing child pornography. So, realistically, Colin hasn't got much of a shot at locating an IP address.'

She glanced across at Ahmed Khan.

'There are plenty of other users on social media making threats against the Khans who are not hidden behind thick digital walls,' she said. 'We can turn Colin loose on them. We can run them down, knock on a few doors, drag them into the light and smack their bottoms to discourage the others.' She looked at me and shrugged. 'But we end up chasing inadequate little morons who don't have a life beyond playing with their mouse. And that doesn't make the Khan family any safer and doesn't make our job any easier. So maybe we should let Bad Moses rant and rave online while we are knocking on different doors.'

We joined TDC Adams in her quiet corner.

'Show him what you showed me, Joy,' Edie said.

I looked over Adams' shoulder at her laptop. It was a YouTube film shot on Borodino Street just after the husband and children of Alice Stone had left. The atmosphere had palpably changed. Grief had given way to rage.

In the middle of a crowd of young men, someone had filmed George Halfpenny on his soapbox, his voice cracking with emotion.

'This is a country where the wicked walk free and the good die fifty years before their time,' he was saying. 'A country where we applaud immigration without integration and then wonder why the newcomers have no respect for us, or our history, or our values. And so we dig our own graves – like the graves we have dug in Lake Meadows and on Borodino Street. And so we place upon the altar the bravest and the best of us. And so children lose their mother, and a husband sacrifices his wife. And for what? So that the scum of the earth can build a funeral pyre for all we love? Here on this street we have to decide – do we let them bully us, betray us and bury us? What do we need to do to finally remember *who we are* – and start fighting back? My friends, I beg you to remember and to never forget – this is *still our country*.'

The crowd roared. The phone's camera jerkily panned to the faces of one hundred young men with their blood up.

'*Still our country!*'

'*Still our country!*'

'*Still our country!*'

'George Halfpenny could tone down the rhetoric,' I told Edie. 'But no court is going to say those words constitute a death threat or even an incitement to violence.'

'I'm not worried about the rickshaw driver,' Edie said. 'It's all the people who are listening to him.'

I looked across at Ahmed Khan.

He smiled gently at me, and rose from the table to join us.

'When can I go home?' he asked.

'Mr Khan,' I said.

'Arnold,' he said.

'Arnold,' I said. 'I'm going to be issuing you an Osman warning. It means we consider there to be a real and immediate threat to your life.' I nodded at Sir Ludo Mount. 'Your lawyer will be familiar with the procedure. You will be given a letter from us telling you that your life may be in immediate danger and you should take all necessary precautions to protect yourself and your family. As an absolute minimum, I strongly advise against any attempt to return to your former home.'

He shook his head. 'I'm going home,' he said. 'And I am returning to work on Sunday.'

'You don't understand,' I began.

'No,' he said. '*You* don't understand. *I have not done anything wrong. And I wish to return to my life.*'

I looked at Edie.

'You've been in a cell at Paddington Green,' she said. 'I don't think you've any idea of what is happening on Borodino Street.'

'People are angry,' he said. 'They hate my sons for all the terrible things they did. And I understand. But their sin is not my sin.' He lightly placed his hand on my arm

135

for emphasis. 'In the end, every parent loses their child,' he said. 'I know now that I lost my sons long ago. But I want my life back. And I will not allow my sons – or anyone else – to steal it from me.'

Sir Ludo Mount joined us, giving me a little nod and completely ignoring Edie and Joy.

The sleek old brief had a curiously offhand attitude to police officers of all ranks, as if we were dimwitted room service waiters who were hanging around for a tip.

'I don't think it is safe for Mr Khan to return home,' I said.

'Mr Khan is going home to Borodino Street as soon as his property is no longer deemed a crime scene,' Sir Ludo told me, as if I had not spoken. 'I understand from my sources that will be formally declared over the next twenty-four hours.' The lawyer waved a well-manicured and dismissive hand. 'Issue your Osman warning and leave us.'

I took a breath.

'Do you seriously want to put this family in harm's way?' I said. 'Because that is exactly what is going to happen if they return to Borodino Street. Is that really what you want?'

A faint flush appeared on Sir Ludo's heavily moisturised chops.

'What do I *want*?' he said. 'Is that your question?'

He gave me the full theatrical blaze of outrage that had wowed a thousand courtrooms.

'I want a complete investigation into the shoot-to-kill policy of the Metropolitan Police,' he said. 'That's what I want. And I want a formal apology to the Khan family. I want a reappraisal of the way firearms are used in this country. I want all of that, and I want it done as soon as possible. And I want your colleague SFO DC Raymond Vann to be brought to justice for the death of Adnan Khan in that basement.'

'I'm just trying to keep your client alive, sir,' I said.

'And I promise you that you will be in serious trouble if you fail to do so,' he said.

He left us, and with an apologetic smile, Ahmed Khan joined Sir Ludo and his well-spoken helpers at the dining table. They were young, eager, hard-working and totally in thrall to their famous master.

The YouTube film was still running on Joy's laptop.

I could hear the anger of the mob and I could feel their appetite for blood.

'What's the drill?' Edie said. 'When someone wants to return home to the scene of a serious crime? To somewhere like Borodino Street?'

I shook my head. *There is no drill*, Whitestone had told me on the Thames Path. Suddenly I was very tired.

'If it is no longer a crime scene, and if Mr Khan wants to go home, then we can warn him, and we can advise him against it and we can hope that he uses common sense,' I said. 'But we can't stop him.'

'That selfish, stubborn old bastard,' Edie said. 'It's not just him going back there, is it?'

And on the other side of that safe house, Layla Khan pushed back her long black hair from her face, looked across at Edie, and I saw her smile for the first time.

13

The noise on a firing range mangles your senses.

The close proximity of continuous live gunfire is the opposite of deafening. When you stand in one of the booths at the Metropolitan Police Specialist Training Centre in Gravesend, Kent, discharging live rounds from a Glock 17, your inner ear does not miss a thing. You feel every shot being fired in your nerve ends. You can hear everything. You can hear the blood in your veins.

Despite the ear and eye protection that we all wore inside our booths, insulating every shooter into his or her own little world, a world that narrows down to you and your gun and your target, and despite every effort to muffle the murderous racket with high, thick panels that divide the shooters, every shot fired seemed to find its own echo somewhere in the back of my brain.

The eye protection that I wore to protect me from flying fragments of spent brass steamed up every few minutes with a fine film of mist. Again and again, I had to – very carefully – place the Glock 17 on the counter before me and swab off the foggy lenses before I picked up the gun and aimed again at the target twenty-five metres away.

'It's amazing how many gun club civilians shoot at a target that is way over twenty-five metres away,' Jackson said, having to raise his voice above the muffle of the headphones. 'You try explaining in a court of law how you shot someone in self-defence who was twenty-five metres away. Good luck with that. This distance is good practice for your hand and eye. But if you want real world, then bring the target in to ten metres or less. That's where they are going to be when you want to make them think again.'

I had heard many shots fired in anger. But that was always sporadic firing that seemed to come out of nowhere, and although it cracked open the very air, it was over before your mind had a chance to register what had just happened. This was different. This was a universe of gunfire. And as I learned to rack the slide back to check the firearm was unloaded, as I learned to load the magazine, and to grip the gun, and to keep my finger off the trigger until I was ready to shoot, I also had to learn to control my heart.

Jackson was having a wonderful time.

We had always been as competitive as brothers, and as he stood with me in the firing booth, his hands sometimes running over the stubby black Glock like a virtuoso tuning an instrument for a novice student – showing me the correct technique for loading or dropping a magazine, demonstrating his steady and unwavering grip, telling me how to pass him a loaded Glock without pointing it at his head – through the nerve-jangling mist that steamed up my eyewear, I saw him smiling with gappy-toothed delight.

'Centre of mass,' he said. 'Think about that, Max. We are training to shoot at the largest part of the body – the torso. We are not learning to kill here. We are learning how to hit our target.'

I spent an hour emptying the Glock at paper targets – a bullseye on a black-and-white image of an armed man's torso. But the actual act of shooting was a tiny part of the lesson, seconds of murderous noise between the longer minutes of learning how to handle my firearm. Jackson talked me through the grind of manually loading the Glock, pushing the full-metal jacket cartridges into the magazine, the rear of the bullet towards the back of the gun, the act becoming physically harder as you loaded more bullets, as if warning of the seriousness of this enterprise.

'There's a speed clip for loading but you should know how to do it yourself,' said my teacher.

Jackson was a patient and good teacher, completely comfortable with a loaded gun in his hands, and always alert when that loaded gun was in mine.

After an hour I left him to it – his aim steady, his demeanour calm as gunfire carved a large black hole in the centre of a target – and I went off to the locker room, sticky with nervous sweat and looking forward to a shower.

The Gravesend training centre was huge, like an abandoned small town, or a large film set. There were make-believe streets with shops, pubs and houses, the carriage of a tube train and the fuselage of a plane.

The live-fire ranges included areas for shotguns, rifles and handguns, like the one where I had left Jackson. The crack and pop of live ammunition filled the air as officers made their way to lecture rooms.

Everywhere teemed with life and action and noise.

But the locker room was silent and empty apart from Ray Vann.

He gave me a tired smile when I walked in. He looked as though he had not slept since the day we went into Borodino Street. I sat down on the bench beside him, remembering Alice Stone singling him out in the jump-off van on the day that she died.

You OK, Raymond?

'You've been shooting with Jackson?' he said.

'He's trying to teach me,' I said. 'But it's hard. I can't imagine what it's like in a live situation. Someone shooting back at you, lousy visibility, your blood pressure off the scale.'

He gave me a rueful smile.

'Yes,' he said. 'That's even harder.'

We sat in silence.

'The IPCC interviewed me about Borodino Street,' I said.

'I know,' he said.

'I wish I could help you more, Ray. But there's no more I can do.'

I'm not going to rat him out, I thought.

But I am not going to lie for him.

'I appreciate what you've done,' he said, not looking at me. Eye contact seemed difficult for him. Today and every day. 'You've done enough for me, Max.'

He said it without any bitterness or sarcasm.

'How's it going?' I said.

'Fine,' he said, when it was anything but fine. 'Jackson told you, I guess – me and him, we were both temporarily suspended because we discharged our weapons. We were both boarded.'

Boarding meant they had gone before an interview board of senior officers on the top floor of New Scotland Yard to justify their actions.

'But Jackson is going back on active duty. There's even talk of him getting the QPM.'

The Queen's Police Medal is awarded to serving police officers for gallantry or distinguished service.

'And I'm not getting a medal,' Ray Vann said. 'But I might get jail time for unlawful killing.'

'Ray,' I said, with more conviction than I felt. 'That's not going to happen. They're not going to do you for unlawful killing. Adnan Khan was a mass murderer. He was a stone-cold killer. He was a terrorist. Adnan and his brother brought down that helicopter over Lake Meadows. His brother murdered Alice Stone. Adnan Khan was not an innocent man.'

'I've been removed from operational duty,' he said, not hearing me, or perhaps unable to believe me. 'There's evidence of unlawful conduct, see, in the trajectory of the GSW.'

Gunshot wound.

'You see, Max, they don't quite buy my line that he was going for a weapon – or maybe those hand grenades that we heard so much about.' He stared at the floor. 'The IPCC have put it to me that I shot Adnan Khan when he was on his knees and attempting to surrender himself to my custody,' he said. 'And even if I don't get done for unlawful killing, there's talk that this big shot human rights lawyer –the one with all the silver hair? – will bring a civil case against me if the IPCC decide that it was a lawful killing. And then there's the DPS.'

The Department of Professional Standards – the internal police complaints unit that investigates all police shootings.

'So – whatever happens – I am going to get whatever they decide to give to me.' And now he finally looked me in the eye. 'They're not going to let me walk away from it, Max.'

He was a decent man. I wished there was more that I could do for him.

'You served in Afghanistan, didn't you, Ray?'

'Yes.'

'Did you know Jackson when you were out there?'

He smiled his shy smile.

'I was regular army. Jackson was something else. Something more. Jackson was playing with the big boys.'

He looked at me to see how much I knew.

'I know Jackson was Special Forces,' I said. 'But I bet it was hard enough in the regular army.'

'We don't talk about it,' he laughed. 'Because we wouldn't know where to start.'

'Tell me,' I said.

He stared at me until he believed that I really wanted to know. Then he took a breath and tried his best.

'Twice a day we went on patrol and I had mates – too many mates – who had their legs and balls blown off by IEDs. Then, when the twice-a-day patrol was over, we went home to a camp with no running water, and no refrigerator, and no roof – all the better for the Taliban to lob in grenades. Our superior officers didn't visit us because it was too dangerous. And then we would go out on another patrol and the legs and the bits of bodies that our mates – living and dead – had left behind would

TONY PARSONS

be tied to trees. And the Taliban knew that we left
nobody behind, living or dead, so they would booby-trap
the bodies – and the bits and pieces – of dead men. Very
young, they were. Very young dead men, Max, their
body parts up there in the trees. It was worse for the
boys they took prisoner, of course. Castration. Scalping.
Skinning alive. The usual Afghan hospitality.'

I looked away because the tears had started and his
face was contorting with fierce effort as he tried to stop
them. There was a choking sound in his throat that was
not from emotion but his struggle to control emotion.

When the terrible sound had stopped I looked back
at him and he was dry-eyed now and smiling at me in
that gentle, diffident manner he had.

And finally I understood exactly why, just before we
went into Borodino Street, Alice Stone had asked him
how he was doing.

It was still just the two of us in that locker room.

I leaned closer to him.

'What happened in that basement, Ray?' I said.

'They brought the war home, Max,' he said. 'And so
did we.'

14

The next day the bulldozers and the skips went in to Borodino Street before first light and behind them a parameter was set up to keep members of the public a mile away from the clean-up operation. Early rising residents were free to come and go but when the first members of the public started arriving, they were politely stopped at the perimeter by uniformed officers and gently relieved of their flowers.

Borodino Street was cleared of flowers with as much respect and dignity as we could muster. Our press office released a statement saying that dying flowers would be used as fertiliser while fresh bouquets would be donated to local hospitals. Condolence cards, poems and letters were all carefully collected for the bereaved family of Alice Stone, should they wish to see them, while teddy bears and other toys would be donated to children's charities.

But it was over.

In the roads surrounding Borodino Street, white vans full of police in riot gear waited for crowd trouble that never came. Their mood was joyful, almost euphoric, coppers who were happy and relieved to learn that they were not going to have anything thrown at their heads in the next few hours. Always a good feeling.

Members of the public were still arriving to pay their respects, and to lay their flowers, and to witness the great festival of mourning, but they did not protest or seem surprised when they were denied access to Borodino Street, and they were grateful when their flowers were taken from them by young uniformed policemen and women with real and unforced tenderness.

There were no photographers around when the bulldozers were filling the skips with their loads of rotting bouquets. By the time the sun was over the rooftops, the first convoy of lorries was already driving away, the battered yellow skips piled high with dead flowers, acres of cellophane flashing in the sunshine. Wary residents woke up and peered from their windows, as if not quite believing what they were seeing. Borodino Street was returning to something approaching normal.

The Met are good at this kind of thing. From Princess Diana to suddenly dead rock and pop stars, we have had a lot of practice. But there comes a point where a city street has to stop being a shrine.

'How can anyone live here now?' Edie said. 'This is no place for a teenage girl to be growing.'

We were standing outside the Khan family home. The place was a ruin. The search teams had torn up the floorboards, ripped open the walls and collapsed the ceilings, dumping the debris in the front garden.

'You saved Layla from care,' I said. 'But you can't save her from her home.'

I suggested we get some breakfast inside us. It was going to be a long day.

Because in the afternoon they were burying Alice Stone.

The police had their own wake that evening.

The Fighting Temeraire is an old-fashioned pub round the back of Victoria, close enough to New Scotland Yard to be annexed by the Met for important occasions.

When I arrived with Edie and Joy at just after six the place was already heaving. One hundred hungry, beer-bleary eyes turned on the two women.

'Or I might just go home,' Adams said.

Edie laughed and took her by the hand.

'We're not scared of this lot,' she said. 'Come on.' They pushed their way into the mob and were lost to me.

The Fighting Temeraire is one of those pubs that prides itself on being untouched by the modern world. There was no music, no dining area, no frills, although it does have giant TV screens for sport.

But tonight they were not showing any sport.

149

The entire pub looked up as they showed a clip from Alice Stone's funeral, the same clip that they had been showing at every news bulletin for the last few hours.

Alice's husband was standing by his wife's coffin, his face a map of a man enduring the unendurable, one small child in his arms and the other holding his hand, the mourners behind them totally silent. Then the clip was gone and the noise level rose. I saw Edie and Joy at the bar. Two young DIs from New Scotland Yard were on either side of them, trying their luck. And I saw that Edie was not interested in this man and, all at once, I understood that TDC Joy Adams was not interested in any man, not in that way.

Edie caught my eye and smiled. I smiled back.

And then a shoulder slammed into me.

I stared into the face of the pale young man with the wispy beard who had carried a shotgun he never used to Borodino Street. I was about to apologise. Then I saw Jesse Tibbs didn't want my apology.

'You've been sucking up to the IPCC,' he said. 'You grassed on Ray Vann. If he goes down for unlawful killing, I will make you crawl, Wolfe.'

I turned to his friends, a silent invitation to intervene before it was too late.

'Leave it, Jesse,' one of them said without much enthusiasm. And that was it. They were letting him off his leash.

'I don't suck up to anyone,' I told Tibbs. 'Why don't you go and have another drink? Not that you need one.'

I made to move past him but he put his free hand on my chest. The other hand held a beer bottle by the neck.

'I heard your mob has been babysitting that murdering Paki bastard,' he said.

I stared at his friends again but they were not going to do me any favours here.

Then Ray Vann was there, staring at me as if we had never met.

I thought I recognised some of the others from the jump-off van but it was difficult to tell now they were not in PASGT helmets and Kevlar.

'Ahmed Khan didn't murder anyone,' I said deliberately.

'Come on, Jesse, have a drink,' said one of his companions. They eyeballed me evenly. It did not feel like we were on the same side tonight.

Tibbs' gaze slid away from me as his mouth twisted with fury.

'Hey,' I said, getting his attention again. 'Did you hear me, pal? *That old man didn't kill anyone.* He didn't kill the people who died when the helicopter came down and he didn't kill Alice Stone. So don't waste your feelings on him. Save it for someone who deserves it.'

Tibbs' friends were putting their hands on him.

He furiously shrugged them off.

He tapped his beer bottle against my chest.

'I'm warning you,' he slurred, and I suddenly saw just how drunk he was. 'You tell me where that safe house is – you tell me where West End Central are babysitting this scumbag – because I'm going round there tonight … '

'Tibbs,' Jackson said, appearing by his side. 'Jesse. Shut it.'

'Why do you always have to watch his back?' Tibbs demanded.

I shook my head. 'Why do you hate that old man?'

'Are you fucking shitting me?' Tibbs screamed. 'Because he raised those evil bastards! Why do you give a toss about him?'

'Because he's an innocent man.'

'Innocent? You really believe that?'

'His sons were poison. He drives buses.'

I pushed past him. His friends half-heartedly tried to restrain him but Tibbs came after me, shouting abuse.

I was not going to do anything unless he put his hands on me.

And that was what he did, his palms slick with sweat and lager on my shoulders, one of them still holding that bottle as he pulled at my T-shirt.

And that was all a bit silly.

He should have just hit me from behind with his bottle.

With his hands on my shoulders, Tibbs was wide open. I half-turned and hit him with a short left hook to the ribcage and he sank down on one knee like someone who had never felt a body shot before.

A wave of sickness and sadness washed over me.

I did not want to fight this man but I knew I might not have a choice. I waited to see if he wanted to take it further.

But he just rubbed his aching ribs as he slowly got to his feet.

'Next time,' he said.

'Next time you better bring your gun,' I said.

I walked back to West End Central.

There were tourists at the end of Savile Row, photographing the outside of number 3, where the Beatles played their last ever gig on the rooftop in 1969, grinning and making peace signs and excited at the proximity of the ghosts of John, Paul, George and Ringo.

I watched one of the tourists pay their rickshaw driver.

George Halfpenny thanked them in Mandarin.

'I heard that you closed down Borodino Street,' he said.

I shook my head.

'We opened it up,' I said. 'We opened it up for the people who live there. Your adoring fans are going to have to catch you at some other venue.'

'I don't have fans. Just some people who listen to what I have to say. Why does that bother you so much?'

'I'm afraid some of them haven't read as many books as you have, George.' I indicated his rickshaw. 'Are you free?'

'Are you making fun of me?'

'No.'

He looked at the Chinese tourists.

'Where you going?'

'Bar Italia,' I said. 'It's on Frith Street.'

'I know where the Bar Italia is,' he said.

I eased myself into the back of his rickshaw.

George Halfpenny stood up on his bike and put some beef into it, transporting me to Soho with real professional pride, as if he wanted to show me that he was far more than a rickshaw driver, far more than a coolie for tourists, as if he wanted to prove that his muscle and sinew and animal strength had been built up over the course of a thousand years.

15

It was still early on Sunday morning when Stan and I strolled across Victoria Park, the time when there was nobody around apart from the serious runners and the dog walkers who rose at the same time whatever the season. Stan sniffed the air with interest, but there was a hint of suspicion in his huge round eyes. These were not the scents of his usual Sunday walk on Hampstead Heath.

It was a short walk from Victoria Park to Borodino Street where a few stray petals were the only reminder of the sea of flowers that had been laid for Alice Stone. But there were no crowds, no reporters, no photographers and no police. Perhaps the press was all waiting at the bus station where Ahmed Khan was going to work the Sunday shift. Yes, that was the money shot for the morning news.

Stan and I walked the length of that small road, my dog delicately sniffing every lamppost and garden gate before cocking his rear right leg and leaving his mark.

He still had one leg cocked in the air when Ahmed Khan came out of his house wearing his London Transport bus driver's uniform and carrying a lunch box. His wife, Azza, and granddaughter, Layla, stared at me over his shoulder.

Mrs Khan tugged at her hijab, gave Layla a push backwards and shut the door behind him without a word.

'Morning, Arnold,' I said.

'They make you do this?' he said. 'They make you watch over me?'

I indicated Stan. 'Does he look like a police dog to you? It's my day off. I'm just checking in on you. Seeing how you're doing.'

In truth there was a part of me that had not believed that he would leave the safe house and return home. I did not believe that anyone would so blithely ignore an Osman warning. I did not believe that anyone could be that stubborn, stupid and brave.

'It's not necessary,' he said.

A police car turned into the street. It slowly passed us, two faces turned towards us without expression, one white and one black, bleary with lack of sleep, clearly at the tail end of the night shift, and then accelerated away.

'They come every few hours,' he said. 'Just drive past and do not stop.'

'I'm surprised they come as often as that,' I said. 'Is it good to be home?'

He gestured at the little front garden. The torn plaster, piles of brickwork and ripped-out floorboards.

'They have destroyed my home,' he said.

I felt something harden in me. 'Blame your sons,' I said.

'I don't blame anyone.'

We stared at each other in silence.

'What do you want from me?' he said.

'I was going to drive you to work. Victoria Bus Station, right?'

'Don't you have a family that needs you on a Sunday?'

'I have a seven-year-old daughter. But she's a very popular little girl. She gets invited to lots of parties and social events. She's doing her own thing. I'm just here to provide a taxi service.'

There had been a sleepover with Scout's Australian friend Mia last night and today Mia's mum was taking the pair of them to an eighth birthday party at the Everyman cinema in Hampstead. I found that I was smiling with pride that my daughter was in such demand.

'Come on, Arnold,' I said. 'I'll drive you to work. My car's parked just by Victoria Park.'

He shook his head.

'I don't need a lift,' he said. 'I will get the tube. Thank you – I know you are trying to be kind. But I just want life to go back to normal.' He hesitated, as if understanding that was asking a lot. 'My colleagues at work – I want

157

to see them. I told you before — I had to win their acceptance when I first came to this country.'

I nodded.

'I remember. Working on all the days when they did not want to work,' I said. 'Working at Christmas. Working on Sundays.'

'And in the end they accepted me. *All right, Arnold, mate?* They called me mate. They called me Arnold. And now I know I have to win their acceptance again.'

'You might have to work a bit harder this time.'

'I know.' He hung his head. 'After everything that has happened on this street. After all the misery and death caused by my sons. But that is them, not me. I have to show my colleagues that I am still the same man.'

I said nothing. It seemed unlikely that he would win hearts and minds by driving the number 73 from Victoria Bus Station to Stoke Newington Common. But what else could he do?

I saw his hands shaking on his Tupperware lunch box.

'The alternative is to hide in shame and fear,' he said, answering my question.

He didn't want me watching his back. He didn't want a lift to work. He simply wanted to return to a life that I knew — and perhaps he did too — had gone forever.

So Stan and I walked with him to the tube station.

He paused at the ticket barrier with his Oyster card in his hand.

'Why are you trying to help me?' he said, his eyes sliding away and then finally meeting mine.

'Because you don't deserve to die,' I said.

And then Ahmed Khan went to work.

Early in the afternoon I waited for Scout outside the Everyman cinema in Hampstead, checking the progress of Ahmed Khan's bus on the news.

The press had been waiting for him at Victoria Bus Station and his return to work was the lead item on the news for most of the morning. But by the time Stan and I were waiting for Scout to come out of a private birthday girl screening of *My Neighbour Totoro*, the interest in Ahmed Khan's return to work had started to wane.

The number 73 is one of the great London bus routes, crossing a vast swathe of the city from west to north and taking in some of the main attractions – Hyde Park, Park Lane, Marble Arch, Oxford Street, the British Library – before veering north at King's Cross for Angel, Islington and beyond, ending its journey at Stoke Newington and then making the trip back across town.

When Ahmed Khan left Victoria Bus Station he was carrying a busload of reporters and photographers. They took their pictures of the slight, serious, painfully thin man settling himself at the wheel of the big red bus, and he could do nothing to prevent that, but when they barked their questions, he resolutely failed to reply.

When I looked at the news on my phone as I waited for Scout, Ahmed Khan was halfway through his Sunday shift. Already the reporters were drifting off, called away by deadlines and a man who, they saw, just wanted to be left alone to do his job.

There were no incidents with members of the public.

Scout came out of the cinema with Mia, breathless with excitement.

'Can I go rowing on the Thames? Can I do that? Is it all right? Is it? I want to do the rowing thing, Daddy.'

Mia's mother confirmed the invitation. The family lived in Pimlico, down by the river, and these sunny, summer Sunday afternoons were spent on the water. So Stan and I found a dog-friendly café – Hampstead was full of them – and he settled at my feet to nibble happily on pieces of toasted buttered bagel.

My ex-wife called just as I was paying the bill.

And I stared at her incoming call, deciding if I should answer it or not, wondering what fleeting fancy it was this time, what new disruption to our daughter's settled life she was planning, and how much more I should take before calling an end to it forever.

Scout was a happy child but it was a happiness that had been hard-won, as happiness is always hard-won for the children of divorced parents.

But I answered Anne's call, reflecting that maybe I should have deleted her number by now.

There was silence, and the sound of a child in the background, echoes from another life in a different home. And then finally my ex-wife spoke.

'I think Scout should live with me now,' she said.

I waited at the tube station for Ahmed Khan, a knot of sick dread in the pit of my stomach. It was early evening now and the heat of the day had built into something oppressive, the dust and fumes of the fag end of the hot weekend in the city wiping away the memory of that crisp clean early Sunday morning.

I heard the screams before I saw him.

The men and women in their summer clothes came before him like heralds, running from the tube station, faces aghast with disbelieving horror. They leapt the ticket barrier and shoved past the ticket collector as if they were fleeing a fire.

And then I saw him.

Ahmed Khan staggered towards the ticket barrier.

A space had opened up around him, as if what ailed him was contagious, as if he was diseased, as if he brought death with him.

His face looked bewildered.

This is how it ends?

The knife had been plunged into the base of his neck where it met his left shoulder blade. It is exactly the point where the subclavian artery pumps blood to the arms and neck. The subclavian is a large artery, difficult to miss if you know what you are aiming at. You cut it when you want to kill. An arterial spurt of blood had drenched Ahmed Khan's left arm and the front of his bus driver's uniform.

And as I reached him, I saw the knife itself.

The blade was buried two inches into his body, but I could still read the inscription on the blade. *Blut und Ehre*, it said. I saw the nickel-plated pommel, and the grip of black Bakelite with the gold-etched black swastika on a red-and-white diamond.

He opened his mouth to speak and a thick bubble of black blood escaped his throat.

'Layla,' he gasped. 'Who will take care of Layla?'

Then he collapsed into my arms and we sank to the ground together, holding each other. I could hear the sirens coming for him above the screams.

They were there in five minutes.

But Ahmed Khan was dead in my arms before then.

It was TDC Joy Adams who saw the graffiti.

The tube station was a murder scene now. The CSIs were all over it. The Divisional Surgeon had pronounced Ahmed Khan dead and the mortuary van had taken his body away. I covered my blood-stained T-shirt with a fleece I got from one of the local coppers. By the time

Edie and Joy arrived there was nothing to do but notify his next of kin. The three of us walked to Borodino Street.

I rang the doorbell and Layla answered, the fear already on her face. It is always the same when someone opens the door and police are standing there. They look at you and they are afraid. And they are right to be afraid. The news we bring is never good.

'Is your grandmother home?' I said.

'What's wrong?' she said, and I was struck by how different she sounded to her grandparents. All I heard in her voice was the accent of the East End, all I heard was the sound of someone who knew no other home. 'I heard the sirens. Is it my Papa-Papa?'

'Please, Layla,' Edie said gently, her face white with concern, her hands resting on the girl's arms. 'Get your grandmother for us.'

Joy Adams had remained on the street. She was staring at debris in the tiny front garden.

'You need to see this, Max,' she called to me.

One of the floorboards had been propped on its side and separated from the rest. There were numbers, five of them, written with some kind of thick black magic marker, carefully etched into the ruined wood. Next to the ramshackle pile, this floorboard looked posed, as if the world needed to see this message. Had I seen those numbers this morning when I met Ahmed Khan as he

163

left for work? Were they there already? Had I stared straight through them?

'You see it?' Joy said.

20:8–11

'What is that?' I said.

Edie Wren, of London-Irish Catholic stock, joined us as Layla went to fetch her grandmother. She looked from the numbers to Joy.

'It's a chapter and verse from the Bible, isn't it?' Edie said. 'What book is that from?'

'It's from Exodus,' Joy said without hesitation. 'The second book of Moses. Chapter twenty, verses eight to eleven.' She looked at me. 'It's the Fourth Commandment.'

'And what's the Fourth Commandment?' I asked her.

'Remember the Sabbath day,' Joy said. She didn't even have to google it. 'And keep it holy.'

From inside the house on Borodino Street, a woman began to scream.

16

My ex-wife still turned heads.

And as Anne walked into the Fleet Street café first thing Monday morning, her husband a faithful half-step behind her, I saw that she would always turn heads.

When we had been together, there had been many furious scenes because some photographer or stylist thought that she was too old, or too fat, or too lacking in some flavour of the month to grace their glossy pages. But what did they know about real beauty? Hers was the kind of beauty that would never fade. Heads turned now, as they would in ten, twenty, thirty years' time.

Her husband – Oliver, I thought, the guy is almost certainly called Oliver – attempted a smile at me. How many times had I seen him in my life? A handful. And I had never seen him dressed for work before. I recognised the Savile Row tailor that had made his lightweight summer suit because I had often stared in their window on my way to West End Central. I saw where their money came from. I saw why, once our little family had started falling apart, I could never compete. Anne had been looking for a life that her fading modelling career and a husband who was a young uniformed cop could never provide.

'This is why Scout is going to live with us, Max,' she said, sitting down. 'Because a child should be with her mother. Because we can provide a better life for her. And because it is what Scout wants.'

I placed my hands either side of a triple espresso. I took a breath.

'What makes you think that?'

'Because she *told* me! When she came to the *party*! I said – Scout, would you like to live here all the time? And she said – she got that serious little look she gets – and she said *yes*.'

'That was the sugar rush talking. That was birthday party politesse. And you should never ask a kid something like that. What's she going to say? She was in your home. She can't say no, can she?'

A nice Australian waiter arrived and we stopped arguing while he took their orders. Green tea for Anne and some complicated milky coffee for Oliver. The waiter left and Oliver stirred in his seat. He placed a comforting hand over Anne's hand, the one with a thin wedding band and a chunky diamond ring. Seeing that familiarity would have hurt me once. Not any more.

I realised suddenly that I no longer cared. Scars are like that. Once the pain stops, you forget they are even there.

'You walked out,' I said. 'You left us to get on with it. And we did. Scout and I have made a life together. I honestly don't get it. Why now?'

She contemplated her fingernails.

'People sometimes ask me how many children I have,' she said. 'They see me at the nursery on the nanny's day off. Or at the gym for my hot Pilates class. *How many have you got, Anne?* And it is hard. Because we have our little boys. But I have three children.'

I smiled at her. 'So you want Scout to live you because of – what? Social embarrassment?'

She flared up. 'Because I – we – can give her a better life. You don't do anything with her! As far as I can tell, all her free time is spent with that flea-bitten old mutt.'

It took me a long moment to realise that she was talking about Stan.

'Stan is part of our family.'

She guffawed. A guffaw is the only word for it – this contemptuous snort of disbelief. Definitely a guffaw.

'Oh, please! Scout's two brothers are her family. Her mother is her family. *Oliver* is her family. Her stepfather.'

I looked at Oliver. As far as I could tell, there was no connection between this man and my daughter. He tried to hold my eye contact but his gaze slid away. His phone beeped importantly.

'Scout should be doing ballet,' Anne said, and I could see that she had it all worked out in advance. 'Horse riding. It's what little girls *do*, Max. She should be learning an instrument.'

We paused as the waiter brought their drinks.

'Cello,' Oliver said, frowning at his complicated coffee. 'Viola.'

'You don't know her,' I told Anne, and I felt the bitter truth of it like a punch to the heart. 'Scout is such a good child. Smart and funny and kind.' I swallowed hard, thinking about the party invitations that filled her diary every weekend. 'But we did something to her, Anne.'

'I didn't do anything to her!' She looked at Oliver for confirmation. 'I fell in love. I made a new life. I was desperately unhappy with my old life. But I left *you* – not Scout.'

'It's the toughest thing in the world to admit,' I said. 'Children pay the price for divorce and they pay it all their lives. But now Scout's happy. She likes her best friend, Mia. She likes her dog. The flea-bitten old mutt, Stan. She likes our home. And when I tell her about the history of Smithfield, I know she's really listening. She likes drawing. When she sees a painting she likes, she buys me the postcard.'

I thought of the postcard of Edward Hopper's *Nighthawks* propped up in the bathroom mirror, Scout's Christmas present to me because she knew how much

I loved that painting, and unexpected tears sprung to my eyes. I blinked them away.

No, I thought. Not in front of these two strangers. No chance.

Oliver glanced at his watch. 'I've got that ten o'clock,' he reminded Anne, with a kind of drawling self-importance. What could possibly be more important in this world than Oliver's ten o'clock?

Anne nodded with understanding. I wondered how long they had scheduled for this meeting about the future of my daughter. Fifteen minutes? A quick cup of green tea?

Oliver signalled for the bill.

'I am not going to let you disrupt her life again,' I told Anne.

She raised her eyebrows and smiled. *'Again?'*

I recognised that gesture with a jolt. The studied amused contempt was one of her signature expressions. She was a total stranger to me now, but there were still gestures that I recognised so well. The worst of both worlds.

'Look,' she said, like the voice of all reason. 'I know you have found it hard to adjust to the failure of our marriage.'

I shook my head. 'It wasn't a failed marriage,' I said.

She looked at her husband and sighed. She thought I was insane.

169

'No marriage fails if it produces a child like our daughter,' I explained. 'We broke up. We got divorced. But – I just can't think of it as a failed marriage, Anne.' I leaned forward. I really wanted her to understand this part. 'You don't know Scout like I do. Our daughter will be better than us. She will be less angry than me. She will be less selfish than you.'

She didn't like that bit.

'Selfish? You don't even know me.'

'And you don't know Scout.' I said, as calm and reasonable as I could make it. 'You can't just come back and ruin everything. I'm not going to let you disrupt her life any more. Scout is staying with me.'

Anne looked at her husband.

He understood tough negotiations. He was familiar with the art of the deal. He knew when it was time to thump tables and jut out his manly jaw.

'We'll have to see what our lawyer says about that,' he said.

It was exactly the wrong thing to say to me, it was the wrong button to push, and suddenly I was on my feet with my hands on the lapels of his £3,000 Savile Row suit, dragging him to his feet, fighting the urge to rip his ears off, enjoying the pure terror in his eyes.

And then Anne was on her feet too and shouting my name.

I quickly let him go. Somehow a cup of herbal tea had shattered on the floor.

But nothing had happened.

He had pushed the wrong button but I had never touched him. Well, perhaps just a little bit.

'Do you think you can bully us, Max?' Anne's voice was shaking. 'Is that what you imagine? That you can intimidate us into going away? You want to punish me, that's what this is about, isn't it?'

'You can kid yourself all you want,' I said. 'I bet every absent parent who ever lived kidded themselves in the same way. But you can't do it, Anne. You can't walk away from Scout and still pretend to know her.'

Everyone was looking at us, enjoying the show.

The Australian waiter was back, pale-faced with fear.

'Leave or I'll call the police,' he told me.

Anne laughed with mocking contempt. That was one more gesture that I remembered from that other life.

'Scout stays with me,' I said.

17

DCI Pat Whitestone held up an evidence bag containing the knife that killed Ahmed Khan and the bright summer sunshine that poured into Major Incident Room-1 glinted on the thick silver blade, and the nickel-plated pommel, and the grip's gold-etched black swastika on its red-and-white diamond.

'Apparently it's the real thing,' I said. 'A Hitler Youth Dagger circa 1937; 26.6 centimetres long, 300 grams in weight. The blade has been sharpened quite recently but it's not a reproduction.'

I had seen hundreds of knives in my job. One night on The Bishop's Avenue, I had been stabbed with one of them. And as DCI Pat Whitestone stared at the knife inside its evidence bag, the old scar on my stomach throbbed with the memory.

Whitestone stared at the inscription on the blade.

Blut und Ehre,' I said, 'Blood and honour.'

'How hard would it have been to kill Ahmed Khan with this knife?' Whitestone said.

'Sharpened like that?' I said. 'Piercing the subclavian artery with it would take about as much effort as you would need for opening a bottle of wine. As long as you knew what you were doing.'

'Forensics?' Whitestone said.

'No prints on the handle,' Edie said, looking up from the report on her screen. 'That was too much to hope for.'

'Then any sign of the gloves the killer was wearing?' Whitestone said.

'Search teams are still looking for gloves, ma'am,' Edie said.

Whitestone looked at TDC Adams.

'Lesson for you here, Joy,' she said. 'As a general rule, killers don't take their gloves home for the weekly wash. They ditch them as soon as they can when they leave the crime scene. And – lucky for us – fingerprints can be found on the inside of gloves, but most villains are too stupid to know that. So if we find the ditched gloves then we are likely to find prints inside and – if we catch a break – those prints will be on IDENT1.'

Adams nodded. She got it.

IDENT1 is the database containing the fingerprints of ten million people who have had contact with the law. If Ahmed Khan's killer had ever been arrested, even if they had never been convicted of anything, then their prints would be on there.

'Who would have access to a weapon like this?' Whitestone said.

'A serious collector,' I said. 'You can't buy them on eBay. Not the real thing.'

Whitestone was still staring at the blade, as if it might reveal its secrets. Inside the evidence bag, the knife was contained in a weapons tube – a hard plastic shell – which was sealed with biohazard tape to prevent contamination of the blood on the blade.

MIR-1 was silent as Whitestone squinted at the Criminal Justice Act label on the evidence bag. The CJA label gave the evidence bag a unique identification number, named the tube station where it was recovered, the name of the CSI who had tagged and bagged it and – most important of all – the chain of custody showing the life of the item from the moment it had been recovered.

'How many CCTV cameras are on the London Underground, Max?'

'Over twelve thousand,' I said. 'But this is all we have of Ahmed Khan in the last minutes of his life.'

I hit my keyboard and the big HDTV screen on the wall of MIR-1 revealed the black-and-white CCTV image of a tube train pulling into a station.

The time stamp in the right-hand corner showed Sunday's date and the exact time I had arrived at the station. The doors of the tube train opened and the crowds emerged. I paused the film. Ahmed Khan was clearly visible in the centre of the screen.

'And this is from the entrance,' I said.

Another CCTV image appeared, sharper this time, with natural sunlight bursting at the edge of the frame. It was from the camera pointed into the station, recording the emerging crowds.

And now they were running.

There was no sound but some mouths were opened in a scream. I saw my back in the foreground, taking a tentative step forward, then halting – men and women rushing past me, some of them looking back with horror – and then there was Ahmed Khan, staggering towards the exit that he would never reach, the knife sticking out of the point where his neck met his shoulder blade.

'I reckon he was stabbed on the escalator,' I said. 'My guess – he was standing on the right-hand side, tired after working a long shift, looking forward to being home, and the killer was on the left-hand side, walking up, and punched in the blade as he passed.'

'Witnesses?' Whitestone said.

'We've got dozens of witnesses who saw him after he was stabbed,' Edie said. 'But nobody who saw the knife go in.'

'Hard to believe,' Whitestone said.

'If it was on the escalator then that's where everyone gets their signal back,' Edie said. 'So they missed the murder because they were all looking at their phones.'

Whitestone gently placed the evidence bag on her workstation. The sound of the traffic down on Savile Row drifted up through the open windows.

'Let me see the graffiti again,' Whitestone said.

TDC Adams called up a CSI photograph of the piles of planks outside the house on Borodino Street. In a tight close-up, the numbers were revealed.

20:8–11

'How many people would get that reference?' Whitestone asked.

Edie shrugged. 'I knew it was a chapter and verse numbers from the Bible. But I couldn't have told you it was one of the Ten Commandments.'

I shook my head. 'Not me,' I said.

Whitestone looked at Adams.

The silver crucifix around her neck shone against her dark skin. 'Of course,' the young TDC said. 'The Fourth Commandment – Exodus version, not Deuteronomy. The laws God gave to Moses on Mount Sinai. How many people would get that reference? There are two billion Christians worldwide and thirty million in this country.'

'Or it could be a false lead,' I said. 'I'm not sure I buy it that this is some Bible-basher. Ahmed Khan wasn't hated because he worked on Sundays. He was hated because his sons were mass murderers.'

'What about the mouthy guy with the funny haircut who was whipping up the crowd down there?' Whitestone said.

'George Halfpenny,' I said. 'No criminal record. And I never saw him advocating violence. But that doesn't mean he couldn't inspire it.'

'Put Mr Halfpenny down as a TIE subject,' Whitestone said.

Trace, Interview, Eliminate.

Whitestone was thinking aloud now. 'Media appeal for witnesses. Get some uniforms from downstairs to help with the H-2-H.' House to house enquiries. 'Interview Mr Khan's colleagues at Victoria Bus Station, Joy, see if he spoke of any direct threats,' she said. 'Edie, make enquiries with local taxi firms to see if any of their drivers had a fare late Sunday with blood on his hands.' She took off her glasses and cleaned them, giving her face that suddenly vulnerable look she got without her specs. Then she put them back on and she was once again the most experienced homicide cop in West End Central.

She looked at me.

'And they never found the two Cetinka hand grenades that were meant to be in that house?'

'They either never existed or they were removed from the premises before we went in,' I said.

'And we still haven't interviewed Ahmed Khan's wife yet?' she said.

'We are waiting for the OK from the doctor,' Edie said. 'Mrs Khan has been too heavily sedated since the murder.'

Adams cleared her throat. She almost raised her hand. 'Ma'am?'

'Go ahead, Joy,' Whitestone said.

'It's a long shot, but there could be images of who was with the victim on that train,' she said. 'There are a lot of websites, Twitter accounts and photo galleries dedicated to fellow passengers.'

We were all staring at her.

We did not understand. Under her ebony skin, Adams blushed.

'People take photographs of other passengers,' she said, spelling it out for us. 'Tubecrush and sites like that.'

'But why would they do that?' Whitestone said.

Adams blushed even more deeply. Edie laughed.

'Because they fancy them, right?' she said, and Adams nodded, grinning shyly.

'Nobody is going to take a picture of a knackered old bus driver,' Whitestone said.

'No,' Adams agreed. 'But someone might have taken a picture of his killer.'

Whitestone's personal phone rang. She listened for a while. 'He's busy,' she said, smiling at me. 'He's working.' Then her smile faded. 'Can it wait?' A beat. 'Understood.' When she hung up, she nodded at me.

'IPCC are back,' she said. 'And they want you down-stairs now.'

The same police Federation rep was waiting at the lift on the third floor, that teak-hard old cockney who cared about his clothes.

This time he looked worried.

'New information about the raid on Borodino Street,' he said. 'That's all I know. Sorry I didn't have a chance to give you a heads-up.'

The same two IPCC investigators were waiting for me, the young blonde and the crumpled old man. We shook hands without warmth or enthusiasm. This time it was the old boy who took the lead.

'I'm Gordon Hunt of the Independent Police Complaints Commission,' he told the tape. 'Also present is my colleague Marilyn Flynn of the IPCC and DC Wolfe of West End Central. DC Wolfe, could you please confirm that you have the appropriate police Federation representation?'

'I do.'

Hunt opened his file.

'This is a follow-up investigation into the two firing officers on Operation Tolstoy on Borodino Street. DC Wolfe – is there anything about your previous statement that you would like to amend, adjust or retract?'

Silence in the room.

I felt my rep shift uneasily beside me.

'No,' I said.

'That's your final answer?'

I stared at him. What was this? A game show?

'I have answered your question, sir.'

'I will remind you, DC Wolfe, that you informed Ms Flynn and I that you were not in the basement and therefore you did not see Adnan Khan make a sudden movement for a weapon and did not see C3 – SFO DC Raymond Vann – discharge his firearm.'

I am not going to rat him out.

But I am not going to lie for him.

'Correct.'

'And you're sticking with that story, are you?' the woman said.

My rep placed a hand on my arm.

Don't lose your rag.

'DC Wolfe has answered your question,' he said.

'As you know, C3 – Specialist Firearms Officer DC Vann – originally testified that you were in the basement and saw him discharge his weapon when Adnan Khan made a movement for a weapon,' Hunt said.

Originally? What did he mean *originally*?

The word hung in the air between us.

You OK, Raymond? You OK?

'Vann has changed his mind,' Hunt said, stripping him all at once of his Special Firearms Officer status, and his rank in the Met, and even his code in this IPCC investigation.

'Vann confessed,' Flynn said. 'He told us the truth.'

'Vann now says that he executed Adnan Khan,' Hunt said. 'Mr Khan was on his knees.'

'Surrendering,' Flynn said.

We stared at each other, letting the weight of this revelation settle between us.

But I was still not changing my story for these people. Even if Ray Vann had ratted himself out, I wasn't going to join in.

These bastards already had enough to put him away for life.

'This of course explains the trajectory of the fatal gunshot wound that killed Mr Khan,' Hunt said, almost smiling, clearly enjoying himself enormously. 'Mr Khan was on his knees. Vann shot him. He is no longer offering any excuses. He does not claim that Mr Khan was reaching for a firearm. He does not even suggest that he was angry about the death of SFO DS Alice Stone.'

'Raymond Vann now says that he killed that man in cold blood,' Flynn said. 'Everything about his version of events has changed.'

'Apart from one thing,' Hunt said. 'He still puts you in that basement.'

18

I came out of the meeting with the IPCC and drove to the East End.

There was a small shrine to Alice Stone under the blue lamp above the entrance to Leman Street Police Station, Whitechapel. The great tide of flowers that had washed up on Borodino Street was a fading memory now but here, at her place of work, they would never forget.

There were cards of condolences, addressed to her husband, on a neat pile of bouquets, some of them dying inside their cellophane, some fresh that morning, and cut from a newspaper there was one of the photographs that had been harvested from the happiest moments of her life.

Alice was on a hotel tennis court somewhere sunny, a baby under one arm. The baby was clearly teething, pressing its pink gums into the tennis ball it was clutching as Alice laughed with joy in her life and delight at her luck.

'People feel they know her,' Jackson Rose said. 'People who never met her. And I suppose they do.'

He must have come out of the station but I had not been aware of his presence until he spoke. There were three new sergeant stripes on the sleeve of his jacket.

'Is Ray Vann inside?' I said.

Jackson nodded, his eyes still on the photograph of Alice Stone.

'What happened to him?' I said.

Now he looked at me. 'Ray came clean,' he said.

'And why the hell did he do that, Jackson?'

He shrugged.

'You better ask him yourself.'

We got the lift down to the shooting range in the basement. Jackson swiped us in with his card. The whip-lash crack of live ammunition filled the air.

There was an armoury desk to the right where weapons were checked in and out and, to the left, a line of firing booths, all of them occupied by officers wearing headphones and eyeglasses, squeezing off shots at paper targets that were as far away as twenty-five metres and as close as ten.

Ray Vann was in the far booth, his firing arm steady as a pool cue as he blew out the bullseye of a paper target of an armed man, his shots placed so perfectly together that the hole in the target could have been put there by a shotgun. There was someone with him in the booth.

Jesse Tibbs.

'You got promoted,' I said to Jackson as we watched Vann squeezing off his shots.

'Yes,' he said. 'When we slot someone we always get a medal or a jail sentence. One or the other.'

There was a TV on the wall behind the armoury desk. Sir Ludo Mount was giving a press conference.

'In the light of fresh revelations, I can reveal that the IPCC will be recommending to the Crown Prosecuting Service that the death of Adnan Khan be prosecuted as murder,' the lawyer said to a forest of microphones. 'My client – Mrs Azza Khan, the mother of Adnan Khan – will also be filing a civil lawsuit against the Metropolitan Police and relevant individuals.'

Jackson nodded at the TV and the uniformed sergeant on the armoury desk hit the mute button.

Jesse Tibbs came out of the end booth, holding the tattered remains of the paper target. His face was covered in the sweat of the firing range, caused by the combination of claustrophobia and tension.

Then Ray Vann emerged, looking calm and relaxed, still wearing eyeglasses but with his ear mufflers around his neck. He was still holding his handgun.

'I dropped you in it,' Vann said to me. 'Sorry.'

'Don't worry about me,' I said.

I had been in a thousand interview rooms and I knew the importance of sticking to your story. Whatever happened in that basement, I intended to keep on insisting that I didn't see him do it.

I was never going to rat him out.

But now he had done it to himself.

I watched Vann's eyes lift to the silent TV screen and then drift away. He did not seem to register that it was his destiny that Sir Ludo was talking about.

'What happened, Ray?' I said.

He stared at the floor, as if he was still trying to work it out himself.

'The IPCC was like a dog with a bone,' he said. 'The old man and that blonde. Hunt and Flynn. They wouldn't let it go. They kept hammering away about the post-mortem trajectory of the gunshot. They knew they had me from the start. They put those autopsy drawings on the table and just left them there. All through all of my interviews, the drawings were always there, as if I had never given a credible explanation for the angle of the shot. And the little man in the profile drawing always had a line entering his chest and leaving around the base of his spine. That's how he died. A single shot entered Adnan Khan's heart and exited from his lower back. The IPCC kept insisting that I must have killed him in cold blood. And in the end I agreed with them. In the end I didn't know what else I could do.'

'You could have backed him up from the start,' Tibbs hissed at me.

Vann looked at him gently. 'It wouldn't have made any difference, Jesse,' he said. 'My story never made sense.'

185

I glanced up at the silent TV screen. Sir Ludo Mount was still talking.

'Listen to me, Ray,' I said. 'That barrister up there will ruin you. He will see you jailed. He will destroy your family. You need to get your Federation rep to produce evidence that you are suffering from adjustment disorder caused by your service in Afghanistan. It is a legitimate defence.'

I looked at Jackson for back-up and he nodded.

'Shrinks talk about the stressors – the stresses, it means – that lead to mental illness,' Jackson said. 'It's true, Ray. PTSD is not an excuse. It's a reason.'

Ray Vann's back stiffened with pride.

'Tell them I'm a nutjob?' he said. 'Because I served my country? You call that a defence? That I killed the bastard because I'm a raving loony?' He shook his head. 'Never, Max. I know you mean well, but that's just not going to happen. You know why I killed him? *Because he deserved to die*. Because he had it coming. Because he deliberately brought that Air Ambulance down on all those innocent people in Lake Meadows. Because him and his brother – and his dad, for all I know, and his mother and the whole rotten lot of them – would dance on our children's graves if we let them.'

'It's war,' Jesse Tibbs said, his face in mine. 'And they started it.'

I put my hand on his chest and shoved him away.

'Are you the one going down for murder, Tibbs?'
I said. 'Then shut your cakehole.'

He came at me and Jackson got between us and seized
Tibbs by the scruff of the neck.

Ray Vann smiled at us like an indulgent parent.

His confession to the IPCC had left him curiously
calm. And I had seen that in a thousand interview rooms
too. The relief that comes with finally having the truth
in the light, no matter how terrible it may be.

'You OK, Raymond?' Jackson said, and it was
an echo of the day we went into Borodino Street, and
I thought about my conversation with Vann in the
locker room at Gravesend, and how the country he
had served would never know of the things he had
seen, and the terror he had endured, and how it felt to
see the body parts of your fallen friends strung from
trees to mock you.

'I might stay a little longer,' Ray Vann said.

'That's a good idea,' Jackson said.

Vann looked longingly around the firing range. I wondered how long it would be before he was under arrest
for murder. He would not be coming down here ever
again and he seemed to know it.

Jesse Tibbs put his arm around Ray Vann. Jackson
and I watched the pair of them return to the booth.

'He's not going to hide behind a plea of adjustment
disorder, Max,' Jackson said. 'Not a guy like that.'

'He wouldn't be hiding behind it,' I said. 'It's what's happened to him. Vann's a damaged man, Jackson. They sent him to their dirty war, all those politicians who never heard a shot fired that wasn't on the grouse moor, and it broke something inside him.'

Jackson shook his head. 'Maybe. But he is just not going to claim to be some kind of victim, Max. He would rather go down.'

'And what do you think they're going to do to him when he tells them that Adnan Khan deserved to die?' I said. 'They're going to put him away for life. Do you have any idea what it's like for a former police officer doing hard time? And then there's going to be a civil case that takes the Met – and his family – to the cleaners. They're going to crucify him, Jackson.'

And then it was all one unbroken moment.

Tibbs shouted, '*Raymond!*' and I saw Vann turn his back on his friend in the end booth, barging Tibbs away with his shoulder as Vann lifted the Glock to his open mouth and tilted his head back and pulled the trigger and the top of his head came off in an explosion of blood and bone.

Ray Vann's body fell as if the life had fled from him like a light going out as Tibbs froze, staring at the splatter on the walls of the booth and down the front of his uniform, the dead body of his friend at his feet.

188

19

As the sun went down at the end of the next day, Edie Wren and I sat outside the gates of Victoria Park in my old BMW X5 and we watched the lights come on in a march that was meant to be a call for an end to the killing.

Peace in the Park, they were calling it.

There were hundreds of lights, perhaps a thousand, the number growing all the time, and they made a universe of tiny stars piercing the soft summer darkness of Victoria Park. They were not the yellow and stuttering light of candles, they were not the kind of lights that looked like they could easily be extinguished. They were the bright and piercing white light of a thousand smartphones held aloft, a hard white light in the gathering twilight that made you think the stars were very close tonight. They looked like the kind of lights that would be burning long after we were all gone.

'It's beautiful,' Edie said. She glanced at me. 'Isn't it beautiful, Max?'

'Yes,' I said, although rallies for peace always made me slightly nervous. I had never seen a peace rally yet where someone didn't get their head caved in. But Edie was right.

All those lights shining in the darkness were beautiful.

I looked at her sharp-faced profile, leaning forward in the passenger seat, a dreamy smile on her face, and for a long moment I just watched her watching the lights shine in the park.

And I had to ask.

'Is that it?' I said.

She looked at me and then back at the lights. She smiled, sighed, took a fistful of quad muscle in my left leg and gave it a squeeze.

And I was amazed that I had waited so long to ask the question that had hung between us since the night – months ago now, just when the dark and cold was finally making way for the first rumour of spring – when I had gone to Edie's home, rung the doorbell and stayed until morning.

One night.

Both of us had been in uncharted territory that night. We were at the end of a gruelling investigation into people trafficking that had begun with the discovery of thirteen passports and twelve young women dead in the back of a refrigerated truck in Chinatown, and ended with the thirteenth woman dying in our arms in a penthouse brothel. I was at a loss, owning up to some kind of loneliness, spending too long on the backstreets of Chinatown, feeling tempted by the invitations from doorways that greet a single man wandering those streets after dark. And Edie was in one of her periodic break-ups with her married Mr Big.

So one Saturday night – the loneliest night of the week, someone once sang – I drove to Edie's flat on the wrong side of Highbury Corner and I rang her bell, ready to take my chances. And she took me in.

Sometimes you wait so long for something to happen that when it does – if it does – you are disappointed. But sometimes it is better. And when that happens, you suddenly know why you are alive. And you want that feeling again, of course you do, you want it more than anything, even if you suspect that it might never happen.

'You were lovely,' Edie said, her green eyes dancing between the lights and me. She tried to lighten the mood. 'It wasn't a one-night stand. It was an all-night stand.'

'So you'll be leaving a five-star review?' I said. 'That's great. But that's not what I'm asking.'

'I know. But – and maybe you noticed – I am back with him, Max. He says he really means it this time – he's going to leave his wife and move in with me and end all the sneaking around that makes me sick to my stomach.' She shot me a desperate look. 'And I have to try, don't I?'

'OK,' I said, feeling foolish for being dumb enough to ask a question when I already knew the answer.

Is that it? Yes, Max, that's it. Of course that was it.

'And you'll be fine,' Edie said. 'You'll be beating the girls off with a big stick. Women love a man who is bringing up a child alone. I've seen the way they look at you when you're out with Scout.'

For I moment I was tempted to tell Edie that Scout's mother had decided that she should bring up our daughter but my heart was closing and I didn't feel the urge to open it up.

'It's true,' I agreed. 'A cute little kid is even better for meeting girls than a dog. And I've got both. So watch out, world.'

We laughed, but there was sadness in it because we wanted different things and nothing could be done to change that fact, not even a beautiful night in a park full of fairy lights.

We had talked about it and now it was time to work.

'What do they want, anyway?' Edie said. 'The Peace in the Park marchers?'

'I guess they just want the deaths to stop,' I said. 'All this never-ending slaughter that we have started to think of as a part of normal life. Maybe they just want us to stop thinking of it as normal. It's not a bad thing to want.'

'What time does Victoria Park close?'

'Dusk,' I said. 'Three hundred and sixty-five days a year. But not tonight.'

More people were still arriving at the park, the only large green space in those crowded East End streets.

We watched the crowds in silence, and I thought of all the other crowds that had been in this park before tonight to see the likes of George Bernard Shaw and Sylvia Pankhurst and The Clash, although not on the same bill, of course.

The marchers were of every age and race and creed but some of the young men walking into Victoria Park had their hair brutally shaved at the sides and back and grown out on top, the Depression-era haircut that George Halfpenny had made popular on Borodino Street. But I saw no sign of George or his brother Richard. More people were arriving. More lights were coming on. A Milky Way of white lights in Victoria Park.

And then finally we saw him. George Halfpenny.

'Ladies and gentlemen,' Edie said. 'Please give a big hand to your pound store prophet.'

The crowd outside the entrance to Victoria Park was parting to allow a rickshaw to enter. George Halfpenny, his face drenched in sweat, acknowledged a burst of spontaneous applause with a curt nod as phones were pointed at his face. Young men with the same brutalist haircut touched the side of his rickshaw, as if the converted tricycle had healing properties. As usual, his brother Richard sat in the back like some stocky, overfed little pharaoh.

A Styrofoam cup of coffee hit the top of the rickshaw. Not everyone was a fan, it seemed.

A small gang of the local youth were jeering and giving the finger to George Halfpenny.

There were perhaps a dozen of them; the boys – and they were mostly boys – were all wispy beards and New York Yankees baseball caps, caught between the faith of their fathers and the sports franchises of the west.

There were two girls with the little gang and one of them was Layla Khan.

She already looked older, taller, her black hair longer and a hard mocking look on her face.

'What's Layla doing here?' Edie said, like an irritated big sister. 'If any of these marchers realise who she is ... '

The locals laughed as Halfpenny pedalled his rickshaw into the park. They followed in a jeering little gang, Layla in the middle of them, looking like she was having a fine old time. Edie watched them go, biting her lower lip.

'You want to give George Halfpenny a tug?' she asked. 'We need to know where he was when Ahmed Khan was killed.'

'Not here,' I said. 'We'll do our TIE on George somewhere a bit less crowded.'

We left the BMW X5 outside the gates and followed the crowds into Victoria Park. Full darkness had fallen now but the park was lit by the white lights of those countless phones and by the orange glow that hovers over the city at night. The press of the people increased the deeper we went into the park. Edie and I tried to stay together but she was slowly being carried away from me by the current of the crowd, as if caught in a riptide.

And then, almost close enough to reach out and touch if I had the room to move my arms, I saw the priest.

And I realised that I knew him.

And I saw that it had always been the same priest on Borodino Street.

The large black priest who had knelt to pray before a dwindling congregation the first time I had seen George Halfpenny. The priest who had prayed by the side of Joy Adams when she brought her flowers to the shrine for Alice Stone.

And the priest who had come to the hospital to visit his brother Detective Inspector Curtis Gane in the final days of his life.

He was Father Marvin Gane of St Anthony's Church, Brixton.

He stared at me now as that great crush of humanity moved deeper into the park, but if he recognised me as the colleague of his dead brother, he gave no sign.

And I saw that Father Marvin Gane, the priest of Borodino Street, was no longer praying.

He was waiting.

The crowd had stopped at the bandstand. The rickshaw was parked beside it. There was meant to be a series of speakers for Peace in the Park but I saw only one.

George Halfpenny had already ascended the short flight of steps and was staring out at the crowds. As his brother Richard stood just behind him, as motionless as a postcard of a Rottweiler, George Halfpenny began to speak.

'Before the other speakers arrive and give you the usual meaningless, virtue-signalling platitudes about how united we all are and how easily medieval religion fits into a twenty-first-century democracy, I would like us to remember a police officer called Raymond Vann,' he said.

Somewhere out in the darkness, someone shouted an obscenity. Heads turned towards the harsh sound, and then back to the young man on the bandstand.

'Raymond Vann was let down by the police, let down by the legal system, and let down by the leaders of this country – all those tenth-rate men with first-class educations.'

'Go back to Soho!' shouted one London voice in the darkness.

'When you go back to Pakistan!' shouted another.

Laughter. Applause. Jeers. Obscenities and heads were turning, ready to take it to the next level. I could feel peace receding into the darkness and looked around for the tousled red hair of Edie Wren.

I could not see her.

But I saw that the heckling was coming from the right of the bandstand. The gang of local youth we had seen at the gates had swollen in number. There were twenty or thirty of them now. Layla Khan was still at the centre of them, a big grin on her face.

'Those leaders did not understand Raymond Vann and they do not understand you,' George Halfpenny said. He looked out at the crowd. 'You are the heirs of a thousand years of freedom, a freedom that has been won by men like Raymond Vann. You—'

And then there was another kind of light in the darkness.

The sudden flare of fire as a rag soaked in petrol was lit.

In the brief flash of light I saw laughing young faces, their eyes shining with hatred, and then suddenly the flaming bottle was arcing through the night. It hit the metal fence that surrounds the bandstand and exploded with a whoosh of air and fire.

George Halfpenny fell backwards.

Richard stared at him, dumbfounded.

And then all hell broke loose.

'Kill the bastards!' someone shouted. 'Kill the lot of them!'

And suddenly the air was full of missiles. The crowd were throwing anything they could find in the vague direction of the gang of locals. Bottles, rocks, cans of drink. Most of it fell well short. But in the sudden flare of light from the fire, I saw Layla in the middle of the locals. She was not laughing now.

'Layla!' Edie shouted.

And I saw that Edie was ahead of me, closer to the bandstand, trying to push her way through to Layla.

'Edie!' I shouted, then something hard and metallic smacked against my neck and sent an ice-cold spray down my back, and when I looked up I had lost sight of her.

There were screams and curses and punches wildly thrown as people struggled to get away from the violence or into the thick of it. Young men with Halfpenny haircuts, their faces twisted with fury, were already lashing out with boots and fists at the local youth. Heavily outnumbered, the locals fought back. Layla stood just behind the frontline, edging away from the violence while sticking up two fingers at the crowd with all the venom of an English archer at Agincourt.

Police in riot gear were shoving their way towards the trouble but they had hung back too far at the start of the evening.

I looked for Edie but I could not see her and cursed.

Then I saw something strike Layla Khan and I saw her go down. I forced my way through the crowd, who were mostly anxious to go in exactly the opposite direction. When I found Layla she was on her hands and knees in the middle of the violence.

I scooped her up in my arms. Then Edie was by my side. She placed her hand high on Layla's forehead and her fingertips came away wet with blood.

'Let's get her out of here,' she said.

One of the locals, a tall youth with a failed beard and last season's Arsenal shirt put his hands on me. Still holding Layla against me, I crisply bounced my forehead off the bridge of his nose. Edie kicked his legs from underneath him and he went down hard.

We joined the crowd trying to get away from the trouble and we did not look back.

Layla twisted in my arms and stared at me bleary-eyed.

'Do you want to get yourself killed?' Edie shouted at her. 'Why the hell are you here?'

'Because *you* –' Layla shouted back, taking in the police, the crowds and everyone with a George Half-penny jarhead haircut – 'are down *here*.'

As the crowd thinned, Edie brushed Layla's hair from her face and winced at the sight of the egg-sized lump on her head, just where the hairline began.

'Hospital,' Edie told me.

'No,' Layla said. 'Not hospital.' She struggled from my arms and swayed unsteadily on her feet. 'Take me home,' she said. And suddenly she was a child again. 'Please, Edie.'

So with Layla holding on to Edie for support we left the park and began walking towards Borodino Street.

'I'm sorry about your grandfather, Layla,' I said. 'He was a decent man.'

She watched me impassively, waiting.

'I held him when he died and I will never forget it,' I said. 'And what I will remember is that he died saying your name. He was worried about you, and full of love for you.'

Her mouth flinched. She looked at the ground, letting that long black hair fall over her face. Edie patted her back.

'And I know that your grandfather wouldn't want this for you, Layla,' I said. 'Whatever you think you are doing tonight. Whatever you're drinking. Whatever you're smoking. Whoever those boys were. Your grandfather would want something better for you.'

It was a nice speech. I was quite proud of myself.

But Layla Khan just laughed.

'My Papa-Papa wanted me to be a part of this country,' she said. 'His generation wanted to *integrate*.' She said it like it was a dirty word. 'Smoking, drinking, fucking.'

'Hey,' Edie said, looking affronted. 'Your mouth, young lady.'

'How do we integrate when you wouldn't want to live next door to us?' Layla asked me, and I had no answer for her.

And then Edie chuckled.

'What have you done to your hair, girl?' she said, stroking Layla's head. Layla tugged at her fringe and now I saw that her jet-black hair was tinged a garish shade of crimson.

'It's Boots own-brand Neon Red,' Layla said. 'That's what it said on the bottle. Don't you like it?'

Edie grinned at her. 'You always look pretty,' she said. 'Neon Red or no Neon Red.'

We were standing outside the house now, the front garden still stacked high with the debris of the search teams. I stood on the pavement and watched as Edie walked Layla to the front door. Layla still clung to Edie, and it was as if she was reluctant to let her go.

Her grandmother opened the door. Behind Azza Khan, I could see that the floorboards and parts of the ceiling were still torn open.

'Layla was in the park,' Edie said. 'There was trouble there tonight. You should keep her home until it passes.'

Edie paused, and I realised that she had never heard the woman speak a word of English.

'Mrs Khan,' Edie said. 'Do you understand what I'm saying?'

Azza Khan looked evenly at her granddaughter.

And then she took the girl's pretty face in one rough hand.

At first I thought the old woman was examining the girl's injury.

But then I saw that she was looking at the trace of lipstick on Layla's mouth, and the cheap red streaks in her sleek black hair and that she was smelling whatever the girl had been drinking or smoking.

'I understand very well,' Azza Khan told Edie.

And then the old woman's open palm cracked hard against Layla's face.

'*Whore*,' she said. 'Just like all the little teenage whores in this country.'

Layla's tears came immediately, and they were the hot and bitter tears that come not from pain but humiliation. She fled sobbing up the staircase.

Edie made a movement to follow her but Azza Khan moved to block her way. The old woman shouted after her granddaughter.

'Remember who you are!' she called up the darkened staircase. 'Remember your father! Remember your uncles! Remember your family! *Remember where you belong, Layla!*'

Then she looked at Edie and smiled apologetically, almost embarrassed by her perfect English.

20

The season was turning.

The days were growing longer and school was winding down for the long summer break. They were watching films in class and clearing their desks. These were the sunny days when Scout came home with sheaves of paintings, poems and stories – 'My work this year,' she would say, dumping it into my arms – carried proudly inside her plain black Kipling City Pack, size small. A big girl's bag.

Scout's school uniform, the blue-and-white gingham dress the girls wore from Easter, still fit her but now it was stained with smudges of paint and grass and ketchup and Cornetto and almost ready to be retired. She would need a new, bigger dress for next year.

And when I took her to school and we stood at the gates, working out the day's schedule with Stan jumping up between us, frantic with farewells, I was struck by the same sweet summer's thought.

We made it through another year.

'What's the plan for the day?' I said, knowing she had it committed to memory.

'Mrs Murphy's picking me up with Stan after school,' she said. 'I can't go home with Mia today but I can at the weekend. You're going to be late from work but not too late.' She looked at me with her solemn brown eyes. 'After dinner but before bedtime, right?'

'Right.'

'You'll read me *Poems for Eight-Year-Olds*?'

I spread my hands. 'But I don't know any eight-year-olds, Scout.'

She was outraged. 'Nearly!'

I leaned down and she lightly pressed her mouth on the side of my face.

All those parents saying goodbye to their children, and all of those kids wanting to grow up fast, all wishing their childhood away, and yet my daughter would still give me a goodbye peck. I knew that would change one day. But not for a while, I hoped.

I watched Scout until she disappeared into school. Parents dressed for the office and the gym drifted back to their cars. A bell rang from deep inside the school building, and that was when I saw her.

Anne was sitting across from the school gates in something large and expensive. A new model Range Rover. Her eyes were hidden behind sunglasses but the curve of her face could not belong to anyone else on the planet, with the exception of our daughter.

If Anne saw me she gave no sign.

If she felt any emotion, then it did not show.

But as I watched Anne gun the Range Rover and drive away, a touch too fast in those streets full of children, I knew with all my heart that I had been wrong about why my ex-wife wanted Scout back in her life.

It is more than guilt, I thought.

It is much more than guilt.

A crime reporter of my acquaintance was waiting at the gates of the Westminster Public Mortuary on Horseferry Road.

'Max,' she said. 'Scarlet Bush of the *Daily Post*. Long time no see. Long time no quote. Maybe not long enough for you, ha ha.'

An unkempt young man was with her. He had a camera slung around his neck. I frowned at him as he took my picture.

'Don't do that,' I said.

He did it again. I stared at him.

'Sorry,' he said, lowering his camera.

'Hello, Scarlet,' I said. 'The *Daily Post*? I thought that rag had closed down.'

She stiffened with professional pride.

'The *Post* is digital only these days, Max. There's no print edition, but you can still find us online. These are difficult times for the newspaper industry. Advertising revenue has fallen off a cliff. So I need you to help me out. I'm writing a piece into what's happened in this city this summer. All of it. The drone bringing down that Air Ambulance on Lake Meadows. The raid on Borodino Street. The death of the Khan brothers and Alice Stone. Now the murder of the father – the old bus driver. Where's it going to end?'

Give it five hundred years or so, I thought.

'This Special Firearms Officer who died in Leman Street – Raymond Vann? Was Vann's death a suicide or accident?'

'We have to wait for the coroner's report.'

'Throw me a bone here, Max. I heard you had become friends with the father of the Borodino Street brothers – is that true?'

'Ahmed Khan was an innocent man. He was as much a victim of his sons as anybody else.'

Scarlet almost smiled. That was good. She liked that.

She was jotting away in a notebook, strange squiggly hieroglyphics that must have been shorthand. Scarlet Bush had all these old-fashioned skills that were slipping into the mists of history. And I saw that being a journalist in the twenty-first century was like being a blacksmith as the first Model-T Ford came over the horizon.

'You don't think that Ahmed Khan bears some responsibility for what his sons did?' Scarlet said, and now I saw that she was wearing a sky-blue ribbon. 'You don't think he shares the blame for Lake Meadows? For Alice Stone's death on Borodino Street?' She looked up from her notebook. 'And for the suicide of Raymond Vann?'

'I blame his sons,' I said. 'And I blame the generations of politicians who allowed ghettos to flourish. And I blame the Internet companies – the ones that are taking your newspaper's advertising revenue – who serve up beheadings of aid workers as if it was family entertainment. And I blame the hate preachers who fill feeble minds with poison. I blame all of them. But Ahmed Khan? I don't blame him. Arnold was a good man.'

'Arnold? You called him Arnold? Wow. You really were friends, weren't you? Can I quote you on all this?'

'Do what you like,' I said. 'Stick it in your digital edition. Nobody's going to read it.'

She called out to me as I walked through the gates.

'What about this Bad Moses character? He's all over social media claiming to have killed your old pal – *Arnold*. Are you taking Bad Moses seriously? Or is he just another social media nutjob?'

I remembered the Fourth Commandment stained on a floorboard outside the house on Borodino Street, and I thought of the Twitter account that Edie had showed

207

me in the safe house, featuring Charlton Heston as Moses in Cecil B. DeMille's *The Ten Commandments*.

But I kept walking.

'Help me out here, Max! For old times' sake! Was the murder of Ahmed Khan a hate crime, Max?'

I turned to look at her from the top of the steps.

'Every murder is a hate crime,' I said.

And then I went inside to look at the dead.

'The dead talk to us,' Elsa Olsen said. 'But they don't tell us everything.

We were in the Iain West Forensic Suite, Pat Whitestone and Edie Wren and I, shivering in our blue scrubs and hairnets, for it is always just a shade above freezing point in this place of the dead.

Ahmed Khan lay on a stainless steel table.

There was a livid Y-shaped incision on his scrawny torso where Elsa had opened him up with the green-handled gardening shears she favoured for her work.

And there was a dark stab wound at the base of his neck.

Elsa, one of those tall, dark-haired Norwegians who defied national stereotypes, like the woman who wasn't the blonde one in Abba, indicated the dead man's legs with a long stainless steel instrument like a conductor's baton.

We waited for our favourite forensic pathologist to reveal what Ahmed Khan had told her after his sudden death.

'There was rigor in the legs but only in the legs,' she said. 'What that means is there was strenuous muscular activity in the legs immediately before he was killed.' She paused. 'Mr Khan was running.'

I thought of the CCTV images of Khan's last moments.

He had bolted from the tube train but I had taken his urgency to be the impatience of a workingman who was keen to get home after a long shift on a Sunday.

But Elsa was telling us it was more than that.

'He was running for his life,' I said. 'He was terrified.'

'Khan must have seen someone in that tube carriage,' Whitestone said. 'Someone he knew was a threat to his life.'

'But we've got witness statements from a dozen people who were in that tube train,' Edie said. 'None of them heard Ahmed Khan being threatened. Nobody saw any threat of violence.'

'Then it was someone he knew,' I said. 'Someone who did not need to say a word because just the sight of him made Ahmed Khan terrified.'

'No defensive wounds?' Whitestone said.

Elsa shook her head. 'When the end came, it came very quickly. He never had time to fight back.'

'So he saw his killer on the train,' I said. 'He ran for his life. The killer caught up with him – my guess is somewhere near the top of the escalators – and stuck the knife in his neck.'

Elsa's stainless steel rod indicated the mark at the base of Ahmed Khan's neck.

'Cause of death was a single wound to the subclavian artery, which as you know is the artery that pumps blood to the arms and neck. If an artery of that size is torn then it's possible that it can contract and stem the bleeding. But a clean cut of the subclavian artery with a blade that has a razor-sharp stabbing point and good cutting edges will kill you in, oh, five minutes.'

The old scar on my stomach throbbed with pain that may have been psychosomatic but felt real enough to me.

'I understand you recovered a newly sharpened 26.6-centimetre knife from the crime scene,' Elsa said. 'That would do the job.'

'The fact that it was sticking out of his neck gave us a clue,' Edie said.

Whitestone shot her a withering look, then turned to me.

'Someone knew what they were doing,' she said.

'Maybe they just got lucky,' I said.

'No,' Whitestone said. 'They knew exactly what they were doing. You don't stick a knife in the subclavian artery by accident. Someone wanted him dead.'

'Time of death you know because he died in your arms, Max,' Elsa went on. She stared thoughtfully at Ahmed Khan and then, almost as an afterthought. 'Manner of death was murder,' she said.

But there were other, ancient scars on Ahmed Khan's body. What looked like a shallow stab wound on his arm. The mottled scarring of broken glass on his shoulder. Dark tissue on his arms where bones had been broken and never properly healed.

'He had a lot of old scars,' I said.

'Yes,' Elsa said. 'When did Mr Khan come to this country from Pakistan?'

'I believe it was the Seventies,' I said.

Elsa nodded.

'Souvenirs of a hard life,' she said.

It was a short walk from the Westminster Public Mortuary on Horseferry Road to West End Central at 27 Savile Row. We cut across St James's Park, glorious in the summer sunshine.

TDC Joy Adams was alone in MIR-1.

She looked apologetic.

'I don't know if this is anything,' she said.

'Show me,' Whitestone said.

'It might be nothing,' she said. 'Just social media drivel.'

Whitestone stared at her hard and Joy Adams stopped apologising.

'I found something on Tubecrush,' she said.

We gathered around her workstation as she scrolled through dozens of images of young men, riding the London underground but dressed for the beach.

211

'Look,' Adams said.

The young man wore cargo shorts and a sleeveless T-shirt. He was turned away from the camera but you could see the strength in his body. The broad back, the pumped-up arms, the thick muscles of the legs. His hair was totally shaved at the side and back, but grew out in a tufty crop on top of his head. In the background, in a half-empty carriage, most of his fellow passengers stared at their phones.

But one man slept.

He wore the uniform of a London bus driver.

It was Ahmed Khan, going home, exhausted by the heat, worn out by the day, on a journey to the home that he would never reach.

'Good work, Joy,' Whitestone said. 'This places Ahmed Khan and George Halfpenny in the same tube carriage just before he was murdered.'

'Wait,' I said. 'Are we sure? The sleeping man is Ahmed Khan, all right. But the young guy with his back to the camera? I don't know if that's George Halfpenny or some kid with the same haircut. A lot of people have got a haircut like that this summer. Edie?'

'I don't know, Max. It *could* be him.'

'It fits,' Whitestone said. 'Ahmed Khan ran for his life when he saw George Halfpenny following him. Why? Because Khan had seen him on TV. And he knew how much he was hated.'

'Five million journeys on the underground every day,' I said. 'On five hundred trains. And we are going to arrest someone for murder because of a haircut?'

But Whitestone had made up her mind.

And I saw how much she wanted it to be true.

21

'*I lie belly-up in the sunshine, happier than you will ever be,*' I read. '*Today I sniffed many dog butts – I celebrate by kissing your face.*'

Scout sat up in bed, smoothing down her duvet and smiling secretly to herself as I read. She liked this one.

'Another dog poem,' she observed.

'*I sound the alarm!*
Paperboy – come to kill us all –
Look! Look! Look! Look! Look!
I sound the alarm!
Garbage man – come to kill us all –
Look! Look! Look! Look! Look!'

She watched Stan, asleep at her feet, as if he might possibly enjoy a poem about a dog. And of course I watched her. My daughter at seven – pink-faced from her bath, her hair smelling of shampoo, sitting up straight for the ritual of the bedtime read.

'*Look in my eyes and deny it,*' I read.

Scout grinned at me, waiting for the punchline.

I closed the book and recited the last line from memory.

'*No human could love you as much as I do.*'

'Who wrote that one, Daddy?'

'That's by Anonymous, angel.'

'He's written some good stuff,' Scout said. 'Old Anonymous.'

I kissed the top of her head and took Stan with me when I turned out the light. Scout's eyes were already closing as she snuggled down. But I knew that sleep would not come that easily for me tonight.

I spread an exercise mat on the floor of the living room and cranked out one hundred press-ups and then one hundred sit-ups in four sets of twenty-five. But although my body was weary my head was still full. I was nowhere near sleep. So I went to one of the big windows of the loft and watched the men at the meat market and the young dancers filing happily into Fabric.

As the time drifted past midnight, and the moon crossed the sky behind the great gleaming dome of St Paul's, the streets below our window seemed to get busier. Smithfield is the insomniac's neighbourhood.

The summer night passed slowly. In the small hours, I lay on my bed for a while but my head was still too full for sleep. So I got up, showered and shaved, and brewed a pot of black coffee. At 4 a.m. sharp Mrs Murphy arrived, bleary from sleep, shivering in the chill of the hour before dawn.

'You'll want your coat on out there,' she told me.

I nodded, and checked in on my sleeping daughter and stroked my snoring dog.

And then I went to work.

The sun would be up at 5 a.m. but it was still pitch-dark when I arrived at the car park of West End Central. The place was already buzzing. Whitestone, in a Kevlar jacket and a PASGT helmet, was briefing a couple of uniformed coppers.

Jackson Rose was standing at the back of a jump-off van, talking quietly to his SFOs.

And a team of paramedics stood in the open doors of an ambulance gulping down coffee they probably didn't need.

Every face in that car park was pulled tight with adrenaline.

Jackson's shots didn't look like police officers at all. With their PASGT helmets, rubber goggles, body armour on knees and elbows and Heckler & Koch assault rifles, they looked like a private army from the next century. Jesse Tibbs shrugged his shoulders, hefted his Benelli 12-gauge shotgun and stared straight through me.

I walked over to Whitestone and her uniforms. They were young, a man and a woman, the man dark and bearded and smiling, the woman younger, stout and dead serious. SYKES, it said on the man's name badge. THOMPSON, it said on the woman's.

'We're looking for shoes,' Whitestone told them. 'If you can find bloodstained clothes, then that's even better. But Halfpenny is likely to have burned or dumped any bloodstained T-shirt or jeans. Because they always do. There would have been a lot of blood on his clothes. You don't get out of the way of an arterial spray. He's a lot less likely to have dumped any trainers he was wearing. He's almost certainly not that smart. Because they never are.'

Edie Wren and Joy Adams, already kitted up, came into the car park. Edie handed me a Kevlar jacket, PASGT helmet and a triple espresso from the Bar Italia.

'Do we really need the heavy mob?' I said, indicating the shots and the paramedics.

'Well,' Edie said. 'Let's hope not.'

My telephone vibrated. NO CALLER ID, it said. And then the message.

I will make you crawl

As I slid my phone back in my pocket, I looked across at Jesse Tibbs, remembering his threat to me in The Fighting Temeraire on the day they buried Alice Stone.

He was staring at his phone, scratching his wispy blond beard with his free hand, before he looked up and gave Jackson his full attention. Tibbs shrugged again, a nervous tic that lifted up the weight of his protective gear and weapons.

It was an unusual threat, I reflected.

People threaten to kill you. People threaten to smash your face in. And they do that all the time, if their blood is up.

But I had never had anyone promise to make me crawl.

I kept looking at Tibbs. He kept staring at Jackson.

Then Whitestone was by my side.

'Ready?' she said.

And as the first rumour of sunlight crept above the rooftops of the city, we went to arrest a man for murder.

The Halfpenny brothers lived above a shuttered pet shop in Camden Town.

There was a ragged FOR SALE sign above the shop. It looked as though it had been on sale for a while. And it looked as though it had been even longer since they sold any pets here. TALKING PARROTS, it said above the shop. TRAINED CHIMPS.

There was a locked metal gate at the foot of the stairs to the flats above the shops. There was some quiet cursing from our mob. Apparently nobody was expecting it to be there, so we crouched down behind recycling bins as Whitestone and Jackson quickly conferred. Some foggy-eyed refugees from the vibrant Camden nightlife were still rolling home and they gawped and leered to see us crouching behind the bins. Then Whitestone and Jackson turned to look at them, Jackson's Heckler & Koch twitching at that 45-degree angle, and the drunks briskly moved on.

Jackson nodded to his team and Tibbs moved forward, lifting his Benelli shotgun to his shoulder, pointing it at the lock on the gate.

I slowed my breathing, telling myself that there was nothing much waiting for us at the top of the stairs, and nothing much behind the next locked door we would go through. But the truth is that you never know, and you can never possibly know, and it is this great unknown that winds you up tight and makes you pray that this is not the day you die.

For one long moment time seemed to freeze.

I looked at the SFOs huddled around Jackson, and I looked at Edie and Joy, and at the two uniformed officers, Sykes and Thompson. And I looked at Whitestone. The sunlight of the new day glittered on her glasses. Then she nodded.

'Go,' Jackson said quietly, and Tibbs fired his shotgun at the big lock on the gate.

The Hatton round took it off as if it was nothing.

Then we were running up the stairs in single file, the sound of the shotgun still ringing in my ears, Jackson and his team of SFOs leading the way, pausing outside the first flat. In one smooth movement Tibbs aimed his shotgun and blew the front door wide open.

Jackson's team poured inside with weapons raised to their shoulders and screaming their warning, the shouts that are there to terrify them and embolden us.

'Armed police! Armed police!'

The flat was tiny.

We fell out of the hall into a box-shaped living room where a teenage boy in a wheelchair was asleep in front of an elderly television set. There was a small coffee table piled high with library books about military history. A. J. P. Taylor and Antony Beevor and Max Hastings. Fat books by thoughtful men on the great wars of the last century.

The boy in the wheelchair came awake with a jolt and gasped with shock at the men with guns. He wore only a T-shirt and boxer shorts. His legs were withered and twisted.

I looked at Whitestone and I saw she was thinking the same thing.

Wrong flat.

It would not have been the first time.

But the boy in the wheelchair had his hair cut in the brutal fashion of that summer, shaved close at the back and side and grown out on top, and there was something about him, the gaunt face that could have come from a photograph of the Depression, that made me realise there were not two Halfpenny brothers.

There were three.

And then George Halfpenny was stumbling into the room in T-shirt and boxer shorts, his gaunt face blurry with sleep, and his brother Richard was behind him, wearing only his briefs, and looking like an overdeveloped strong man in one of those old ads about not getting sand kicked in your face when you go to the beach. Only their haircuts were the same. They stood there staring at the men who had entered their home and at the assault rifles that were pointing at their chests. The boy in the wheelchair was between us.

'*Armed police!*'

'*Raise your hands!*'

'*On your knees! Now! Do it!*'

The brothers did not move.

Jesse Tibbs took George Halfpenny by the scruff of his neck and forced him to his knees. Richard followed suit without being prompted. The boy in the wheelchair began to cry.

'Edward,' George Halfpenny said to him. 'Please don't cry.'

George, Richard and Edward, I thought.

Poor boys named after kings.

'Tell them you didn't do it!' the boy in the wheelchair – Edward Halfpenny – shouted at his brother, his mouth twisted with effort, the words sounding as though they were coming from underwater. 'Tell them you didn't kill anyone!'

'George Halfpenny,' Whitestone said. 'I am arresting you on suspicion of the murder of Ahmed Khan.'

The two uniformed police officers, Sykes and Thompson, approached the boy in the wheelchair. Thompson crouched down beside him, trying to calm him down, while Sykes placed his hands on the back of the wheelchair, ready to move him from danger.

And that is when George Halfpenny went berserk.

He was on his feet and coming forward, throwing wild punches at Sykes. One of them connected with the point of Sykes' chin and the young officer went down hard, cracking his temple on the side of the coffee table before he hit the worn-out carpet.

There was a sickening fraction of a second when we all stared at Sykes. The officer was not moving. A tiny sliver of blood pulsed from a vein on his forehead.

Then someone was screaming into their radio for medics.

They were there almost immediately.

222

Jackson stepped forward and almost casually bounced the butt of his Sig Sauer assault rifle off George Halfpenny's forehead and hands grabbed him as he sagged to the floor.

He was dragged away.

'Tell them! Tell them!' Edward shouted at his remaining brother, his thin arms and wasted legs writhing with anguish.

Richard Halfpenny was still on his knees with his hands in the air, a powerful young man whose strength had been confiscated. He cast an anxious look at the door. He was lost without his big brother.

The flat was quickly cleared and then I was alone with the two brothers.

Richard Halfpenny was still on his knees, hands raised, trying to understand what had happened. Edward was weeping, bent sideways in his wheelchair.

'Tell them!' he moaned. 'Tell them!'

'You can get up now,' I told Richard.

He stood up slowly, glancing towards the door.

'Don't they have to release him after twenty-four hours?'

'Not if they plan to charge him with murder,' I said. 'And they can hold him for ninety-six hours if they do that.'

'Edward,' Richard said gently, placing one of his thick hands on his brother's shoulder. 'Please stop crying.'

With some effort, Edward Halfpenny moved his wheelchair closer to the coffee table. He picked something up in his clawed hands. I saw he was fumbling with a phone.

'Show him, Richard! Show him, show him!'

'What do you want to show me, son?' I said.

Richard took the phone from his brother.

He hit some buttons and handed it to me.

'This is what he wants to show you,' Richard said.

And I saw George Halfpenny laughing in a swimming pool as he held up his crippled brother on his back in the water. It was a public pool, impossibly crowded in the summertime. They were both laughing.

And even without that same hobo haircut, I thought, you would have known they were brothers.

'When did Ahmed Khan get topped?' Richard said. 'It was Sunday afternoon, right?'

I nodded.

He laughed bitterly.

'Stupid, stupid coppers,' he said.

In the bottom right-hand corner of the film there was a time and date stamp.

The date was Sunday.

The time was exactly when I had been waiting outside the underground station for Ahmed Khan to come home.

I closed the phone.

George Halfpenny had the perfect alibi.

He could not have killed Ahmed Khan.

'George takes Edward swimming every Sunday afternoon,' Richard said. 'It's their time together.' He looked at his brother in the wheelchair. 'The doctors and the physios all say that swimming is best for him.'

I looked at Edward Halfpenny. His mouth struggled to form the words, and his head jerked back, pulled by forces that I could not imagine. He struggled to exist inside his skin. And he would always struggle. I knelt by his side, the phone in my fist.

'We go … *swimming*,' Edward said. 'My brother George works six days a *week*. But he would *never* work on a Sunday.'

Down in the street the sirens started, as loud and empty as canned laughter.

22

Only Whitestone was in MIR-1 when I got to West End Central.

'There's something you need to see,' I said.

I had placed the phone in an evidence bag. There was a Criminal Justice Act label on the side, with a unique identification number and my name, rank and the location where the phone had been recovered. I put on a pair of blue nitrile gloves, took out the phone and called up the film of George Halfpenny in the swimming pool with his brother Edward.

Before it had finished, Whitestone had turned away, unimpressed. She settled her spectacles on the bridge of her nose.

'Is that going to be his alibi?' she said.

'You don't think it's a pretty good one?' I said.

'They've always got an alibi,' Whitestone said. 'Every villain I ever met. Nobody was guilty. Not one of the dealers, the muggers, the wife-beaters, the pimps – and the murderers, Max. They were all somewhere else.' She nodded briefly at the phone. 'It's good you bagged and tagged it, but let's see if it stands up for more than five minutes before we make him a free man, shall we?'

I put the phone back in the evidence bag and sealed it.

'So you think the film is fake?' I said.

Whitestone shrugged. 'The film is real. I'll give him that much. But I think the time and date stamp are likely to be fabricated.'

I shook my head.

'It's a perfect alibi and you know it,' I said.

The anger flared.

'And has he got an alibi for assaulting a police officer, Max? PC Sykes is in an ICU in an induced coma with a cracked skull and a blood clot on the brain. Does he have an alibi for that, Max?'

Edie and Joy Adams were standing in the doorway.

Both of them had their breakfast with them.

'Sorted?' Whitestone said.

'Ma'am,' Edie nodded, coming into the room. She watched Whitestone warily for a moment and then gave Joy the nod. The pair of them settled down to some breakfast from Bar Italia.

Nothing much would happen in West End Central for a while.

George Halfpenny was being processed in the custody suite. He would be cautioned, searched, relieved of his possessions, read his rights by the custody officer, fingerprinted, photographed, mouth swabbed and hair root plucked for DNA, visited by the station's duty solicitor and then, after this initial flurry of activity, all the meticulous, well-oiled bureaucracy of arrest, he would be left to stew in his cell before we got around to questioning him.

'Is that team of shots still here?' I said.

'In the car park,' Edie said.

So that's where I went.

Down in the underground car park below West End Central, Jackson's team of Special Firearms Officers were hanging out behind the back of their jump-off van, all feeling pretty good. Drinking coffee, yakking it up, eating bacon sandwiches, grinning with relief that it had gone down the way it did.

There was a murder suspect in custody, no weapons had been discharged and the only casualty was the uniformed police officer who had got a nasty bang on the head when George Halfpenny decked him. But the job was done and the bacon sandwiches were hot and the sun was shining and nobody was dead.

Jesse Tibbs had a big dopey grin on his bearded face that disappeared when I threw my PASGT helmet at him and knocked his carton of tea all over him. He turned away, cursing, PG Tips dripping down his body armour.

'Hey, top gun?' I said. 'Look at me, top gun, will you? You going to make me crawl, are you? Come on, top gun – let's see you make me crawl.'

I had my hands around his throat before I was gripped from behind, and my arms locked by my side. What you should always do when someone does that to you is lift your feet off the ground and drop your centre of gravity before throwing your head back in a kind of reverse headbutt that – with a bit of luck – scatters a few of their front teeth to the wind. That always makes them let you go.

But I knew who was pulling me off. And so I resisted the urge.

'What is wrong with you?' Jackson snarled in my ear, and I heard years of resentment in his voice, years of it, decades of it, the seasoned bile of brothers.

He dragged me away from Tibbs, still gripping me from behind, my arms still pinned to my side.

'Ask him,' I said. 'Ask your man Tibbs. He reckons he's going to make me crawl because he blames me for Ray Vann topping himself – don't you, top gun?'

Tibbs delicately shook his arm, sending off a spray of English Breakfast tea.

'You know what you did,' he said darkly.

'He reckons he's going to make me crawl, Jackson,' I said, and I was suddenly sick of being held.

I lifted my feet from the ground, dropped my body weight, and thrashed like a dying rat in a dog's mouth until Jackson let me go.

He put his hand on my chest and looked at Tibbs.

'Are you making threats to this man, Jesse?' Jackson asked him.

Tibbs snorted. 'Anything I want to say to him, he'll know because I'll be standing on his doorstep.'

Which was the wrong thing to say to me.

I am very fussy about who I have standing on the doorstep of my home where I live with my daughter and my dog.

It was another threat, and the worst kind of all.

'Let's have it then,' I said. 'I'll shove that shotgun right up—'

Jackson pushed my chest, shoving me backwards. And he did it again, knocking me back another step. And then I stood there and I shook my head and it was just my oldest friend and me and I was not going to let him push me back any further.

'Don't,' I said.

And he didn't.

We stared at each other, our fists clenched by our sides.

I turned away, heading up the ramp for the exit, fresh air and daylight blazing ahead of me. It was going to be another beautiful day. I turned at the top of the ramp.

'He didn't do it,' I told them. 'George Halfpenny. They're going to have to let him go. He was nowhere near Ahmed Khan when he was killed.'

'So what?' Tibbs shouted. 'Nobody cares about that old Paki. Only you.'

But there was someone else who cared about Ahmed Khan.

I walked round to the front of the building and found Layla sitting outside under the big blue lamp that marks the main entrance to West End Central.

It was still ridiculously early. Uniformed coppers were still coming off the night shift. The bespoke tailors on Savile Row were all still closed. A few dead-keen office workers were carrying coffee to their offices in Mayfair but these were still the hours of cleaners doing their minimum-wage work before the day began.

'Is that him inside?' Layla said. 'The murderer?'

'What are you even doing here?' I said.

'Is that the man who killed my grandfather? The one you've got locked up?'

'Did some journalist call you?'

'Edie,' she said. She glanced at the doors. 'Edie sent me a text. Edie said you got him.' Her eyes shone with tears. 'She thought I'd be happy.'

I sighed and shook my head and sat down on the steps next to her. I was still wearing my stab-proof vest.

231

I undid the straps and exhaled as though I hadn't breathed all night.

'Edie shouldn't be calling you about this stuff.'

'She's trying to be kind.'

'I know. She cares about you. She still shouldn't be doing it.'

And then Edie was there.

'Hey,' she said softly, leaning over Layla and pushing back her long black hair from her face. There was a fading red scuffmark high up on one cheekbone where her grandmother had slapped her after we had brought her home from the park.

She sat down on the other side of the girl. Edie took her hands.

'And is it him?' Layla said.

Edie looked at me and I shook my head at all of it. Her sending text messages to this kid. The young man we had down in the cells. The wrong-headed certainty of Whitestone.

'They *think* it's him,' Edie said carefully. 'The SIO – Senior Investigating Officer – thinks it is him.'

Still holding hands with Edie, Layla studied my face.

'And what? You don't think it's him? Why not?'

'We'll see, OK? The man they brought in, he is going to say that he was somewhere else when your grandfather died. And then we are going to see if it's true or not.'

'And if he didn't do it, then we will keep looking until we find the man that really did murder your grandfather,' Edie said. 'I promise you, OK?'

'OK, Edie.'

'But go home now, Layla,' I said. 'Nothing is going to happen quickly today.'

'It's the man who was always outside our house, isn't it?' she said to Edie, and I saw how terrifying it must have been for this teenage girl to look out her window at the crowds that gathered every night on Borodino Street.

'The one with the haircut,' Layla said. 'The one who was making the speeches every night until they cleared the flowers away. They put him on television and You-Tube and all that, and then there were more of them.'

She let go of Edie's hands and ran her fingers through her hair, the streaks of red dye reminding me of the face-painting of young children, it was as playfully inept as that, and that is when I saw the marks on her wrists, the thin white cuts that had healed and been opened again and again and again, the tell-tale bracelets of self-harm. And Edie saw them too.

She seized Layla's hands and would not let her pull them away, dragging the sleeves of her cheap leather jacket halfway up her forearms.

'This,' Edie said, 'is not what your grandfather would have wanted for you, Layla. To see you hurting yourself

233

would have broken his heart. And you know that, don't you?'

A big sergeant came out of 27 Savile Row, yawning widely in the bright new day. He glanced at the three of us sitting on the steps and then slowly walked away, ready for his bed. Layla Khan hung her head, the tears rolling down her face.

'Did he really say my name at the end? Is that true?'

'It's true,' I said.

'You were the best thing in his life, Layla,' Edie said. 'His sons – your uncles, your dad – caused him nothing but misery and grief and pain. But you made him happy, Layla. So wipe your nose. You were the good thing in his life. OK?'

'OK.'

They smiled at each other.

I looked at the red scuffmark on Layla's face and I wondered what the hell was going to happen to this child.

23

I was home before Scout woke up.

The meat market was over for the night. The dancers at Fabric were all tucked up in bed. The first of the office workers were loading up with fuel in Smiths of Smithfield. And maybe it was my imagination, but among the locals I felt a palpable sense of excitement.

It was the last day of the school year.

I collected our mail – *Boxing Monthly*, *Your Dog*, offers of free pizza and an official-looking letter from a firm I had never heard of – and took the steps to our loft two at a time.

Mrs Murphy and Stan were foggy-eyed. The Cavalier stretched like a little furry four-legged lord and idly smacked his lips as Mrs Murphy prepared his breakfast.

'Everything all right?' she said. 'Everybody still in one piece?'

I thought of the young bearded copper with a cracked skull. PC Sykes.

'No fatalities,' I said, and she was happy with that.

Scout was not up yet so, after Stan had wolfed down his Nature's Menu breakfast, Mrs Murphy took him for his walk while I brewed myself a pot of strong black coffee.

Anthony Joshua was on the cover of *Boxing Monthly*.

'The Misunderstood Staffie' was on the cover of *Your Dog*.

And I confirmed that it was really my name and address on the envelope that said *Butterfield, Hunt and West – Solicitors*.

Scout bounded into the room, barefoot and still in her pyjamas, her long brown hair flying. She was grinning from ear to ear and suddenly I remembered exactly what the last day of the summer term felt like when I was that age.

'So is today better than Christmas?' I asked her, scooping her up, and smelling that Scout scent of sugar and shampoo.

She laughed. 'It's very close!'

She squirmed away from me and I gently put her down.

'We're all going to do our hair!' she said. 'Because it's a special day! We're going to do our hair like – you know – the Angry Princess.'

'But I thought you grew out of the Angry Princess.'

'I did. We have. But we thought it would be fun if we all did our hair like the Angry Princess for the last day of the year. Can we? Can I?'

The nostalgia of seven-year-old girls. They could feel the world turning, too. Even at that age they could sense the seasons slipping by. To me it only felt like five minutes ago since we were watching *The Angry Princess* in a packed cinema. But Scout and her friends missed her already as a long-lost part of their childhood.

'Sure, Scout.'

I was reaching for the cereal, milk and cutlery. Scout was looking at me expectantly. A small cloud passed across her face.

'Daddy?'

'Angel?'

'But you have to do it for me. You have to do my hair. Like – you know – the Angry Princess.'

My spirits sank. The Angry Princess was animated royalty. As I recalled, Her Majesty wore her hair up – an impossible pile of golden curls and swirls sitting on top of her head that was then allowed to drop into her eyes in carefully tousled tendrils.

So it was sort of up but falling down. I looked at Scout's tangled mess of long brown hair, with just a slight natural kink in it. And I did not know where to begin.

'OK,' I said.

Scout brightened.

'I'll get the hairclips, comb, brush and all that stuff,' she said, and disappeared into her bedroom.

By the time Mrs Murphy returned, my daughter was white-faced with shock. She was sitting in front of the mirror with what looked like a small collapsed hedge on top of her head. My attempt to replicate the coiffure of an animated princess had failed miserably.

Mrs Murphy laughed. 'Let me,' she said.

Scout and I smiled with gratitude. Mrs Murphy combed Scout's hair straight, deftly piled it up on top of her and, as if by magic, pinned it in place. Scout was a dead ringer for the Angry Princess.

I was smiling as I opened the letter from Butterfield, Hunt & West.

Dear Sir,
Our client, Mrs Anne Lewis (née Wolfe), has instructed us to obtain a child arrangements court order pertaining to the residency of her daughter, Scout Wolfe. The court will arrange a directions hearing which you will be obliged to attend. You will shortly be contacted by the Children and Family Court Advisory and Support Service (Cafcass) for an interview prior to the court hearing ...

I didn't understand what I was looking at.

I didn't understand what any of it meant.

None of it. Not a word. Who were these people? What did they have to do with our life?

Mrs Murphy was putting the finishing touches to Scout's hair.

Scout smiled at me and I smiled back.

'I like your hair,' I said.

'Thank you.'

We had breakfast and then Scout brushed her teeth and got into her grass-stained summer dress without one hair on her head even moving. We both thanked Mrs Murphy for her hairdressing skills and then I took Scout to school.

Some people have said to me that I was both mum and dad to my daughter. But the truth was that every day of my life I was confronted with the hard fact that I would never be a mother to her.

It was tough enough just trying to be a father.

I went up to Room 101 of New Scotland Yard, the Crime Museum of the Metropolitan Police, also known as the Black Museum.

Visits to Room 101 were meant to be strictly by appointment only – the happy days when Sir Arthur Conan Doyle was given his own set of keys were long gone – but over the years I had often come here when I did not know where else to turn.

TONY PARSONS

The Crime Museum is cold, dark and full of secrets, ranging from the casework on the Jack the Ripper investigation to the remains of the drone that brought down the Air Ambulance helicopter on Lake Meadows. The faces of the dead stared at me from the darkness. Some of them were familiar – the old gangs of London, the Krays, the Richardsons and the Warboys – and some were the smiling faces of victims, who the world rarely remembers so well.

One living face loomed out of the Room 101's twilight. Sergeant John Caine, curator of the Crime Museum, was a detective with thirty years' service on his face and not a gram of flab on his body.

'Put the kettle on, son,' he told me. 'I'll just finish off here.'

John was showing around a dozen young recruits from the police academy at Hendon. They were about to finish their training and there is no place better than the Crime Museum – valued as much as a training facility as a museum by the Met – for an understanding how every day at work would put them in harm's way.

'We call it The Job but it's not a job,' John was telling their serious young faces. 'You will run towards danger when others are running away from it, and your training and your trust in your colleagues will enable you to do this without hesitation. You will put yourself in harm's way to protect people you will never

240

know and you will do it every day of your lives. We call it The Job but when one of us falls then we mourn like a family.' He paused to smile at them. 'Take care of yourself and each other out there. Thank you and goodbye.'

They gave him a round of applause.

When they had filed out he came into the small office that acts as a lobby to the Crime Museum proper.

'I've got some chocolate digestives,' he said. 'What's on your mind – this nutter Bad Moses?'

I shook my head and gave him the letter from Butterfield, Hunt & West. I knew that John had his own grown-up children and I knew that not all of them had managed to keep their marriages together. And I didn't know who else to ask.

'What does it mean, John?'

He read it through and handed it back to me.

The kettle began to boil.

'Your ex-wife wants your daughter,' he said. 'And she is going to fight you like hell for her.'

'Thanks for joining us,' Whitestone told me when I walked into the MIR-1. 'We're charging George Halfpenny and I would like you to do the honours, Max.'

Whitestone and I got the lift down to the custody suite.

She did not say much.

But she said enough.

George Halfpenny was sitting on the little bed that is built low to the ground so you can't fall off and hurt yourself. That struck me as bitterly ironic as the custody sergeant locked the door behind us.

'George Halfpenny,' I said.

He was on his feet, shaking his head.

'No,' he said. 'I didn't kill Ahmed Khan. Please believe me. I was swimming with my brother.' He sank back on the low bed, his face crumbling. 'I'm innocent,' he said.

Whitestone laughed, a short bitter bark of loathing.

'I'm not arresting you for the murder of Ahmed Khan,' I said. 'I'm arresting you for the assault on PC Simon Sykes.'

'Remember him?' Whitestone said. 'The police officer you dropped?'

'The cracked skull caused a blood clot on the brain,' I said. 'PC Sykes is still in a coma. He may never wake up. And if he does, he may never walk again.'

'Unlucky for him,' Whitestone told Halfpenny. 'And unlucky for you, too.'

I took a step closer to the man on the bed.

'George Halfpenny, I am charging you with inflicting grievous bodily harm with intent against a police officer executing his duty within the meaning of Chapter Five of the Criminal Justice Act.' I rattled it out: 'You do not have to say anything but it may harm your defence if you do not mention when questioned something you later rely on in court.'

He looked up at us with his mouth half open but he said nothing and he did not need to say a word because at this moment they are all thinking exactly the same thing.

What will they do to me?

How long will I get?

'Life,' Whitestone told him, so softly that it was almost a sigh.

24

Stan loved meeting new people.

Our small red dog was indiscriminate with his affections, although in these hot summer days he showed a definite preference for the builders that thronged the city because they were often wearing shorts, and a pair of bare legs always had Stan's nose twitching with interest.

He perked up the moment the woman from the Children and Family Court Advisory and Support Service appeared on our doorstep.

'Mr Wolfe? Ms Vine.'

She was not wearing shorts but had on a long, swishy skirt above stout walking sandals but it was enough to have Stan's nose testing the air and his tail wagging. He padded out of Scout's bedroom, where he had been napping, crossed the room and delicately inserted his nose just under the hem of the skirt. All I could see of him were his ruby-coloured hind legs and that feathery tail swishing like windscreen wipers.

I said what I always said when Stan was thrusting his attentions on someone.

'I hope you like dogs.'

She froze, looking down at the creature that had inserted itself under her skirt.

'Not really,' she said.

She was a large woman in layers of vaguely ethnic clothing – a flowing scarf, peasant blouse, that long hippy skirt that had enveloped Stan. He took another tentative step inside and she jerked away.

Stan blinked with surprise in the sudden sunlight.

'Could you?' she said. 'Bit allergic.'

'Sure,' I said. 'Sorry.'

I picked up Stan, carted him to Scout's bedroom, shut the door and returned to the loft.

The woman from Cafcass was staring out of one of the big windows.

'Coffee?' I said.

'I'm good.'

As we settled ourselves awkwardly on the sofa, half facing each other, I realised that our conversation was being conducted in monosyllables.

But then Ms Vine began to speak.

'As you probably know, my department looks after the interests of children involved in family proceedings,' she said. 'We interview the concerned parties and then advise the court on what we consider to be in the best interests of the children.'

She had a thin green file in her hands.

I stared at it.

Was that it? This thin green file? Were our lives in there?

Scout. Me. Anne.

The old life. The new life. The future life.

Did something as big as all that really fit into such a thin little green file?

Ms Vine seemed to take my lack of response as a sign of incomprehension. And perhaps she was right. The man in front of her did not have a clue what was happening to his family.

'So my role,' she said, speaking slowly to help me get it, 'is to look out for the child's interests in care, supervision or placement proceedings.'

Is that what this was – a placement proceeding?

I thought we were talking about Scout's life.

'So are you a social worker?' I said.

She bridled at such a prosaic description.

'When working on care cases we are known as a "children's guardian". It's my role – as children's guardian – to be the independent voice of the child in court. Do you have any questions, Mr Wolfe?'

'I don't really understand what's happening,' I said. 'What exactly you're trying to find out. What might happen next. I know there has to be some kind of court hearing—'

She cut across me, pursing her lips with impatience.

'You haven't been advised by your solicitor?'

I shook my head.

'I am here to ensure that a court makes decisions that are in the child's best interests,' she said.

She still had not said my daughter's name.

I waited.

She peeked at the thin green file.

'Scout,' she said. A smile of recognition. 'Like the little girl in *To Kill a Mocking Bird*. The guardian's job is to be Scout's voice in court. I'm on *her* side.' She patted her thin green file. 'Scout's side. Usually there's mediation in a case like this before we get to a family court hearing, but because of the special circumstances, there will be no mediation.'

'Hold on. What special circumstances?'

She met my gaze levelly. 'Because of the violence.'

What? There's never been any violence! I would never hurt Anne! I would never hurt any woman! That's not the way I was raised. That's not who I am.'

'You didn't assault Oliver Lewis?'

The husband.

The bloody husband.

I laughed.

She sat up straighter, her mouth flexing.

'You find me amusing, Mr Wolfe?'

'I find you misinformed, Ms Vine. There was nothing resembling violence between myself and ... ' *The new guy*, I thought. 'Mr Lewis,' I said. 'Some voices may have been raised. A chair may have been knocked over. But it was all handbags – sorry, man bags – at ten paces.' I shook my head. 'I was never arrested, never charged and never found guilty of harming a hair on this gentleman's moisturised head.'

We stared at each other for a bit.

'The law,' I said. 'It's sort of what I do.'

'Yes, Mr Wolfe,' she said. 'Me too.'

She got down to the heart of the thing.

'It's unusual for a daughter as young as Scout to be living alone with her father.'

I waited. I didn't feel like telling her my life story.

She was still waiting.

'Families come in all shapes and sizes,' I offered.

'Hmm,' she said, as if we might have to come back to that one. 'Perhaps you would like to tell me something about Scout's current arrangements at home? Childcare and so on. Your network of support. That's a question, Mr Wolfe.'

'I have a lady called Mrs Murphy who helps me. She lives on the other side of the meat market. Very close. Mrs Murphy loves Scout.'

There was a notebook in her hands.

'So this Mrs Murphy is a relation?'

'No.'

'Employee?'

I shrugged. Mrs Murphy was so much more than that. 'She is,' I said. 'But that doesn't cover it. You see, Mrs Murphy has a big family and they—'

'Your parents? Do they help with Scout?'

'My parents are dead.'

'Siblings? Do you have brothers and sisters, Scout's aunts and uncles, who help you?'

'I'm an only child,' I said.

She wrote for a while. Her eyebrows arched at this strange man who had so few people in his world. As she jotted down these details, I thought I should make some point about how well we were doing, Scout and I, how it had been desperately hard at first but now we were doing fine. But I said nothing. I was afraid of what was going to happen next.

'And how – in your opinion – did the current arrangements come about, Mr Wolfe? Why – in your opinion – is Scout living with you and not her mother?'

'It's not my opinion,' I said. 'It's what happened. My ex-wife left the family home. She had a new life with a new man who is now her husband.'

'The man you didn't assault.'

We stared at each other. The man I didn't assault. That was a good one.

249

'That's the guy,' I said. 'My wife – ex-wife – Anne – was busy with her new life. I don't know how else to explain it – to excuse it. I think when people start a new life – new home, new partner, new children – there's not enough *space* in their life for the old life. The life they left behind.'

I looked towards the big windows of the loft, the July sunshine streaming down as if from heaven.

'I've thought about it a lot over the last few years,' I said. 'Trying to understand it. Trying to make sense of what happened. And that's the best I can come up with. There is only so much room in someone's life. And I know men do that sort of thing all the time.' I looked back at the woman from Cafcass. 'But women do it too. My daughter and I were left to get on with it. And that's what we did.'

'Your ex-wife maintains that you froze her out.'

I put the brakes on my anger.

'After my ex-wife left, my daughter didn't get a birth-day card from her mother. That's how busy she was. That's how cruel she was. My ex-wife wasn't frozen out. She opted out of her family. And Scout and I carried on.'

As always in our home, there was a scattering of toys and playthings on the floor that belonged to my daughter and our dog. A Konk toy. An old Angry Princess doll. And an extra-small-sized boxing glove.

Ms Vine stared at it, as if in disbelief, and then picked it up.

'Scout's,' I said.

'Boxing?'

I smiled.

'My daughter enjoys banging the pads.'

For a moment she was speechless.

'You don't think it encourages violence?'

'I think it encourages my daughter to believe she can stand up for herself in this rotten world. I want her to be a confident little girl. I want her to be a strong young woman. I want her to be ready for whatever life throws at her.'

'So she punches things?'

'Hard and often,' I said, rising to the bait.

She was writing this down.

Don't lose your rag.

'There have been – let's see – nine afternoons when you were late to pick up your daughter from school, Mr Wolfe?'

'Who's counting?'

She gave me a smile as thin as her little green file.

'The school was very understanding,' I said. 'They've been great—'

'This is not about how *understanding* the school are, Mr Wolfe. It's about the welfare of your daughter! It's about how capable you are of facing up to your responsibilities as a parent. I am trying to ascertain if your job is compatible with Scout's best interests.'

'It's not a job. It's a calling. And it's not nine to five. It's twenty-four seven.'

I did not know how to explain it to her. There was so much that I found hard to explain.

'Did you ever see photos of 9/11?' I asked her.

She looked at me as if I was speaking some unknown language.

'One of the most famous 9/11 photographs is of an NYFD fireman called Mike Kehoe when he was running into one of the towers as everyone inside was trying to get out,' I said. 'Everyone thought Mike Kehoe must have died in there when those towers came down. Because so many of his colleagues died that day. Three hundred and forty-three NYFD firemen. Sixty police and eight paramedics. But Mike Kehoe made it out.'

She was resisting the urge to sigh.

'What's your point, Mr Wolfe?'

'My point is that the world is divided into the people who run away from life-threatening trouble and the people whose job it is to run towards it. That was Mike Kehoe's job – to run towards trouble. And I like to think that I'm like Mike. At least, I aspire to be a man like Mike Kehoe. And you need people like us. Because if someone is kicking down your front door in the middle of the night, then you will pick up the phone and call for one of us – the people who run towards trouble – to come and put ourselves, without thinking, without asking questions, between you and whoever is kicking down your front door. But – and this is my point – it's hard to schedule the trouble, so sometimes people like me are late for the school pick-up. And sometimes we never make it home at all.'

She was unimpressed.

She looked at me as if that was all just a pile of – what would she call it? – patriarchal macho bullshit.

She glanced at her watch as if I was wasting her precious time.

'And what happens to your daughter if you never make it home?'

'I hope that she will be proud of me.'

She raised her unplucked eyebrows.

'So what happens next?' I said.

Scout would be home soon. And I wanted to be alone by then.

'It's the court's job to decide what will happen to your child,' Ms Vine said. 'The judge will listen to everyone involved in the case before she or he comes to her or his decision.'

'But you don't *know* Scout,' I said. 'None of you *know* her.'

She slammed the little green file shut as if that was an irrelevance.

253

'Well, I think that's it,' she said, standing up.

'Not quite,' I said.

'I beg your pardon?'

'Ms Vine,' I said. 'Please – I don't want any of this for my daughter.'

'Excuse me?'

'I don't want Scout to be interviewed by you – or anyone like you. Please don't be offended. It's nothing personal. I know you are just doing your job. And I understand your job is to stick up for the child. But please – please, Ms Vine – I don't want Scout's happiness poked and probed and pushed around. I don't want her life in a courtroom. I don't want her questioned.'

She barked with laughter.

'Why on earth not?'

Because we – my beautiful ex-wife and I – have already stolen too much of her innocence, I thought.

Because Scout has already paid too high a price for the mistakes that two adults have made.

Because it would hurt and confuse and upset her.

But I didn't say any of that.

'Because I love her,' I said.

We were on the way to the door. I could hear Stan scratching to get out of Scout's bedroom. He knew there were bare legs walking about in the loft. He wanted to get at them. He wanted to get his head up that hippy skirt. He wanted a good sniff.

'I don't have the contact details for your legal representative, Mr Wolfe.'

'I don't have one,' I said.

'Get one,' she said.

Scout was exhausted when she came back from the long afternoon with her friend Mia.

It was more than a passing fancy. Rowing was her thing that summer. Rowing on the Thames. Rowing on the Serpentine. And it was exhausting.

Stan and I waited by her bed as Scout wearily brushed her teeth, got into her pyjamas and crawled under her duvet.

Her eyes were closing before I opened the book of poems at random.

'On Waterloo Bridge with the wind in my hair
I am tempted to skip. You're a fool! *I don't care.*
The head does its best but the heart is the boss —
I admit it before I am halfway across.'

I closed the book and kissed the top of her head.

'Sleep now, Scout,' I told her.

But she was already sleeping.

My phone vibrated as Stan and I padded from Scout's bedroom. It was a message from an unknown number.

I will make you crawl

I flew to the window as if I would see him waiting for me in the street.

And there he was.

He was long and lean, fit and hard inside athletic gear. If you didn't see him coming it would be over before it began. And even if you saw him coming, he looked like he would hit you with maybe more than you could handle. He was wearing running shoes. At his feet there was a kitbag that could contain anything. A hoodie was pulled up, shielding his face. He was loitering at the start of the Grand Avenue, the great central passageway through Smithfield meat market.

And he was looking up at our loft.

I stared at Scout's bedroom door.

All my instincts were to stay here with her.

But I knew that would never make us safe.

Settle it now.

I put down food and water for Stan and triple-locked the front door behind me as I quietly let myself out. And I thought of that social worker.

You're not my daughter's protector, I thought.

Because I am.

I could not leave by the front door on Charterhouse Street without him seeing me so I went up to the roof.

The view caught my breath and held it. The meat market was getting ready for the night. There was a wash of moonlight on Wren's great white cathedral, the old high-rise towers of the Barbican and the newer, far taller towers of glass and steel that soared everywhere across the city.

From the roof I could see that the man in the shadows was still down there, and he was still staring up at the loft. There was good cover for him in the Grand Avenue.

A convoy of refrigerated lorries and white vans lined the street. Men in white coats were everywhere, hauling their loads of meat into the market. An easy spot to get lost in the crowd.

I crossed to the back of the building and clanked down the old iron fire escape. The emergency exit door at the back of the building was never locked. It took me out on to Cowcross Street, one of those old winding backstreets in Smithfield. I walked down it quickly and paused at the start of Charterhouse Street.

He was still there. Of course he was still there.

I turned right, walking away from home, away from the main entrance where the dark figure was waiting, and I entered the Central Market from the far end.

The place was roaring with shouts and catcalls and threats and laughter. The meat market is long and narrow in here and I walked the full length of it, four hundred metres, and on either side of me there were the men in white coats in the stalls expertly working on huge slabs of bloody meat.

And everywhere there were potential weapons.

I walked quickly, never pausing, never looking from side to side, my eyes always straight ahead and fixed on the exit that would take me out on the Grand Avenue and the man waiting in the shadows.

And as I walked I selected a weapon.

I first picked up a five-inch narrow boning knife and then, a few stalls further on, put it down and picked up a ten-inch chef's knife and carried on walking, my hands held loose at my side, the chef's knife in my right hand.

And then, just before I emerged from the central aisle, I saw what I was really looking for.

A meat cleaver and cut gloves, the hand wraps that butchers use to avoid losing their fingers.

I put down the chef's knife and scooped up the cleaver and cut gloves, pulled them on to my hands without breaking my stride, keeping the meat cleaver down by my right side and my gaze fixed ahead. The cut gloves were moist with the blood of fresh meat.

I stepped out into the night.

He was still there, looking up at the loft, but he sensed me behind him and turned just as I raised the meat cleaver to bring it down where the shoulder meets the neck.

'Jackson!' I said, slowly lowering the meat cleaver. 'What the hell are you doing?'

He did not answer and I did not need him to answer because I knew that he was doing exactly what he had been doing since we were children.

Jackson Rose was watching my back.

'Someone's coming for you,' he said.

25

In the small hours before dawn we sat at my kitchen table with a pot of black coffee between us.

Jackson took a folded sheet of A4 paper from his jacket and spread it on the table. It was the digital front page of the *Daily Post*, the photograph taken outside the Westminster Public Mortuary on Horseferry Road on the day I went to see the body of Ahmed Khan. It was a big close-up of my face, the moment I turned away from Scarlet Bush. *Every murder is a hate crime*, I had told her, and that is what they had used as their headline.

My eyes were missing in the photograph.

Because someone had shot them out.

I grinned at Jackson. 'Is this what they're using for target practice at the firing range now?' I said.

Jackson was not smiling.

'This was left inside my locker,' he said. 'My locked locker, Max. Some shot has got it in for you big time. And I don't think you can laugh it off.'

'Tibbs?'

Jackson shook his head. 'It's not Jesse's style. He's a hothead and a big mouth. But he will say it to your face. You've seen that. A lot of them up there resent you, Max.' He hesitated. 'They blame you for the death of Ray Vann. For not backing up his side of the story. For not going along with his version of events to IPCC.'

'They blame me for not lying,' I said.

He shrugged.

'And how about you, Jackson?'

'I'm on your side,' he said. 'Even when you're a stubborn bastard who is in the wrong.'

'Thanks for that. What I saw of Ray Vann, he was a decent but seriously damaged man. I'm sorry that he's dead. *But he made a mistake*. He shot a man he should have handcuffed. He executed a man he should have arrested.'

Jackson winced. He was still wearing his sky-blue ribbon in memory of the dead at Lake Meadows. The colour was fading now.

'Ray Vann shot a terrorist, Max. Adnan Khan might have been genuinely surrendering or he might have been bluffing. Either way, he was a mass murderer. Who knows what was in his tiny brain in that basement? But he was exactly the kind of murdering bully who, out there in the wicked world, is allowed to put a bullet in a little girl's brain for the sin of wanting to go to school. Or who will use a drone to bring down a helicopter on the heads of people he has never met and who have done him no harm and might even worship the same god as him. So – whatever we do – let's not get too sentimental about the scumbag he slotted. Ray Vann put down a rabid dog.' Stan stirred between his feet and Jackson scratched him behind the ears. 'No offence, Stan.'

I wasn't going to argue with him.

'You know why I wouldn't lie for Ray, right?' I said. Jackson nodded.

'I can guess. Because if you got caught in a lie then you would lose your job.' He indicated the closed bedroom door. 'And then you would probably lose Scout.'

And now maybe I was going to lose Scout anyway.

I pushed away the photograph of my face with the eyes shot out.

'It's too late to save Ray Vann,' I said.

'But it's not too late to defend yourself.'

Jackson hefted his kitbag on to the table, unzipped it and took out a faded Lonsdale T-shirt that had once belonged to me. Wrapped inside the T-shirt was a handgun.

He placed it carefully on my kitchen table.

'It's a Glock 19,' he said. 'A 9 mm semi-automatic. Polymer-framed, short recoil. The Glock Safe Action Pistol.'

I said nothing.

'Don't worry,' he said. 'It's not from the Met.'

I stared at the stubby black firearm.

'That's a relief, Jackson,' I said. 'Because for a moment there I thought you might be getting me into trouble. Is this a souvenir from your service days?'

He shrugged.

'How much kit did you bring home with you?' I said.

'Nothing the British Army will miss.' He nodded at the Glock. 'You know how to use it, right?'

I didn't touch it. I thought that if I ever touched it in my life, I would make sure I was wearing a brand-new pair of blue nitrile disposable gloves.

'Is it traceable?' I said.

'Only if they catch you with it.'

We both looked at the Glock.

'The serial number has been removed,' Jackson said. 'I'm going to show you how to clean it. Cleaning is simple but important. There are only four parts to your Glock. Frame and barrel and slide and recoil spring. That's it. And the magazine, of course. Important safety tip to remember when cleaning your Glock – make sure you haven't left one in the chamber. That's how people die cleaning their weapon. They remove the magazine but they didn't know there's one still in the chamber. And that's the one that kills them. You got all that, Max?'

I said nothing.

He looked towards the window. The sun was coming up. It was going to be another glorious day. He stretched and yawned.

'I just don't want you to die, Max.'

'Me neither.' I stared at the Glock on the table between us. 'That's not army-issue,' I said. 'You didn't steal this from the army. You stole it from somewhere, but it wasn't the army.'

'How would you know?'

This is what I knew.

This is what I remembered from when we were two boys who were closer than brothers.

My friend Jackson Rose was a thief.

When we were kids, I had seen his thieving – a compulsive shoplifting, as likely to happen in a local newsagent as a giant department store in the West End – as a symptom of his wildness.

And for the first time I realised that a thief never grows out of the habit.

'Who did you steal it from, Jackson?'

'Someone who doesn't need it any more,' he said.

I believed him.

But still I did not pick up the gun.

George Halfpenny sat with his head bowed in an interview room at West End Central.

The career criminal slips into the zone when they are in an interview room, the tape running, their bored lawyer by their side. An almost Zen-like calm descends upon the professional villain. They know that we are in there to build the foundations of their prison walls. They know it takes time. They know they need patience and guile.

George Halfpenny was not like that.

He seemed like a man who had already been broken.

'You intended to inflict serious physical harm on PC Sykes,' Whitestone told him. 'Look at me when I'm addressing you, will you?'

Halfpenny's eyes slid to Whitestone's face. But he could not look at her for more than a moment. He knew that she wanted to see him locked up for life.

She nodded at the file before me and I pushed it across to her. She picked it up, began flipping through it.

'Before your job as a rickshaw driver, you were in the Territorial Army for five years. Apparently you took your training seriously. Good grades for unarmed combat, it says here. A big strong boy who lost his temper – is that what you are, George?'

Halfpenny finally looked at her, and when he spoke his voice was hoarse and cracked.

'It all happened so fast. I didn't mean to hurt him. I am not a violent man.'

'You hated the officer you put in a coma,' she said. 'Just like you hate all cops.'

'I don't hate anyone.'

'Come on, George,' Whitestone said, laughing easily. 'You don't hate anyone? Really? We have hours of footage of you preaching outside Ahmed Khan's house on Borodino Street. Whipping the crowds up. Night after night after night. You're the man who single-handedly turned that peace rally in Victoria Park into a riot. You're *full* of hatred. You're full of rage.'

'I hated Ahmed Khan's sons – no, even that's not right. I hated their acts. I hated what they did to the people in that helicopter. And the people who were on the ground when it came down. And I hated what they did to Alice Stone.'

Whitestone erupted. 'Don't you mention her name to me, you piece of filth! Not after what you did to PC Sykes!'

His lawyer perked up.

'My client—'

Whitestone waved him away.

'Your client is going to say he never meant to hurt anyone. Yeah, I can guess. And I am sure that will be a great comfort to PC Sykes' two-year-old daughter and his pregnant wife. It was all a dreadful accident. So what? So what? *So fucking what?*' She shook her head at George Halfpenny. 'And don't think you're off the hook for the

killing of Ahmed Khan.' She tapped the file before her.
'I see that when you were in the Territorial Army you
took Advanced First Aid. So you know enough about
human anatomy to know exactly where to stick a knife
if you want a man to die.'

Halfpenny looked at me.

'You know I was nowhere near Ahmed Khan on the
day he died,' he said. 'You saw my phone. You know
I was swimming with my brother.'

'Our tech guys don't buy it,' I said.

I addressed his lawyer. 'Colin Cho of PCeU – the
Police Central e-crime Unit – maintains that time and
date stamps are extremely easy to fake. They're running
tests right now. PCeU will tell us if it's genuine or not.'

'But *you* believe me?' George pleaded.

'It doesn't matter what I believe,' I said.

Whitestone stood up. 'Even if it's not a phony time
and date stamp, and even if I don't charge you with the
murder of Ahmed Khan, you're still looking at life for
putting my young officer in a coma. And a lot of rough
jail sex.'

'I really must object,' the lawyer said.

'Your client assaulted a young police officer who now
has a blood clot on his brain,' Whitestone said, suddenly
calm. 'That's a hard thing to bounce back from. Your
client has ruined the life of one of our own. The judge
and jury can calculate intent. But – some advice that

you would do well to take – save your professional outrage for someone who gives a damn.'

Whitestone and I rode the lift to the top floor.

'You know he didn't kill Ahmed Khan,' I said.

'I want him put away for life, Max,' she said. 'I don't care what label they stick on it.'

I did not argue with her. Because whatever we charged George Halfpenny with, and whatever conclusion a judge and jury one day arrived at, Whitestone was right.

Sykes' young daughter had been robbed of the father she had known and his wife had been robbed of the man she married. I had seen injuries like the one afflicting that young copper. And I knew they always changed more than one life.

A young woman with a small baby got into the lift. You don't see many babies in West End Central and Whitestone and I both grinned goofily at it – a fat little baldy thing of about six months – and we remembered when our own children were that age.

The woman was dressed for the gym but with a milk stain down the front of her Sweaty Betty top, a good-looking woman who was trying to stay in shape but clearly run ragged by the demands of her life.

She got out on our floor, the baby falling asleep in her arms, gently rocking it and looking around as we edged past her. She eventually started following us down the corridor to MIR-1. I thought she must be lost. But it turned out she knew exactly where she was going.

Edie Wren and Joy Adams looked up from their workstations as we walked into the room.

And suddenly the blood drained from Edie's face.

The woman with the baby was staring at her, shaking so badly that the baby was waking.

'Stay away from my husband, you fucking whore!' the woman shouted.

She hovered in the doorway, her baby crying now, her face clenched tight with fury and grief, her eyes shining.

'He is *a married man*. You are wrecking our home. Just stay away from him, can't you!'

And then she was gone.

Edie turned towards her workstation. She seemed to have stopped breathing. She hung her head. One teardrop fell on her keyboard. I wanted to put my arms around her and hold her close. I wanted to get her out of this room. But I made no move to touch her.

Apart from the rolling news on the big TV, there was total silence in the room.

'Joy?' Whitestone said.

'Ma'am?'

'Try to get a statement from Halfpenny's Commanding Officer from his time in the Territorial Army. I want something on the record about any obsession with knives, blades, and bayonets. Anything on an unhealthy interest in weapons is good, but we are looking for a sick interest in sharp objects. If that date and time stamp on his phone turns out to be fake, we are going to be charging him with murder.'

'Yes, ma'am,' Adams said, reaching for the phone.

'Edie?'

Edie turned towards her. Her pale Irish face had red blotches on her cheeks as if she had been slapped.

'Ma'am?'

'Nobody cares about your broken heart, Edie,' Whitestone said quietly. 'I need you to save the tragedy for outside the office. Have a broken heart on your own time. OK?'

Edie nodded and wiped at her face with the back of her hand.

'Yes, ma'am.'

Whitestone turned to give me some instruction but I was no longer listening.

I was watching the breaking news on the big screen.

'Look,' I said.

The house on Borodino Street was burning.

26

It was the kind of fire you see when an accelerant like petroleum distillate, like kerosene, gasoline or diesel fuel is poured or sprayed through a letterbox and then torched.

The kind of fire the police see all the time.

The call to the emergency services must have been made quickly because the blaze was fierce but confined to the ground floor. Flames spumed from the collapsing front door and the nearest ground-floor windows, wreathing the house on Borodino Street in billowing black clouds of noxious fumes.

Half a dozen fire engines lined the street by the time we got there.

Layla Khan was with her grandmother and a young female lawyer from Ludo Mount's chambers. They stood in silence as they watched their home burn. It was the first time that I had ever seen Azza Khan seem subdued. The stout old woman stood there tugging at her head-scarf, and if she heard the mocking cheers of the crowd who were being kept behind police tape at the end of the street, then she gave no indication.

'If it had happened at night,' Whitestone said, 'they would have burned in their beds.'

Fire Officer Mark Truman stood with Whitestone and me watching the men from the giant six-wheel rigs directing snaking hoses a hundred metres long and unloading thousands of litres of water.

'Any chance it was accidental?' I said. 'A faulty boiler? Dodgy wiring? A frying pan left on the stove?'

Truman smiled grimly.

'Always a chance,' he said, wiping his forehead with the back of his hand. 'Not my call to make.'

There were already small groups of specialists whose job it would be to make the call. A senior fire officer from the Fire Investigation Team had arrived and CSIs were getting suited and booted, including a chemist who would take the lead identifying samples of fire debris for analysis in the lab. But all of them would have to wait until Mike Truman and his men had put out the fire.

The flames were at their most ferocious around what remained of the front door. As we watched, the burning door peeled from its hinges and seemed to melt away to nothing.

'There's the seat of the fire,' Whitestone said.

Mike nodded. 'We will have to wait for the FIT's report, but the front door certainly looks like the point of origin.'

'And fires don't start accidentally on the welcome mat,' I said.

Joy Adams approached us. 'Most of the street's residents have been evacuated,' she said. 'They're bedding down for the night in local churches, synagogues and mosques. Edie and some uniforms are taking witness statements. Nobody saw anything, as far as we can make out.'

Whitestone indicated the crowd at the end of the street.

'And who's talking to them?' she said.

The crowd was different now. When the sea of flowers was laid in memory of Alice Stone, those who came to Borodino Street seemed to come from every corner of society. Men from the City. East End pensioners. Young women with sunbed tans. Schoolchildren and their parents.

Now the crowd was predominately young and male and angry. At each fresh eruption of smoke and flames from the windows and front door of the house on Borodino Street, the firemen hunched and braced themselves for the worst before immediately returning to their work, while the crowd roared their approval. Most of them, I noticed, had their hair shaved completely bald at the sides and a short crop on top in the manner of George Halfpenny.

But not all of them.

Father Marvin Gane was standing to one side of the crowd, watching the fire from the end of the street. Joy Adams saw me staring at him.

'Father Gane is offering a camp bed in St Anthony's to anyone who needs it,' she said.

I looked at her.

'You know Father Gane?'

'He buried my father,' Adams said. 'He married my sister. He christened me. He taught my brothers to box. I see him for most of his Sunday services, if I'm not working.' Her face was impassive. 'I know him, yes.'

'You know Father Gane is the brother of one of our colleagues who died in the line of duty?'

'His brother Curtis,' she said. 'I didn't know Curtis.' She smiled. 'He wasn't much of a church-goer. I knew Mrs Gane, their mother. She was friendly with my mum.'

'Why does Father Gane keep coming here, Joy?' I said. 'He's a long way from Brixton.'

She looked genuinely shocked.

'He comes to pray for those who have been separated from God,' she said.

Adams went off to help Edie.

And then Scarlet Bush was standing by my side.

Together we watched the fire.

'Those Khan brothers certainly started something, didn't they?' she said.

I did not reply. I was watching the girl. Layla Khan was standing stiffly by her grandmother's side and together they stared at the fire, trying to make sense of something that made no sense at all. A young woman

274

from Sir Ludo Mount's chambers stood to one side, speaking into two hand-held devices at once.

Scarlet Bush was still talking.

'Don't you wonder where it comes from, Max? The medieval violence that started all this hatred and violence? Don't you wonder where this nihilism comes from? The poison that the Khan brothers took into the world? Someone pumped their brains full of all this toxic waste. It has to start from somewhere, doesn't it? Some Internet chat room. Some raving Iman. I don't buy the notion that it is just a cumulative effect. It has to come from somewhere, Max. Just as that fire had to be lit by someone. Who poisoned the Khan brothers? Somebody did.'

'That's your next story, Scarlet. Maybe it will save your paper. Maybe it will save your industry.'

I glanced at my watch. I had to be in a lawyer's office in Chancery Lane in thirty minutes. I realised I was going to have to put the blues and twos on if I was going to make it.

'It's not my job to worry about where the mess comes from,' I told her. You could smell the stink of the fire on Borodino Street. 'It's my job to clear it up.'

Scarlet nodded, unimpressed.

'And how's that working out?' she said.

My lawyer looked far too young for the job. Sergeant John Caine of the Black Museum had recommended her – she had represented two of John's grown-up children when their families fell apart – and that should have been good enough for me. John Caine never gave me anything but sound advice.

But my heart dipped as she showed me into her tiny, box-like office, indicating one of the two chairs that faced her jumbled desk.

Maria Maldini, Family Law LLB (Hons), looked as though she was not yet out of her twenties. Her name was Italian but everything about her calm, confident manner suggested one of those London private schools that cost £18,000 a year, where they guarantee you come out with iron-clad confidence. My dog Stan could get four good A Levels at a school like that. But she did not look old enough or experienced enough to keep my family together.

And then she began to speak. And made me think again.

'I don't think your ex-wife has a chance of custody,' she said. 'There are four hundred thousand single fathers in this country now. Yes, single fathers are still a minority – around 13 per cent in the UK the last time I looked. But there are *one million children* being raised by single fathers.' She gave me the kind of smile you know has made some orthodontist a rich man. 'And I was one of them,' she said.

Her male PA appeared in the doorway.

'Coffee?' she said.

'Espresso?' I said.

'Of course,' she said.

'Triple,' I said.

She grinned. 'Two triple espressos, Matthew,' she said, leaning back in her chair.

And then Maria Maldini told me her story.

'My father raised me after my mother left the family home when I was thirteen,' she said. 'And if you think *that's* a cliché – the pre-menopausal mother having a mid-life crisis brought on by her pubescent daughter – then who do you think Mother ran away with?'

I had no idea.

'Her tennis coach,' she said, shaking her head, the contempt still raw after the best part of a couple of decades. The door opened and she paused while Matthew carefully placed our triple espressos before us.

I sipped mine.

Maria Maldini bolted hers down in one go, like a vodka shot.

'I never saw much of my mother after that,' she said. 'Rather like your daughter – Scout.'

She did not need to look at my file to name my daughter.

'My mother was too busy concentrating on improving her groundstrokes with her tennis coach to devote much time to me or my younger brother,' she said. 'It is the oldest and saddest story in the world. The absent parent who does not have enough time for children they leave behind. Usually it is men who behave with such ... '

She searched for the phrase she was looking for.

'Selfish cruelty,' she said. 'But not always. As you know.'

Now she glanced at my file.

'You had your interview with Cafcass?

'Some social worker came round ... '

'Don't tell me. I can imagine. Some sour old battle-axe who thinks that all men are rapists. Don't worry about her. I'm the product of a home where the father was the primary caregiver, Max. And we are not going to let any of them stand in the way of you bringing up your daughter. Now tell me your story.'

It felt like there wasn't that much to tell.

'My ex-wife fell in love with someone else. She started a new family with him. Scout and I were left to get on with it. And we did.'

'No problems at school? No mental health issues? No wailing for her missing mother?'

I shook my head, almost laughing at the thought.

'Scout's a happy, intelligent, loving little girl.' I shrugged. 'She's just a great kid.'

Then I hesitated. I could not pretend that Scout was untouched by divorce. We all like to pretend that children are unharmed by divorce. We all lie to the world and to ourselves because it hurts too much to admit the truth.

'Go on,' my lawyer said quietly.

'There's a seriousness about Scout,' I said. 'I don't know how else to describe it. I feel that we – my ex-wife and I, because it is my fault too as I was part of that marriage – robbed her of something. She's different from the little girl she would have been if my ex-wife and I had stayed together. It's a hard thing to admit – that you have inflicted this lifetime wound on your child. But it's true.'

'And what does she say about what happened between you and your ex-wife? What does Scout have to say about being brought up by her father? What does she say about the mother who has only had sporadic contact with her since she left?'

'We don't talk about it,' I said. 'We don't talk about any of it.'

Maria Maldini was not remotely surprised. She nodded briskly.

'Custody and residency proceedings were always meant to be in the best interests of the child. The reality is that for fifty years they were in the best interests of the mother. But that has finally begun to change.'

'Look, I don't want to get into a war about this,' I said. 'I want Scout to stay with me. But I don't want to get into some ugly custody wrangle. I don't want

TONY PARSONS

her hurt more than she has been already. I want to protect her.'

Maldini sighed.

'It's an adversarial game, Max. Because sharing doesn't work. Sharing is a myth. There is no such thing as joint parenting. It doesn't work for practical reasons – a child needs to go to school somewhere. And it doesn't work for emotional reasons – most divorced couples would be very happy to never see each other again. But you have to put up a fight, Max. And most fathers *don't* put up a fight. No doubt there are some men who are too busy with their new lives to fancy the school run every morning – but there are other fathers, good fathers, who feel they simply haven't got a chance. So they don't even put up a fight.'

She leaned forward.

'Another triple espresso?'

'I'm good.'

She nodded.

'You deserve to be the primary carer. You've *earned* it. Your daughter is *happy* with you. It is in her *best interest* to stay with you – not be dragged off to some hideous house in the suburbs by – what does she call herself these days? – *Mrs Anne Lewis.*'

She made it sound like an alias. She made it sound as if my ex-wife did not have a hope in hell of taking Scout away from me.

'Who knows if your ex-wife is even going to stay with her latest husband,' my lawyer said.

'They seem pretty settled,' I said.

'OK – maybe they'll live happily ever after. But my mother's tennis coach had a very short shelf life. After all that disruption in all those lives – and my brother has never really got over the divorce – the tennis coach soon found himself unseeded. And my guess is that your ex-wife – Anne – might find that real life intrudes on every happy ending. To your knowledge, is she working?'

'I don't think she's worked since we were together. She has had a couple of kids with the new guy.'

Was I still allowed to call him the new guy?

I could in this room.

I could call him anything I liked in the chambers of Maria Maldini, Family Law LLB (Hons).

'Anne was a model,' I said.

My lawyer grinned at that. 'And did she make a living as a model?'

I shrugged. 'It was feast or famine.'

'And her latest husband is some kind of banker in the city?'

Her *latest* husband! I had to smile. And she made *banker* sound like an insult.

'Yes. He's in the finance industry. A rich guy. Oliver.'

'We're going to bury them, Max. No wonder they're fighting dirty.'

'How are they fighting dirty?'

She carefully pulled a letter from the file.

'They know how many times you were late picking up Scout. They keep bursting into tears because you raised your voice to Oliver.' She looked at me levelly. 'And they say you are not capable of being the primary care-giver, even though any reasonable judge would say that you have already proved yourself to be a responsible and loving father.'

She slowly stood up.

My time was nearly over.

'But if they want to fight dirty, then we can fight dirty too,' she said.

We stood up and shook hands.

'I don't mind fighting dirty,' I said. 'But I am not using my daughter as a weapon.'

Maria Maldini waited for more.

'I don't want Scout involved,' I said. 'I just want her to have a happy childhood. A stable childhood. A normal childhood.'

'It's too late for that,' my lawyer said, glancing at her watch.

27

High summer on Hampstead Heath.

It is the time of year when the regulars – the dog walkers and the serious runners who are out on those 800 acres of forest, meadow and rolling hills whatever the season – share all that wild open space with the rest of the city.

Scout and I came out of the long shadows of the lime trees and into the dazzling sunshine of Parliament Hill, Stan padding ahead of us, his nose twitching at all the picnics that were being enjoyed across that steep green hill. He swerved at the scent of some sausage rolls and Scout called him back.

'Stan,' she said in her best stern voice. 'They're not for you.'

'Sausage roll walks into a bar,' I said.

'Barman says – *sorry, we don't serve food*,' Scout said. 'Oh my God, Daddy, everyone knows that one.'

We climbed Parliament Hill, our pace slowing, and even at the end of the long summer day, we were so high above the city that up here the air was alpine fresh.

We crested the summit and stopped, and all London was spread out below us, from the North Downs that mark the southern border of the City, to the Shard and Canary Wharf to the East, and to St Paul's Cathedral, marking our home in Smithfield.

Usually we would turn right at the top and make our way down to the string of ponds that would lead us out of the Heath, but today I indicated the lone wooden bench that waits for the weary traveller on the summit of Parliament Hill.

'Sit down for a moment, Scout.'

She gave me a questioning look but parked herself on the bench, Stan chewing the grass between her feet to aid his digestion or maybe just because he liked the taste.

We stared at our beautiful city bathed in the haze of a blazing summer and it looked like a sweet dream that would evaporate upon waking.

'We never sit down on a walk,' Scout pointed out, swinging her legs, and lifting her chin in the direction of the neighbourhood that waits beyond the Heath. 'Not until we get to Hampstead High Street. That's how we do it.'

'That's true,' I said. 'But I've been thinking, Scout.'

'OK,' she said, as if there was a first time for everything.

'We don't really talk about what happened, do we? With our family. With your mother.' I looked away from the city spread out below us and I concentrated on my daughter. 'We never talk about it, Scout.'

'We mostly talk about Stan.'

I smiled at her. It was true.

We did not talk about her school. We did not talk about my work. We certainly did not talk about what had happened to our family. Almost all of our conversations revolved around our dog.

'And there are a few good reasons for that, Scout.'

'I'm still young,' she said, swinging her legs.

'There's that, angel. You're right. But there's other reasons too. We don't talk about it because we're doing all right, you and me. And we don't talk about it because I guess we don't know where to begin. And most of all, I think, and this is the way I see it, Scout — we don't talk about it because it still hurts. It's painful for us, Scout. All of it. Our family being together and then coming apart. All that time when you never saw your mum.'

'She was very busy.'

'That's right. But we do need to have a bit of a talk about it now, OK?'

She nodded.

'Your mother didn't leave you. She left me.'

'But you're nice.'

285

'Thanks, Scout. I appreciate that. It's really kind of you to say so. It means a lot to me. It means the world. But here's the thing, Scout – I know you miss her.'

'No,' she said. 'Oh, no, no, no.'

I ploughed on. 'And I know you miss having your mother around. And I think you deserve a chance to be loved by her. And I think that you might like to try but you don't want to hurt my feelings.'

Scout thought about it for a while.

Stan sighed, lifted his head to sniff her trainers, and fell asleep.

'I'm sort of *forgetting* her,' Scout said. 'My mum. I don't remember – really remember – when we were all together. And sometimes I don't know if I remember a time or if I just saw a photograph of it.' She reached down to scratch the fur of the sleeping dog. 'Or maybe I imagined it. You know what I mean?'

My heart ached for this beautiful child who did not want to betray me.

But the forces pulling her away from me seemed irresistible.

'I know exactly what you mean, Scout. I think you miss your mum. I think you have missed her more than either of us – you and me, I mean – want to admit.'

We were silent.

I had to find the words.

And I knew the words.

The difficult part was saying them.

'Your mum wants you to live with her,' I said. 'And she wants it very much.'

'I know.'

'You know?'

'She told me. And she showed me where my bed would be and where I would keep my stuff and she told me that it wouldn't be like before. She told me that I would still see you. And that I would have all of the summer holiday before I had to think about going to a new school. And that everything would work out fine.'

I choked down something hard and bitter.

'I will be there for you forever,' I said. 'Whatever happens, Scout. With me. With your mum. When you are a kid. And after you are all grown up.' I grinned at her and she smiled back. 'I'm not going anywhere, kiddo,' I said. 'I'll always be there for you. All my life. And after my life is over. If there's anything else, some kind of heaven, then I will be there and I will be watching out for you. Because nothing is more important to me than you, Scout. But you know all of that already, right?'

'Right.' She chewed her lip and scratched her sleeping dog. 'But what about *you*? What would happen to you if I go? And when will I see Mia? And what about Stan? And what about all my *stuff*?'

She was seven years old. Scout cared about me. But she also cared about her stuff. And her friend Mia.

And her dog.

I swallowed hard and indicated the city that was spread out below us, that beautiful silver city shining in the dreaming summer sunshine.

'Everything that you have here in London will still be here for you. Your friend – Mia. And your dog – Stan.' I fought to find the words and felt them sting my eyes. I didn't know how else to say it. 'And my love, Scout,' I said.

We stared out over London.

'OK then,' she said, and it was somehow all settled in that moment.

Scout would live with her mother. It was not the decision of the lawyers and the social workers and the judge. It was not even the decision of my ex-wife and me.

It was her choice.

And that was the way it had to be.

'Shall we go?' I said.

'Pancakes sitting outside the Coffee Shop?'

I grinned at her.

'Sounds good,' I said. 'And Scout?'

'Yes?'

'Nothing changes between us,' I said. 'Not now and not ever. And you know something else, kiddo?'

'What?'

I touched her lightly on the shoulder.

'I'm proud that you're my daughter,' I said.

28

Stan didn't like to see you go.

Even if I was just nipping down the shops to get some bagels and milk, or if Scout was being dropped off for a sleepover, our dog would groan as if his heart was breaking into a billion tiny pieces to see part of the pack going its own way. And so Scout and I smiled at each other when he began to whimper when we parked on the street where it looked like nothing bad had ever happened.

Because seven days after we talked on Parliament Hill, with the summer and our city and her lifetime all before her, today she was really leaving.

'Dogs don't change, do they?' Scout said.

'That's right,' I said.

Dogs don't change, I thought. Even when everything else changes. Dogs stay the same.

'Oh, Stan,' Scout said. 'You best boy. You little red rascal. I will see you very soon.'

We left him in the car and carried her things up the path. Some of her things. Enough to get her settled, enough to remind us that the loft in Smithfield would always be there.

Anne and Oliver opened the front door as we came up the garden path. Their two small children milled at their feet.

Oliver stepped forward to help me, taking the suitcases I held and placing them in the hall. Then he shook my hand. How could I still think of him as the new guy?

This was Scout's life now.

Scout was listening to her mother telling her about exciting times that were ahead. I didn't catch all of it.

Pizza for dinner. A trip to the cinema to see *The Angry Princess Two*. All good stuff. The two children peered at Scout shyly from between their mother's legs.

I looked at Oliver and for the first time in my life, I felt a pang of feeling for the man. I was touched that he was here for Scout's arrival. 'How's work?' I said, feeling like I should say something to him.

His mouth twisted into something between a grin and a grimace.

'The bank let me go,' he said.

'Oh,' I said. And that was the end of that conversation.

The handover had the feel of a sleepover. It didn't feel real. It did not feel *final*. It was only when they all went inside and the door closed behind my daughter that I felt a sense of loss as acute as an amputation.

My daughter was gone and yet it felt like she was still there.

As if she would always be there.

Stan was sleeping when I stopped the car by the side of Richmond Park. A giant red stag stared at me from the tree line. I had thought that nothing could replace having Hampstead Heath as your back garden.

But perhaps I was wrong. There were wild open spaces everywhere.

Still watching the red stag, I finally returned the voicemail message from my brilliant young lawyer, Maria Maldini.

She was not angry with me and I was grateful for that.

'As you can imagine, I just took a rather triumphalist call from Mrs Lewis' lawyer at Butterfield, Hunt and West,' she said.

Mrs Lewis. The mother of my child. What a mess we make of our lives, I thought. And it is always the children who pay the price.

'I didn't do it for my ex-wife,' I said. 'And I didn't do it for myself. I did it for my daughter.'

'Well,' my lawyer said brightly, as if she already understood something about this world that I had yet to learn. 'Let's hope it works out, shall we?'

When Stan and I got home, Edie Wren was standing outside my front door, trying to call me. And Layla Khan was sitting on my doorstep.

Edie and I stepped away while Layla fussed over the dog.

'Layla's run away from home,' Edie said. 'Turned up at West End Central. She wouldn't tell me everything but her grandmother sounds like a nightmare. She can't keep doing it, Max, because social services will take her into care.' Edie chewed her bottom lip, looking at Layla and Stan. 'That's why I brought her here. If she hangs around West End Central, someone's to call social services just to get shot of her. What are we going to do with her?'

'What can we do, Edie?' I said. 'We're going to take her home. Going into care isn't going to bring her any joy, is it?'

Edie leaned closer, lowering her voice.

'But her grandmother knocks her about, Max,' she said. 'Calls her a whore for mucking about with her hair and make-up. She's a sixteen-year-old girl growing up in London, for Christ's sake.' Edie shot a protective look at Layla. 'I'm really concerned about her, Max. There's other stuff going on that she doesn't want to talk about. Apparently some cousin's turned up from Islamabad. She's got all these family members laying down the law.'

'Edie,' I said. 'It's good that you care about the kid. But you can't change her world. What else can we do with her apart from take her home? Do you really want to hand her over to social services? You think that's going to sort out her life? A few years being abused in care and then chucked on to the streets to fend for herself? Living with her family has got to be better than that, doesn't it?'

'But how can I send her back, Max? She trusts me. I was tempted to take her home with me. Just until we worked something out.'

'Then you would have both been in trouble,' I said. 'There's nothing to work out, Edie. Apart from the least worst option.'

We all went up to the loft.

Layla picked up a Frisbee and zipped it too high and hard across the room, as if Stan was a Labrador.

He gamely went after it anyway.

'Layla?' I said. 'We are going to have to take you back to your grandmother. The alternative is to let social services take care of you. In the eyes of the law, you're still a child.'

Layla glared at Edie with tears in her eyes.

'You said he would think of something.'

'I said he would try.'

'I thought you were *my friend*. I bet you think you support women's rights, don't you? Well, what about my women's rights? Or are you too scared of looking racist to stand up for *my* rights?'

'I am your friend,' Edie insisted. 'And I'm going to keep an eye on you. And I am not going to let anyone—'

293

But Layla wasn't interested.

'You tell me to fit in!' she said. 'You tell me to integrate! You tell me to assimilate! Then you send me home to a place where I have to turn the clock back five hundred years.'

We had no answer to that.

'Maybe my family were right about you,' Layla said, looking at both of us now. 'You hate the lot of us. *We destroy your buildings because you destroy our countries*. And we hate you right back.'

'That's not you talking,' Edie said. 'That's your father or your uncles talking. That's some dick with a beard on YouTube. But it's not you, Layla.'

'You don't know me,' Layla said, and stormed off to use the bathroom.

We watched her go. Stan belatedly returned with the Frisbee, disappointed the game was over so soon.

'I promised her that we would work something out,' Edie said.

'And you did,' I said. 'Layla goes home and you keep an eye on her. Explain to dear old granny – and anyone else that's hanging around – that nobody's allowed to knock a child about in this country.'

Edie dragged her fingers through her hair.

'Layla doesn't really hate me, does she?' Edie said. 'She's a teenager. Hormones all over the place. Reminds me of me at that age.' She smiled ruefully at me. 'You've got all that to look forward to, Max.' She looked around the loft. 'Scout's got a sleepover?'

I took a breath. 'Scout's living with her mother now.'

Edie took that in.

'I'm sorry, Max. That must have been hard.'

'It's hard but it had to happen. And how are you, Edie?'

'I'm fine. I'm good.' She hesitated. 'I bailed out of the thing with Mr Big after the wife turned up at work.' She shuddered at the memory. 'I should have done it years ago. She was right. I should have known better. And he was never going to leave his wife. But it's OK. Most relationships don't end too soon. Most of them go on too long.'

She ran her fingers through her red hair as we stared at the bathroom door and waited for Layla to come out.

'I just wish I could sleep,' Edie said.

I nodded.

'Me too,' I said.

We drove Layla home.

At the far end of Borodino Street a crowd was gathering behind police tape and a short line of uniformed officers. At the other end, where we showed our warrant cards to a hefty uniformed sergeant, there were three police vans. Two of them were full of more uniformed coppers, drinking tea and laughing as if they were not expecting anything too arduous in the shift that lay ahead.

Most of the houses on Borodino Street were boarded up now. The locals were moving out. The developers were moving in. Building work was everywhere. A scaffolding lorry was parked halfway down the street. In a year or two Borodino Street would be full of luxury apartments for young professionals.

I stared at the crowd waiting beyond the police tape.

There were still some George Halfpenny haircuts but their numbers were swelled by local youths and perhaps not so local. They were white, black and Asian, with little in common apart from their age and their boredom.

The boys of summer, I thought, and I could smell a riot in the warm air.

'How many have you got up here, Skipper?' I asked the sergeant.

'A full PSU.'

A complete Police Support Unit consists of an inspector, three sergeants, eighteen officers and three drivers for the three vehicles that every PSU is split into. So there were a couple of dozen officers to manage a crowd of perhaps a hundred.

'It might not be enough,' I said.

'Oh, it will be enough if these little herberts keep it quiet,' the sergeant said confidently. 'And if they don't, we'll just bell for some back-up.' He indicated the crowd. 'They think they've got a big gang?' The sergeant chuckled. 'We've got the biggest gang in town.'

We walked down the empty street to the house.

There were jeers from the crowd when they recognised Layla.

'They really hate us, don't they?' she said. 'All of us. They just want us gone.'

Edie put an arm around her shoulders. 'Nobody's going to hurt you, OK?' she said.

Layla snorted with disbelief. But she made no attempt to shrug Edie off.

The ground floor of the house on Borodino Street was an abandoned ruin. There was blackened brickwork around the boarded-up windows. The old wooden door was gone and had been replaced by what looked like a stainless steel slab behind a locked metal grille.

A few dim lights were burning upstairs. A Porsche 911 was parked right outside.

'I'm surprised they didn't move you out,' I said to Layla.

'My grandmother wouldn't move,' she said.

'I thought the council would tell her to move,' Edie said.

Layla laughed with something like pride. 'They don't tell her what to do. She tells *them* what to do.'

A man opened the door. He was young, fat, with the scant remains of his hair plastered across his gleaming skull. He said something to Layla in Urdu.

She brushed past him without replying and went upstairs.

We showed him our warrant cards. He stared at them blankly. He tapped his chest.

'Husband,' he said. 'Husband.'

Edie and I exchanged looks.

The grandmother came shuffling down the stairs.

'Husband,' the man said, indicating the stairs. 'New husband.'

'You're getting married again?' Edie said.

Mrs Khan showed us her teeth. 'Yes, yes, yes,' she laughed. 'Taking a new husband now the old one is gone. Ha, ha, yes!'

There was suddenly a roar from the crowd beyond the police tape. They were surging forward, trying to get past the line of officers. The tape had already been shredded. A policeman's helmet careered like a skittle across Borodino Street. The cops from the vans were racing down the street to reinforce their colleagues.

'Inside now,' I said.

The fat young man locked and bolted the stainless steel door behind us.

I went into the front room. It still stunk of fire and sodden wood and blackened brickwork although the worst of the damage was all close to the hallway and front door. All three of the bay windows at the front of the house had been boarded up but there were gaps in the wood where shafts of light came in. I pressed my face against the largest crack in the boards that covered the middle bay window and saw it afforded a good view of the full length of Borodino Street.

A few dark figures with their faces obscured by ski masks and hoodies were already moving around the abandoned convoy of police vehicles.

As I watched, one of the empty police carriers suddenly burst into flames. One of them must have sprayed something on the side of the burning vehicle before it was torched because it was suddenly there in rough black characters, the single word and the four numbers, shining out of the flames like a thought for the day.

EXODUS 20:13

Edie was on the phone calling for back-up as Sir Ludo Mount came into the room.

'This continuing campaign of intimidation against my clients is outrageous,' he said. 'The institutionalised racism of the Metropolitan Police must—'

'Do you believe in Bad Moses, Sir Ludo?' I asked him.

He stared at me.

299

'I beg your pardon?'

'Do you think this Bad Moses is real? Because if Bad Moses exists, then he is here tonight.' I indicated the boarded-up window. 'Look out there.'

He pressed his smooth pink face against the crack in the boards and I saw his body stiffen. When he turned away from the window, I saw the terror in him.

'I'm getting out of here,' he said.

'I strongly advise against it,' I said.

'This Bad Moses will lynch me from the nearest lamp-post if he gets a chance!'

'That's why you are better off staying in here,' I said. 'There's back-up on the way—'

But Mount was no longer listening to me. He was screaming at the fat young man who still held the keys in his hand.

'Open it! Open it!'

The fat young man opened the front door and Sir Ludo pushed roughly past him. The door was quickly locked and bolted again. From the boarded-up window Edie and I watched Mount get into his Porsche and gun the engine.

'Is this a good idea?' Edie said.

'If he makes it,' I said. 'And if he doesn't, it's a lousy idea.'

The police were pushing back the crowd at the far end of Borodino Street and the Porsche containing

Mount sped off in the opposite direction, towards the abandoned police vehicles, swerving up on to the pavement to avoid the blazing van with the word and the numbers sprayed on its side.

But suddenly more dark figures were at that end of the street, as if drawn by the fire, faceless shapes with their features hidden by ski masks and scarves. There were a dozen of them, then twenty, then too many to count.

The engine of the Porsche gave a throaty roar as it hurtled towards them, but they blocked his exit now and Sir Ludo did not have it in him to plough through them.

He jammed on his brakes and began reversing down the street. Then he stopped and fell out of the car, on his hands and knees and then rising and running, as if it was his car that they wanted and not his skin, not his head, not his life.

And perhaps he was right because the masked crowd cheered as Sir Ludo fled but they did not give chase as he ran back towards the house.

The outnumbered police had fought the crowd to a standstill at the far end of the street while at the other end, the faceless figures capered and danced and cheered as they began rocking the abandoned Porsche, attempting to turn it over.

And then there were sirens in the distance, getting closer with every second, and at both ends of the street, the mob was melting away as if of one mind. Cursing them, the bruised and battered Police Support Unit gave chase.

Borodino Street was suddenly deserted.

Sir Ludo was standing bewildered in the middle of the empty street as Edie and I came out of the house.

'Is it safe?' he said. 'Is help on the way?' And then he squealed with pain. 'My bloody car!' he said, marching towards it. 'Those animals!'

The Porsche had been flipped on its back.

I looked at Edie Wren and she smiled at me with the relief that comes when you know you are finally safe and sound.

And then my phone vibrated.

NO CALLER ID, it said.

And then the promise.

I will make you crawl

And at that moment the headlights of a scaffolding lorry came on at the end of the street.

'We've been set up,' I said as the scaffolding lorry's engine fired up.

It was coming towards us, moving rapidly down the deserted street, gaining speed with every second, the headlights dazzling, the big diesel engine roaring.

Sir Ludo Mount was standing by the side of his flipped-over Porsche, looking at his phone.

The scaffolding lorry struck him a glancing blow, catching him low on the back, and it was enough to spin him around and toss him screaming into the air, his hands clawing at his broken spine before he even hit the ground.

And it just kept coming.

'Go,' I said, but Edie did not move. And for a long sickening moment, neither did I.

Then I shoulder-charged her off the pavement and over a low, scrubby bush into a neighbour's garden that had long ago exchanged its grass for concrete. And when I saw her feet in the air and I knew she was out of harm's way, I ran. I ran for my life.

And I ran for my car, that big Bavarian tank, as if it was my only hope of walking away. The scaffolding lorry was gaining on me, the driver leaning on the horn, one long scream of blue murder, but I threw myself behind my old BMW and then it was tearing past me and gone, hurtling out of Borodino Street.

I slowly got up off my knees, the smell of diesel in the back of my throat.

All at once the street was full of vehicles and people. The world had filled with blue lights. Edie was climbing out of the bush and numbly staring at Sir Ludo Mount.

At first I thought he was roadkill. But then Edie was on her knees, pumping his chest, pushing out the thirty compressions before lifting his chin and tilting his forehead and pressing her mouth against his mouth as she blew air into his lungs.

The fire had burned itself out in the police van. Most of its white paint had curled and dissolved, revealing the steel beneath. But you could still just about read the message.

EXODUS 20:13

'What does it mean?' a woman's voice said beside me.

I turned to look at Scarlet Bush.

'It's the Sixth Commandment,' I told the reporter. I knew them all by heart now. '*Thou shalt not kill.*'

Then Edie was there. Paramedics were all around Sir Ludo Mount, lifting him on to a gurney and loading him into the back of an ambulance.

She hugged me. I looked at her face. Her fabulous face.

We broke away from each other.

Scarlet Bush had approached the back of the ambulance and started taking photographs of Mount's mangled body being secured for transportation to hospital. One of the paramedics furiously cursed her and she backed off, checking her phone to see what she had.

'Get any good shots?' Edie said, her voice ripe with contempt.

'A few,' Scarlet said. She lowered her phone and looked at us. 'Sir Ludo was really hated, wasn't he? Because he stood up for the Khan family after the brothers killed all those innocent people. Because he went after the Met after Alice Stone died.'

'Yes,' I said. 'Sir Ludo Mount was hated.'

She held her phone nearer to me. There was a little red light that told me she was recording.

'And would you say he was the most hated man in England?'

I nodded. 'There's your story, Scarlet,' I said, and she hurried off to write it.

Edie was staring at me. 'But they weren't trying to kill Mount, were they?' she said. 'They were trying to kill *you*. He just got in the way. *Exodus 20:13*. Who do they think you killed, Max?'

Ray Vann, I thought. Someone thinks I have to answer for Ray Vann.

But I said nothing.

'Look,' Edie said, and we stared up at the house on Borodino Street.

Mrs Khan and the man who called himself *husband* were watching the street from the top floor.

And from an unlit window at the other end of the house, Layla Khan also looked down at the street.

I hardly recognised her because the girl's head and face were now covered by a hijab. And I understood that the bald young man from Islamabad was not here to marry Mrs Khan.

He was here to marry Layla.

Then Layla Khan turned her head, as if someone was calling her name, and she stepped away from the window and Edie Wren and I saw her no more.

29

It was high summer now, the blazing days of August, and Stan and I were on Hampstead Heath, making our way up Parliament Hill, ascending the steep climb to one of the highest points in the city when all you can see ahead of you is hill and sky, and there's a tingle in your blood because you know that the moment you reach the top all of London will suddenly be displayed below you.

And then I realised that Stan was no longer by my side.

I jogged back down the hill to the wood, calling his name, waving a pack of Nature's Menu treats, and feeling a sense of rising panic. And then deep inside all the bright greens of summer, I saw a smudge of ruby-coloured dog concealed in the bushes and then those shining black eyes.

But my smile fell away as I went deeper into the bushes.

Stan was not moving.

I got out some treats, still calling his name, but the most food-motivated dog in the world did not budge. He was not interested in food.

'Anaphylactic shock,' a passing dog walker said as his elderly Retriever gambolled on Parliament Hill. 'Something stung her or bit her.'

Strangers always thought that Stan was female. There was something about the extravagant curls of his ears that made him look like a girl. I retrieved him from the bushes and held him to my chest. He was a dead weight in my arms. The dog walker looked at me impatiently.

'Get her to a vet,' he said. '*Now.*'

I stumbled from the bushes with Stan in my arms.

And then I ran.

Christian, our vet, confirmed the dog walker's diagnosis.

'But anaphylactic shock covers a lot of ground,' he said as Stan closed his eyes and curled up on his examination table, wanting only to sleep, wanting only for the world to go away. 'He's certainly had some kind of extreme and rapid allergic reaction.' Christian's hands searched the red fur for clues. 'I'm guessing it's a sting from a bee or a wasp.'

I clutched Stan's worn old leather lead like it was a set of rosary beads.

'Anaphylaxis is as serious in dogs as it is in humans,' Christian said. 'Leave him with us for forty-eight hours.

We'll give him epinephrine to get his heart rate up, antibiotics to prevent infection and some fluids to kick-start his blood pressure.'

Stan looked at us with mournful eyes. They were not completely black, I saw, but etched with a thin ring of deepest brown. And those eyes were round as marbles and as huge as the eyes of a hero in a Japanese comic. I felt my own eyes flood with tears and lightly touched his red fur.

There was nothing to say.

'He's a fit young dog with a thin layer of fat,' Christian said. Then he looked at me with a kind of clear-eyed compassion. 'But as you know, they're a delicate breed,' he said.

I nodded. Stan was not moving. There was nothing more I could do. I left him with Christian. And this dog who hated to see anyone he cared for walk away did not even look up.

As I walked to the door of the examination room, he was as still as when I found him hiding in the bushes on that hill between the city and the sky, like a creature who had all at once had enough, like an animal who had crawled away to die.

I called Scout at nine o'clock sharp.

She answered the phone herself. I was relieved that I did not have to talk to anyone else. And no doubt everyone else was happy that they didn't have to talk to me.

'Ready to rock and roll?' I asked her.

'Indeed,' she said.

'Are you sitting comfortably?'

'I'm sitting on the stairs by the landline.'

'Then I'll begin. 'High Flight' by John Gillespie Magee. He was a pilot in the war.'

> *'Oh! I have slipped the surly bonds of Earth*
> *And danced the skies of laughter-silvered wings;*
> *Sunward I've climbed, and joined the tumbling mirth*
> *Of sun-split clouds — and done a hundred things*
> *You have not dreamed of — Wheeled and soared and swung*
> *High in the sunlit silence ... '*

And nothing but silence on the other end of the line.

'Are you all right, Scout?'

'I'm listening very carefully.'

So I continued.

> *'Hovering there, I've chased the shouting wind along, and flung*
> *My eager craft through footless halls of air.'*

'Wow,' said Scout.

'Scout?' shouted her mother from another room.

But I went on.

'Up, up the long, delirious, burning blue
I've topped the wind-swept heights with easy grace
Where never lark, or ever eagle flew —
And, while with silent lifting mind I've trod,
The high, untrespassed sanctity of space,
Put out my hand ... and touched the face of God.'

Scout sighed. 'That's a good one,' she said. 'What happened to John the poet?'

'John died in the war, angel. Just after finishing that poem.'

She thought about it.

And then she was tired of thinking about it.

'I need to brush my teeth now.'

'You go and do that and I'll call you again tomorrow.'

'How's Stan?'

This was going to be hard.

This was going to be the hardest thing of all.

'Stan's sleeping now. He's resting.'

'Good. Here's Mummy.'

I heard my ex-wife take the phone and felt her waiting until Scout had scampered up the stairs to brush her teeth. I could hear noises in the background. Family noises. Children getting ready for bed, music coming from somewhere. Some kind of late-night, chilled-out cocktail jazz that was not a perfect fit in a house full of young children.

311

These domestic noises fascinated me. I had never thought about my ex-wife's home life. And now that Scout was living with her, I thought about it all the time.

Then Anne was on the line. 'Do you have to read her a poem *every* night?' she said.

I was dumbstruck.

'Well, it's our bedtime poem,' I said, as if that explained everything. 'Scout always has a poem before she sleeps.' I thought about it, struggling to find a compromise. 'I could buy Scout her own phone so that we don't—'

But the total stranger at the other end of the line sighed with infinite weariness and slowly hung up.

I stared at the phone for a bit and then got down on the floor and did twenty-five quick press-ups. Then I did another twenty-five, thinking about my form, cranking them out more slowly. Out in the main room of our loft I could hear Mrs Murphy, totally lost without Scout and Stan to take care of. I flexed my right knee. It felt almost as good as the other knee. Fred's intensive rehab had worked wonders on the injury from Lake Meadows and the gaps between the flare-ups of pain were getting longer. And then I did a third set of twenty-five press-ups, the lactic acid building up nicely in my arms and shoulders now, making them burn with an aching kind of pain. And then I caught my breath and slowly pumped out the final twenty-five, pushing myself to go on when I wanted to stop and rest.

Then I checked my gun.

I stood on the bed and pushed back a panel in the ceiling, the only place in the loft where Mrs Murphy never cleaned. I pulled down Jackson's old kitbag and unzipped it, smelling the gun oil. I unwrapped the T-shirt inside and stared at the glint of the Glock 17 in the night-time. Then I wrapped it in the T-shirt, put it back in Jackson's kitbag and stored it again in the ceiling.

Mrs Murphy looked up at me as I came out of my room carrying my own kitbag.

'Off to the gym?'

'Yes.' I was going to leave it there but I didn't like to deceive her.

'But not Fred's gym,' I said. 'I'm going to a different gym tonight.'

'And how are they?' she said. 'How's my Scout?' she said. 'And how's my Stan?'

'No real change,' I said, hoping that would cover it.

She nodded.

'They lead such accelerated lives, don't they? Their lives just rush past us.'

'Dogs or children?'

'Both,' she said sadly.

It was a busy night at the Muhammad Ali Youth & Leisure Centre.

Teenage boys and girls were shadow-boxing, banging the bags and doing sit-ups, press-ups and planks. There was a small boxing ring with sagging ropes and Father Marvin Gane stood in the middle of it with a pair of battered Lonsdale pads on his hands. A line of children of assorted age and size queued up to throw three-punch combinations at the pads.

He saw me and nodded.

It was the first time I had seen him in the gym. Even in his clerical gear, he looked like a giant of a man. But in a sweat-stained T-shirt and tracksuit bottoms, shouting instructions – 'Double Jab! Right cross! Don't let that right hand fade away! Get it back to your chin!' – he looked like something else.

Father Marvin Gane looked like a fighter tonight.

I found an empty bench and kept out of the way until he was ready for me. After the children in the ring had all thrown their combinations, he slipped between the ropes.

'Shadow-box!' he told them. 'Three three-minute rounds! Ten burpies and ten press-ups between rounds! Keep it neat! Think about your form! Hard work and dedication! Defend yourself at all times!'

The children began bouncing about in the ring, their faces dead serious, dancing around their imaginary opponents.

Father Gane shook my hand and eased his large body on to the bench beside me, his handsome black face gleaming with sweat. Someone had once told him he looked a bit like Marvin Gaye on the cover of 'What's Going On?' and he had grown a neat beard to encourage the comparison.

'I'm sorry I didn't come to your mother's funeral,' I said. 'She was a lovely woman.'

He nodded briskly, a gesture that suggested we skip the small talk. 'How can I help you, Detective?'

'Sir Ludo Mount was hit by a truck in Borodino Street last night,' I said. 'He is going to live but he's never going to walk again.'

'I saw the news,' Father Marvin said. 'Very sad for his family. But I imagine he had many enemies.'

'I was there when it happened. There was another message – a Biblical reference. This one was sprayed on the side of a cop car. Exodus chapter 20, verse 13: *Thou shalt not kill*. The Sixth Commandment.'

'Yes, I'm familiar with it.'

He stared at me, waiting.

'I know you had an interest in Borodino Street,' I said. 'Because I saw you down there a few times.'

And now I waited.

He looked out at his gym. 'I'm interested in anyone who has been separated from God,' he said. 'I prayed for the Khan family.' He looked at me levelly. 'Are you asking me for my theological opinion on the killer's use of the Commandments?'

'I'm trying to work out if it's a false lead,' I said. 'If the use of the Ten Commandments is designed to send our investigation down a dead end.'

'I see – you're wondering if you should be looking for a religious maniac or if the use of the Commandments is just a con?'

'Exactly.'

'The Ten Commandments are the basis of God's law and establish timeless, universal and unequivocal standards of right and wrong,' he said, watching the children as they stopped shadow-boxing and began their burpies. 'But they're not, as many believe, specific to Christianity. Ethical principles exist in every religion. You'll find something like the Ten Commandments – we call them the Decalogue in the trade, from the Greek for "ten words" – in Islam and Judaism. As a Christian, I believe that what's unique about the Ten Commandments is that only they were written with the finger of God.'

He stared at me, unsmiling.

'Will you excuse me a moment?' he said.

A tall, gangling youth had entered the Muhammad Ali Youth & Leisure Centre with a small kitbag in his hand and a large spliff dangling from his mouth. He was pulling out a pair of worn red Cleto Reyes gloves when Father Gane turned him around and slapped him hard across the face.

The spliff fell to the floor.

Father Gane crushed it underfoot.

'Pick it up,' he told the youth.

The youth meekly picked it up.

'Now get out of my gym. And that garbage with you.'

The youth did not move and in a flash Gane had him by the scruff of his neck and he was carrying the boy to the exit door.

Not dragging but carrying.

The youth's feet did not touch the ground.

'Come back when you're sober,' Father Gane said, and tossed him into the night as if he was a rag doll with the stuffing knocked out of it.

Gane came back to the bench, as every child in there watched him out of the corner of their eye.

He clapped his hands.

'Keep working!'

He sat down beside me as if nothing had happened.

'But I thought you had arrested this – what do they call him? – Bad Moses?' he said.

'My boss thought so too,' I said. 'My SIO – you remember DCI Pat Whitestone?'

'Of course.'

Whitestone and her brother Curtis had both been DIs when I started in Homicide at West End Central.

'She liked this George Halfpenny for the murder of Ahmed Khan,' I said. 'Maybe you saw him on Borodino Street.'

'I saw him talking but I wasn't listening,' he said. 'Because I was praying. Our paths did not cross.'

'But – between you and me – it was wishful thinking that Halfpenny was Bad Moses. He seriously injured a policeman when he was resisting arrest so there was a desire to see him go down. Many of my colleagues *wanted* George Halfpenny to be Bad Moses, including my boss. But Halfpenny was locked up in HMP Belmarsh when Ludo Mount got crippled. And I have spoken to George Halfpenny. The man's an atheist.'

'Then I shall pray for him, too.'

We watched the children training.

'There was a famous murder case in the Seventies,' I said. 'The press called the killer Black Moses. A married white woman who had been playing around was strangled and they arrested her black husband. He was a lay preacher out of Trinidad and that fit very well because the killer wrote the chapter and verse number of the Commandment about not committing adultery on the bedroom wall. And he wrote it with her blood. Did you ever hear about that case, Father?'

'Double up that jab, Lewis!' Gane shouted.

'The husband did ten years,' I said. 'But the murderer turned out to be the woman's father, who was white and angry that his daughter had married a black man. Today we would call it an honour killing, even though there's never any honour in them. The real killer, the woman's father, let it slip to a workmate a decade later. They usually have to talk about it to someone in the end. It must drive you nuts, trying to keep that kind of secret. But the law missed the real killer at the time because he wrote the Commandment about not committing adultery on the wall.'

'Deuteronomy,' Gane said. 'Book 5, verse 21.'

'Although the way the killer wrote it was Exodus 20:14. He used Exodus rather than Deuteronomy. Like our guy now – like Bad Moses. He uses Exodus, doesn't he?'

'Does he?'

Gane was not looking at me. But I knew he was listening.

'And I don't get it,' I said. 'Why would you use one set of Commandments and not the other? How would you choose between Deuteronomy and Exodus? What's the difference?'

'None. Personal preference.'

'But when *you* talk about the Ten Commandments, you use Deuteronomy, don't you, Father Gane? Bad Moses quotes Exodus. But you look me in the eye and you quote Deuteronomy.'

He turned to face me. 'And do you think that might be a false lead, Detective? Me using Deuteronomy when the man you are seeking quotes Exodus?'

I could smell his sweat now.

I had not noticed it before.

'Do you think I am capable of killing a man?' he said.

I didn't think Father Marvin Gane was capable of taking a life.

I knew it.

'We never really talked about your brother,' I said. 'We never really talked about what happened to Curtis, did we?'

I had seen a lot of Father Gane in those last days of my colleague's life. In truth, his brother Curtis and I had never been close friends. Curtis was too far ahead of me when I joined Homicide and Serious Crime Command for a real friendship to develop early on and when we grew closer, after he broke his back, the time was always running out.

But I had been there the night we busted a paedophile ring in an abandoned mansion on The Bishop's Avenue, and I had watched DI Curtis Gane take one step back from a man holding a black carbon lock knife with a four-inch blade and I had seen him fall two storeys, breaking the vertebrae that connected his head to his spine.

I had been there when Curtis Gane's life changed and I was there in those long hospital nights when he begged me to end his life.

I could not do it.

But I had always known that Father Marvin Gane had it in him – the physical strength, the moral certainty – to hold a pillow over his brother's head until the pain and suffering was over.

'My brother was in unimaginable pain,' he said. 'In the end his death was a mercy. For him. And for my mother. God took him.'

'I saw you – and your mother – the day we scattered Curtis' ashes from the roof of West End Central. But I didn't see you again after that. Not until Borodino Street. And I still don't understand what you were doing there. I could understand why all those people came to pay their respects to Alice Stone and to leave their flowers. But some people couldn't stay away from Borodino Street. Some people were drawn back to it again and again. And you were one of them, weren't you?'

He watched the children springing around the ring, throwing punches at their invisible foes.

'*Your iniquities have separated you from your God, your sins have hidden His face from you, so that he will not hear,*' he said. 'Isaiah chapter 59, verse 2. *That's* why I went to Borodino Street, Detective, because it was a place without God. That seems totally absurd to you, I know. In a godless society, faith always seems insane. The idea of being separated from God seems raving mad to the man who does not believe in God. Of course it does. But you didn't really come to talk to me about theology, did you? You came to see me because you

321

mistakenly believe that I murdered my brother and you are wondering who else I might have killed.'

For a long moment there was only the sound of leather hitting leather, and gasps of effort, and the sound of breath running out.

'Where were you last night, Father Gane?'

For a moment I thought he was going to put his hands on me.

I thought he was going to kick me out of the Muhammad Ali Youth & Leisure Centre just as he had violently ejected the stoned young man. I did not doubt that he could do it. Of the two of us, he was by far the more powerful man. But he wrung his huge hands, as if in prayer or perhaps restraining himself.

'I was home alone,' he said.

'So I shouldn't look for you on the CCTV around Borodino Street?'

His mouth flinched.

'I wasn't anywhere near Borodino Street. And I didn't run down that lawyer. And I didn't kill the father of those two mass murderers.'

I waited for him to mention his brother.

I waited for him to tell me that he had not placed a pillow over the face of Curtis Gane.

But he was standing up.

'Are we done?'

I got up and held out my hand. 'For now,' I said.

He took my hand and he did not let it go and, with the slightest of motions, he pulled me towards him.

And once again I felt the power of this man.

'Be careful out there,' he told me.

When I got back to Smithfield, the meat market was in full swing, the club kids were coming out to play and my favourite Criminal Informant was waiting for me, watching the night go by and giving his pale frail body what it craved.

Nils was standing in the shadows, eating a sponge cake with his fingers, a streak of jam running down his leather trousers, relishing the sudden hit of sugar the way only the career heroin addict truly can.

'You still looking for those hand grenades?' he said, licking his fingers.

30

'Rapid entry, dig out and dominate,' Jackson Rose told his team of Specialist Firearms Officers.

The young men and women of SC&O19 sat in the front two rows of the briefing room of Leman Street Police Station, Whitechapel. They wore grey body armour and expressions that were pulled tight by adrenaline.

'Then back here for tea, biscuits and medals all round,' Jackson grinned. 'How's that sound?'

They smiled back at him.

There were murmurs of amusement and assent.

It sounded pretty good.

We were back in the place of legends. This was the police station where murder detectives once hunted Jack the Ripper. And this was the police station where DS Alice Stone had led the raid on Borodino Street that resulted in the death of the Khan terror cell and herself. Now Jackson Rose stood on the low stage of that dimly lit room, telling his young shots how it would go down, and trying to inoculate them with his own quiet confidence.

Because somebody always had to go in.

And because you never knew.

You never really knew what was waiting beyond the door.

My mob sat to one side in the front row. Whitestone. Joy. Edie. And me on the aisle, waiting for Jackson's nod to come on stage. All of us trying to get comfortable inside the stab-proof Kevlar. PASGT helmets resting on our laps, apart from Edie Wren, who was already wearing hers.

She leaned in.

'How you sleeping?' she whispered.

'Good,' I said. 'Yeah. Good, good.'

She leaned back with a knowing smile, her green eyes sparkling with amusement under the rim of her PASGT helmet. There were freckles on her nose that would always be there now.

'As bad as that?' she said.

Then Jackson was looking at me, giving me my cue with a small nod.

I got up and walked on stage.

'DC Wolfe of West End Central,' Jackson said.

I looked out at the briefing room. Beyond the SFOs in the front rows, I could see a Specialist Search Team from SO20, the Counter Terrorism Protective Security Command, dog handlers with firearms and explosives search dogs from DSU, the Dog Support Unit, and teams of paramedics. And right at the back, resting his great bulk against the wall, Flashman of Counter Terrorism Command and his team.

Once upon a time they called them the bomb squad.

We might need them today.

There was a laptop on a lectern. I hit a button and a face appeared on the big screen behind me. A police mugshot, face-on and profile of a white man in his late twenties.

'This is Peter Fenn,' I said. 'AKA Ozymandias. He sells weapons. Mostly small firearms to gang members and drug dealers south of the river but lately he has been expanding. We believe he has established a connection with the Balkans. It was believed Ozymandias sold two twenty-year-old Croatian hand grenades to Asad and Adnan Khan. This was the initial intelligence that took us to Borodino Street. As you know, we found the brothers but not the grenades.'

I hit another button.

Two hand grenades appeared on screen. Black, lattice-faced spheres with a gold-coloured handle and ring pull, identical to a key ring. You could clearly read the name of the manufacturer on the side.

Cetinka, it said.

'But we have finally located our Mr Fenn. Ozymandias has been off the radar for a while. Our CI – a regular buyer at one of the crack houses in the estate where Fenn lives – tells us he is back in town after a prolonged bout of sex tourism in Pattaya, Thailand.'

Another button. A derelict council estate of pre-fabricated blocks, five storeys high, dark steel sheets covering many of the windows and stairwells.

'The Elphinstone Estate,' I said. 'An open sewer of drug gangs, crack addicts and rats the size of unneutered toms. Developers have been trying to tear it down for ten years to build luxury flats but some of the residents have refused to move out.' I looked at the blighted block of flats. 'It's as close as this city gets to a no-go area. And it is home to Peter Fenn.'

Jackson stepped forward.

'Expect firearms on the premises,' he said. 'It's what Ozymandias does. There is also the strong possibility of explosives. So look after yourselves and each other in there, as I know you will. You've already got plans of the building. Any questions?'

Jesse Tibbs raised his hand.

'MOE, skipper?'

'Our Intel is that Fenn has a stronger front door than the Bank of England,' Jackson said. 'So method of entry will be you blowing it off its hinges with your Benelli shotgun. But you might have to knock more than once. Good with that, Jesse?'

Tibbs nodded.

Jackson was no longer smiling.

'Then gun up,' he said. 'And let's go to work.'

We arrived at the Elphinstone Estate at first light.

But for some people the night was not yet over.

As our unmarked jump-off van pulled into the court-yard, four blocks of flats facing a no man's land where someone had dragged a sofa and then set fire to it – I could hear distant laughter, screams, crying – and music. Lots of music. The sounds of Detroit and Jamaica and Ibiza, all swirling around the rotting estate, like the soundtrack to a party that was over in some other lifetime.

We had left Leman Street in a small convoy but the rest of the vehicles – the ambulances, the dog units, Flashman and his team – were left in neighbouring streets with their engines idling by the time Jackson's shots and my mob piled out of our jump-off van.

Led by Jackson, we headed for the far block of flats and sprinted up three flights of stairs before he raised a hand and we crouched in a stairwell. Wind whistled down the bleak corridors and stairs. Wind would always whistle down them.

And then suddenly we were being watched.

The tiny child must have wandered out of one of the flats. He was wearing just his pants and a filthy T-shirt. He was perhaps two years old, with all the chubby roundness of that age. He gripped a can of fizzy drink and stared wide-eyed at the shots with their Glock 17 handguns, Black Mamba Sig assault rifles, M26 Tasers, the body armour, their faces hidden by black balaclavas, three holes for mouth and eyes.

Edie pushed her way forward.

'*Go home*,' she hissed at the child.

He did not move.

I waited to hear the voice of an adult calling his name, desperately trying to find him. It did not happen. The children were left to wander in the Elphinstone Estate. The kid slurped his fizzy drink and showed no sign of moving.

So Edie picked him up and carried him away.

Jackson was conferring with Tibbs.

'Go,' Jackson said.

Tibbs began walking down the long windy corridor with the Benelli M3 Super 90, his youthful face impassive. We followed him and I was aware of eyes watching us from the other blocks. And then Tibbs was directly outside Peter Fenn's front door.

It was a mesh metal grille over a slab of steel.

Tibbs considered the door for a moment, then shouldered his weapon and began to fire. The day cracked with sound, again and again and again. Spent brass flew.

It was a strong door. But the semi-automatic shotgun went through it like a machete through margarine.

TONY PARSONS

The shots poured inside. We followed them.

'Armed police! Stand still!'

'Show me your hands!'

'Stop! Armed police! Stand still!'

'Stop! Armed—'

And then there was that moment of total stillness when we were inside the target building and nobody was trying to kill us. There were two large Samsonite suitcases in the hallway. *BKK–LHR* said the baggage tags. Bangkok to London.

The shots were moving into the flat, still shouting the commands, until they suddenly stopped and I heard someone mutter an appalled curse.

They had found Ozymandias.

The weapons dealer had been crucified.

He was naked and unmoving on the floor of the living room, pinned there by some kind of knives or short swords that had been driven into his hands and feet. Both his hands were pulled high above his head, in a gesture of surrender, and his feet had been placed on top of each other.

He looked as though he had put up a fight because there were perforations to his hands and arms after some unsuccessful early efforts to nail him to the floor. There was a lot of blood but most of it had come out of his right wrist where the sword – no, it was a bayonet – that held him to the floor must have nicked his radial artery.

'No pulse,' one of the shots said. 'No heartbeat.'

Jackson got down on his hands and knees and began pumping the crucified man's chest.

'Max,' Whitestone said, pulling on a pair of blue nitrile gloves.

She was indicating the writing on the wall.

The letters were a foot high, daubed with the weapon dealer's blood.

The blood had been drying for long enough to turn black.

Exodus 20:16

I looked at Joy Adams.

'The Ninth Commandment,' she said, pulling on white baggies over her shoes. '*Thou shalt not bear false witness against thy neighbour*. Someone thinks he was a grass.'

The shots were searching room to room, their blood still pumping.

'*Armed police! Stand still!*'

'*Show me your hands!*'

'*Stop! Armed police! Stand still!*'

'*Stop! Armed—*'

But there was only the dead man here now.

The room swam into focus. In contrast to the squalor of the Elphinstone Estate, the flat had an almost suburban cosiness to it. It had the mustiness of a place that had not been lived in for a while but the cushions on the leather sofas were almost prissily arranged. Peter Fenn aka Ozymandias had been proud of his home.

There were framed photographs on a desk with a large iMac. I stepped closer to look at them.

They were displayed like family portraits.

But they were not family portraits.

Boy scouts, long dead, in shorts and khaki shirts smiled for the camera. No, not boy scouts. *Hitlerjugend (HJ)* said the caption. Hitler youth.

The next photograph was of an unsmiling man in a black uniform.

Waffen Schutzstaffel der NSDAP (SS).

And finally, in the largest photograph, there was a sea of helmets for as far as the eye could see, staring at a distant stage.

Overview of the mass roll call of SA, SS and NSKK troops, Nuremberg, 9 November 1935.

I stepped back. I had wondered what kind of mindset you needed to make a career out of selling weapons.

And now I knew.

'It's a shrine,' Whitestone said beside me, pulling off the PASGT helmet.

'So Bad Moses killed Ozymandias,' Adams said. 'And Bad Moses killed Ahmed Khan and crippled Sir Ludo.'

Whitestone looked uncertain.

'This could be the work of a fan of Bad Moses,' she said. 'The Ten Commandments are right on trend these days. Bad Moses never wrote on the wall in blood before.'

'No,' I said. 'This is not a copycat kill. It's not just the Old Testament Bad Moses likes.'

I remembered Ahmed Khan dying in my arms, and the name of his granddaughter escaping with his final breath, and I remembered the knife that had been plunged into Ahmed Khan's subclavian artery, and the motto on the blade.

'Bad Moses likes knives,' I said. 'And he likes *these* kind of knives. Third Reich blades. The knife that killed Ahmed Khan was bought from Ozymandias. And whoever bought it believed that Ozymandias — Peter Fenn — had ratted him out.'

We stared at the naked man on the floor.

I got on my knees beside him and I saw the blades that had been driven through his hands and feet clearly now.

A long rusty bayonet had been thrust through his feet and the short sword that fixed his left palm to the floor looked medieval. But the dagger that pierced the palm of his right hand had a black wooden handle with a runic

SS symbol and an eagle above a swastika. There were faded words on the blade.

Meine Ehre heißt Treue

'My honour is loyalty,' I said. 'Motto of the Waffen-SS. Currently banned in all the European countries that still remember.'

The blades all looked as though they were from the same collection as the knife that killed Ahmed Khan, the Hitler Youth dagger with *Blut und Ehre* – Blood and honour – on the blade.

'How long has he been dead?' someone said.

Jackson shook his head, on his hands and knees, still pressing Fenn's chest, but slowing now. Then he stopped and got to his feet.

For a long moment all you could hear was the chatter on the Airwave radios.

And then the crucified man screamed.

I bent by his side as they shouted for the paramedics on the radio.

'Listen to me, Fenn,' I said. 'Listen to me. What happened to those two Croatian grenades? What happened to them?'

'The brothers ... '

'It's true? You sold them to the Khans?'

'*Help me.*'

Jackson was dragging me away.

'Christ, Max! Talk to him at the hospital!'

'He's not going to make it to any hospital!'

Jackson shoved my chest. His shots were on their knees, trying to get the blades out of Fenn's hands and feet.

'Get away from him, Max!'

I went into the bedroom, trying to control my breathing.

There were footsteps behind me.

Jesse Tibbs had followed me. He was still holding the shotgun.

'So someone did this Fenn creature because he was an informer, right?' he said. 'Lesson for us all. What does it say in the Bible? *Thou shalt not bear false witness.*'

'Someone did him because he was a scumbag who made a living selling weapons to other scumbags. That's what happened. It's not difficult, Tibbs. Even you should be able to grasp it.'

'No,' Tibbs insisted. 'Fenn bore false witness against his friends.' He leaned against the doorway, the Benelli shotgun cocked at that 45 degree angle. 'Like you with Ray Vann.'

And suddenly I had had enough of him.

'Is it always all talk with you, Jesse, or are you ever going to do something? You're like one of these little boys on social media — all mouth and Apple mouse.

Be a man, Jesse. If you are going to do it, then get it done.'

He smiled, and we both nodded, as if something had finally been decided.

He slowly raised his shotgun.

And then Jackson Rose was standing behind him.

Tibbs turned away.

'Any weapons?' Jackson said, addressing Tibbs but looking at me.

'There's enough firepower to start a small war under the floorboards in the kitchen,' Tibbs said. 'But no sign of any grenades. Croatian or anything else. Maybe the search team will dig them out.'

Jackson nodded and stood aside to let Tibbs leave the room.

'You can talk to Fenn as soon as they've stabilised him at the hospital, Max.'

'That's going to be too late, Jackson.'

He shrugged.

'Best I can do, Max,' he said. 'You can't interview a man when he is being crucified.'

I barged past him. The paramedics were giving Fenn oxygen in the living room when I walked out. Edie Wren was waiting down in that fly-blown courtyard, sitting on the sofa that someone had set fire to. She was still wearing her PASGT helmet but she had pushed it on to the back of her head.

There was a can of fizzy drink in her hand. She had found the child's parents, or at least she had found the one that was still around.

'A kid that age shouldn't be drinking this crap,' she said, pouring it on the ground and then kicking the can away, and I smiled for the first time that day.

The shots went back to Leman Street.

We went back to West End Central.

Peter Fenn died on his way to the hospital.

The search team tore his neat little two-bedroom shrine to Nazi Germany to pieces.

And they still did not find those grenades.

31

'So is Stan going to die?' Scout said.

She was home for the weekend. And I think to both of us the loft in Smithfield still felt like Scout's home.

We stood in the doorway of my bedroom, watching Stan as he huddled in his basket where I had placed it by the side of the bed. He was unmoving but his eyes were open and shining, and he appeared to be waiting for whatever happened next.

'I don't know,' I said. 'Something bit him when we were on the Heath and his body reacted against it.'

'Anaphylactic shock,' Scout said. 'I saw it online. What does Christian say?'

Scout and I both trusted Christian. Our local vet had looked after Stan since our dog was a capering puppy, wild-eyed with joy and agog with wonder at the world, stunned by the scents of the meat market, relieving himself with gay abandon in every corner of our loft. These are the things that you remember when you think your time with a dog is coming to the end.

GIRL ON FIRE

'Christian says rest, water and a bland diet,' I said. 'Although right now he's not eating anything at all. Give him time, Christian says.'

Scout sat on the floor with her dog and she ran her hands through his fur. Stan lifted his head as if to acknowledge her presence, his black diamond eyes settling on her face before he curled up again.

'Can't you put him in your bed?' Scout said.

'The bed's too high for him if he needs a drink of water.' In the distance I could hear the sounds of a summer day in the city. 'I was going to take you rowing on the Serpentine today. But I don't like to leave him when he is like this.'

'Me neither,' Scout said.

So we stayed home all day. Me and Scout and Stan.

The sun crossed the sky and we did not stir from our loft. As the hot, lazy day drifted by, Stan's condition did not change but our sadness seemed to lift a little.

There were visitors.

Scout's friend Mia was delivered by her mother and the two girls sat side by side on the floor, drawing for hours. Mrs Murphy came round to see Scout and check on Stan. Smiths of Smithfield sent up sandwiches.

In the afternoon Stan made a guest appearance in the main space of the loft when I carried him wrapped in a blanket to his favourite sofa. He still didn't move but he seemed to be happy surrounded by all the familiar faces.

Stan's love for people, especially children, was gleaming in those eyes.

And then my ex-wife came to collect Scout and the day fell apart.

Anne was dressed for the gym and she was pressed for time, throwing anxious glances at her iPhone.

'How was the rowing?' she said. 'I bet Hyde Park was crowded, wasn't it? Come on, Scout. Get your things.'

'We stayed home,' Scout said. 'And we took care of Stan.'

'All day long? On a beautiful day like today, you stayed inside this loft with a sick dog?'

She made it sound like a crime against nature.

'Yes,' Scout said, her voice getting smaller.

Now Anne was looking at me, struggling to hold her temper.

'Unbelievable,' she said. 'One day of the week you get her and she spends it locked up in here with a flea-bitten mutt.'

She cast a contemptuous glance at Stan, bundled up on the sofa.

The dog blinked, looking sorry for himself.

Scout gave him a brief peck on the forehead and I was never more proud of her.

'Don't kiss the bloody thing,' Anne said.

'He's not a bloody thing,' Scout said, finding her voice. 'He's Stan and he's a living, human creature!'

Not quite human, of course.

But I took her point.

Anne's iPhone came alive in her fist. She listened, sighed, held the phone away from her.

'Just stick it in the bloody microwave, Oliver!' she bawled.

I was glad that Mrs Murphy and Mia had gone home. I did not want them to see this angry woman in her gym kit who did not comprehend how loving a dog could break your heart.

'You don't understand,' I said. 'Stan is very ill.'

But why should she understand? Stan had come into our life after Anne had left it. When she was on her leafy suburban street where nothing bad ever happened, with a new man and a new home and a new baby growing inside her, I had attempted to replace the hole in Scout's life – and my life – with a puppy.

Something Scout and I loved had been lost forever and we did our best to replace it with something that would love us with the unconditional, unchanging love that we both missed and craved.

And it had worked. We were a rescue family.

And the dog saved us.

Anne touched her daughter's hair.

'Don't be sad, darling. They don't live forever, do they? We'll get you a hamster or – I don't know – a goldfish. I'm sure you can get them online.'

'I don't *want* a hamster.'

341

Scout was struggling to put on the new rucksack I had bought her and Anne instinctively helped her, the gesture of a woman who was used to being around much smaller children.

I wanted to explain what was happening here. I wanted to tell Anne that love and illness and death are never small things, that they can never be treated with contempt and disdain. Not even in a hamster. And certainly not in a dog.

I wanted to tell her something that she seemed yet to learn – that there is always a price to pay for loving something or someone.

But I did not have the words.

I did not know where to begin.

Because I realised that I did not know this woman collecting my daughter. We were strangers now.

No, it was worse than that.

We did not even like each other.

Married for a while, I thought. Divorced forever.

'You have to understand,' I said. 'Stan is part of our family.'

'No,' my ex-wife told me. 'Scout has a new family now.'

Then they were gone but I felt closer to my daughter than ever.

We choose to love, I thought. We choose to open our hearts and pay the price of having them smashed to pieces.

And it is worth it, I thought.

The bill is always worth it, even if it cripples us, even if it scars us, even if it kills us.

*

I was sitting on the sofa with the new issue of *Boxing Monthly* and my sick, sleeping dog when my doorbell rang.

It was close to midnight. The neighbourhood was jumping. But nobody should have been ringing my doorbell at this hour.

I went to the door and looked on the monitor that showed the street.

Edie Wren was standing outside my front door.

And somehow I was not surprised.

It was as if I had been waiting for this moment for years.

I buzzed her up.

We stood there looking at each other for a moment and then it was as if we made up our minds at exactly the same time.

She crossed the threshold and she came to my arms and our mouths found each other and they fit, they fit in a way that very few mouths will ever fit your mouth in the course of a lifetime.

Then I held her against me, filled with wonder, and she was warm from the day and the heat was rising in me and I wanted to kiss her again right now.

My green-eyed girl.

'Max?'

'What?'

'I know how we can sleep tonight,' Edie said.

32

We walked into MIR-1 and TDC Joy Adams was sitting on a workstation looking up at Scarlet Bush.

Edie jabbed a finger at the journalist.

'She can't be in here,' she said. 'Are you nuts, Joy? We're conducting an active murder enquiry in here.'

Joy jumped down from the workstation.

'You need to hear this,' she said.

We all stared at Scarlet Bush. She looked older than I remembered. The strain and stress of working in a declining industry, I guessed.

'I know where the poison comes from,' she said.

And we let her talk.

'The Khan brothers were thugs,' Scarlet said. 'All three of them. Adnan, Assad and Ahmed, the one who died in Syria, Layla's father. Thugs and losers. Their digital footprint on social media suggests non-stop party animals and petty criminals. And then suddenly they are joining the global jihad. And then they are bringing down a helicopter in London. And dying in shoot-outs in the East End with armed police officers. And Ahmed – the one we never met – is dead in some bloodstained sandbox in Syria. It doesn't add up, does it? One minute they are sucking on a spliff in Ilford and knocking back the vodka shots and wondering if their benefits will stretch to one more pole dance. Then all at once all three of them are willing to kill and die for jihad? It makes no sense.'

'No, it makes perfect sense,' I said. 'In fact, it's shockingly common. Life's losers latching on to something far bigger than themselves – it happens all the time, Scarlet, especially if there's a history of violence, drug use or mental illness.'

'True. But I stick to my original theory – the poison still has to come from somewhere, doesn't it?'

I shrugged. 'Sit in front of your computer for long enough every day and you can convince yourself of anything,' I said.

She shook her head. 'It's more than that. And I can prove it.'

There was a manila envelope on the workstation.

She took out a photograph of three men.

A westerner in a suit and two men in *shalwar kameez*, the traditional long shirt and baggy trousers of the northwest frontier of Pakistan. One of the Pakistanis was in his sixties. The other was around thirty, and cradling an assault rifle.

'This was taken in the Services Bureau in Peshawar, Pakistan in 1981, around a year after the Soviet Union invaded Afghanistan,' Scarlet said. 'It appeared next to an op-ed in the *New York Times* predicting that Afghanistan was going to be the Vietnam of the Russians. The westerner is from the US Embassy in Islamabad and, I would guess, CIA. The older Pakistani is from the ISI, the Pakistani secret service, who backed the rebels who were resisting the Soviet invasion and occupation. And the younger man is one of the rebels.'

'The mujahideen,' I said.

'The mujahideen – Arabic for those who struggle and strive for a cause worthy of praise. Those engaged in holy war. *Because they weren't terrorists back then*. They were plucky freedom fighters taking on the wicked Reds. They were our brave Muslim allies. That's why these three men are smiling for the camera. The west couldn't help them enough.'

She touched the old photograph.

'All of this is hotly denied now, of course,' she said. 'Because one of the mujahideen who helped set up this Services Bureau was a Saudi Arabian called Osama bin Laden. But the ISI and the CIA provided arms, money and training to anyone who resisted the Russian invaders. Anyone. They didn't ask for character references. Radical Muslims were not a threat to the west back then – they were on the same side as us.'

She placed her fingertip on the image of the man with the assault rifle.

'That's an AK-74 assault rifle captured from *Spetsnaz* – the Russian Special Forces. The AK-74 was a big status symbol. Bin Laden had one just like it. It's the gun you see with bin Laden in every photo opportunity. People think it's an AK-47. But the AK-74 was designed thirty years later.'

'And who is he?' I said.

'His name is Hamid Jat. He had a sister who came to London to get married in her teens. And her name is Azza.'

'Azza Khan?' I said. 'The man with the gun is her brother?'

We stared at the photograph.

'So you're suggesting the Khan brothers took up terror because their dear old Uncle Hamid fought the Russians in Afghanistan?' I said. 'Sorry, Scarlet. I don't buy it.'

'I am saying that it is an unbroken line,' she said. 'I am saying this family has armed resistance in their DNA, Max. I am saying that the poison was in them from the start. But they wouldn't see it as poison. They would see it as – I don't know. Defending their faith. Standing up to the non-believers. A cause worth dying for. Look, modern terror has its starting point in the fight against the Soviets in Afghanistan. But now they don't wait for your commanding officer to give you your orders to attack a Russian tank. You buy a drone online, fly it above a shopping mall that's on a flight path to Heathrow, and cross your fingers. But the mujahideen are the vanguard of modern terror, the roots of jihad without borders. And the Khan brothers would have known all about Uncle Hamid because it's like having a war hero in your family. Their mother – Hamid's sister – would have told them all about him. And they would have been proud of him.'

'You know who I blame for all that death and destruction, all those broken bodies and lives?' Edie said. 'I blame *them*. The bastards who killed Alice Stone. The scumbags who stuck that drone in the sky.' She nodded at the photograph. 'Not some beardy old bloke wearing a dress in 1981.'

Scarlet shook her head, and I wondered if she had written her story already. And I wondered why she had come to us before running it.

'This man Hamid Jat – and all the men like him – were an inspiration to the Khan brothers and their kind,' Scarlet said. 'Because they believed that the mujahideen inflicted the death wound that killed the Soviet Union. And they believe that if they can draw America into another war just like it, then the United States – and the western world – will die too.'

We thought about it in silence.

'It's not complicated,' Scarlet insisted. 'The Khan brothers believe the end is nigh for the wicked west. They believe we will fall just as the Russians fell. Their worldview is a virus that has been around for decades. We think it's a modern phenomenon but there is nothing remotely modern about it. The nature of the beast changed, that's all. In the Eighties it was a conventional army, fighting the Russians. And now it is leaderless resistance, sustained by an idea, fighting the west. And the mother of the Khan brothers is the link between then and now.'

'Hold on,' I said. 'Azza Khan is the widow of a London bus driver. I knew the man. The crimes of his sons had nothing to do with their father. Why should they have anything to do with their mother?'

'Because Azza Khan is the sister of a mujahid who fought the Russians in Afghanistan. And she is the mother of the terrorists who brought down that Air Ambulance over Lake Meadows. The mother of the men who killed Alice Stone. It might not be a crime to be that sister, to be that mother, but forgive me – at the very least, it's a great story. And do you know what I think, Max? That it wasn't the Internet that radicalised them. And it wasn't some hate preacher that filled them with poison. *It was their mother.* Azza Khan is jihadi royalty. And she passed the torch to her sons.'

Suddenly Whitestone was standing in the doorway of MIR-1.

'This woman shouldn't be in this room,' she said.

'You need to hear this,' I said.

DCI Whitestone listened to the story in silence.

'What happened to Hamid Jat?' she said.

'When the Soviets finally pulled out in 1989, the muja-hideen started slaughtering each other. Hamid Jat slips off the radar for a while but we know he survived the civil wars and in the Nineties he joined the 055 Brigade, also known as the 55th Arab Brigade. They were the elite of al-Qaeda – one hundred of them were bin Laden's personal bodyguards. They fled to the Tora Bora caves in the White Mountains of eastern Afghanistan that the Americans built in the Eighties and then bombed in 2001. Hamid Jat died in the battle of Tora Bora.'

'And do you have proof that Azza Khan's family name was Jat before she was married?' Whitestone said.

'I've had every intern on my paper digging into it for weeks. I have a copy of the marriage certificate. I have immigration and naturalisation records from the Home Office. I have a copy of Azza Khan's British and Paki-stani passports. And I have a source that I can't disclose.'

'And is the source you can't disclose in the police or the intelligence community?' Whitestone asked.

'I am not at liberty to say.'

'Maybe you're being played by someone, Miss Bush. Did that ever occur to you?'

'My story all checks out. Even my paper's lawyers are happy.'

'But maybe Azza Khan was just some woman who got caught up in the tides of history,' Whitestone said. 'A woman who happened to live her life at a time when the men in her family were in a nihilistic death cult. How about that for a theory?'

'It's a stretch, isn't it?' Scarlet said. 'Look at her brother. Look at her sons.'

I looked at Edie and I could see she felt it too.

We believed her.

Whitestone sighed. 'But so what?' she said. 'Whatever her beliefs, whatever her brother or her sons have done, Azza Khan hasn't committed any crime. We're not the thought police. It's still a free country. You can believe whatever you like – no matter how crazy. We can't lock someone up because they dream of black flags flying over Buckingham Palace and Downing Street.' Whitestone gestured at the ancient photograph. 'This is not enough to charge her with anything,' she said.

Scarlet Bush looked surprised.

'I'm not suggesting you charge her with anything,' she said. 'But what do you think will happen when I run my story?'

'Bad Moses will stir,' I said. 'Bad Moses will look at Azza Khan and he will see the enemy.' I looked at my boss. 'And he will come for her.'

'You're asking me to use an innocent woman as live bait to apprehend a murderer?' Whitestone said. 'That's not going to happen.'

Scarlet's face hardened.

'I'm not asking you for a damn thing,' she said. 'Apart from this one small favour as a courtesy for bringing you this information: I want to be embedded with your officers when my story goes live.'

'But maybe Bad Moses will stay away,' Whitestone said. 'Maybe he'll smell a rat trap. Maybe he's had his fill of blood.'

She looked at me.

'No,' I said. 'I think he'll come after her.'

'Can't you see the significance of this?' Scarlet Bush said, as if we had still failed to grasp her central point. 'The poison is not from some raving Iman. And it's not from the dark corners of the Internet. The Khan brothers didn't need any of that stuff.'

She tapped the old photograph and Hamid Jat smiled at us across the years, proudly cradling his Russian AK-74.

'They had it all at home,' Scarlet said.

There is a small supermarket near Victoria Park and most of its façade is covered in the satellite dishes of the flats above. *Groceries – Fruit & Veg – Money Transfer* says the worn blue awning.

Layla Khan was sitting at the shop's cash register. The hijab she wore covered her hair and revealed her face. There was a raw red scuff mark near one eye. It was new.

She wore no make-up. Her make-up days were done.

She stared wearily at Edie and me when we walked in.

'What now?' she said.

'We wanted to warn you,' Edie said. 'There might be some trouble on Borodino Street.'

Layla laughed bitterly.

'Taking care of me now, are you? Watching out for me? It's a bit late for all that. *You sent me back.*'

'I'm sorry,' Edie began, but I cut across her.

'We're not social workers, Layla,' I said. 'And we're not your parents. We sent you back because we had no choice. The options were to put you into care or send you back to your family.'

'But I thought you were my *friend*,' she said to Edie, and I felt her flinch. 'You should have *been there* for me. You shouldn't have sent me back to that house.'

'Layla,' Edie said. 'Please. We just want you to be careful. We just want to warn you – it's not over yet. Is there somewhere you can go?'

Layla laughed bitterly. 'Look at me,' she said.

The doorbell dinged and Edie and I turned. The fat young man with the hair slicked across his bald spot came into the store carrying a box of fizzy drink.

'Unloading van,' he said.

We watched him stagger to the back of the store.

'*Look at me*,' Layla repeated.

We looked at her and I saw it at last. Something in her eyes had already died. They had beaten her in every way imaginable. And we had done nothing to help her. She still had her East End accent. But the rest of her old life was gone.

'I go where my husband tells me to go,' she said.

33

Near the end of the night, in one of those moments when the first of the sunlight is creeping into the room and you are not sure if you are asleep or awake, I felt Edie slip from the bed, then pause and briefly place her mouth on my forehead.

'Sleep more,' she whispered. 'Busy day.'

I stretched, I turned and I reached for her, wanting to hold her again. But she left the bedroom and I must have slept because when I reached out for her again there was full sunrise streaming through the skylight.

It was still very early. When I got up Edie was in the main space of the loft, sitting on the window ledge in just her T-shirt and pants, her legs tucked up beneath her, clutching something to her chest. I stood in the doorway of the bedroom and watched her for a while, enjoying watching her, that pale face lost in its own thoughts, the red hair that was never entirely tamed and the slim, muscled limbs of Edie Wren.

She is the woman I see, I thought. *And she is the only woman I will ever see.*

I went to her at the window. Our mouths still fit. They would always fit. I felt like the world had suddenly thrown its arms around me. It was a good feeling.

Outside, the market was winding up for the night. The sunlight was dazzling and Edie shielded her eyes.

'Everybody let her down,' she said, and I saw that it was thoughts of Layla that had disturbed her dreams. 'The authorities. Her family. And me.'

I placed a hand on her shoulder, still warm from our bed.

'You didn't let her down,' I said.

'Have you seen her wrists, Max? Have you seen what she does to herself?'

'I've seen them.'

'And now she's in a marriage to some creep she can't stand. And now she has to cover her pretty hair ... '

I took her in my arms. There was nothing I could tell her. Edie had done nothing wrong apart perhaps from believing that she could rescue Layla from the culture she came from.

And now I saw what she was holding. *The Angry Princess* rucksack that I had been replacing on the day the plane came down, that old, outgrown rucksack stained with paint and ice cream and who knew what else?

She laughed and wiped her eyes.

'Don't you love a good office romance?' she said.

'It's my favourite,' I said.

'Are we really going to take a chance on each other, Max?'

I smiled. Because there was not a cloud in the sky above our city, because we had got here in the end, and because I had waited so long for this woman.

'Yes,' I said. 'What else would make any sense?'

I looked at the rucksack and a memory of Borodino Street stirred.

On that first day.

The man and the woman and the girl on the floor of the kitchen, terrified for their lives. I remembered telling them they were safe, but they had to go, they had to go immediately. And I told them – it was very important – to have their hands raised and palms showing as they came out of the house so they were not shot.

I remembered them running, Ahmed and Azza and Layla Khan, running as people only run when they think that this is probably the minute they might die, grabbing a pink and purple *Angry Princess* rucksack just like this *Angry Princess* rucksack, and fleeing for their lives with their hands in the air as I had showed them. From the moment we met them, I thought, we had done all we could to protect that family.

'And what about Scout?' Edie said. 'What happens when Scout visits and finds me here? How does she feel then?'

I took Edie in my arms again, pushing Borodino Street from my mind, sick of thinking about that place, and I kept holding her.

I needed to stay close to her now that I had found her.

'Then Scout will be happy,' I said.

Leman Street Police Station, Whitechapel.

Jackson Rose clearly felt like this was a long shot. His smile always got bigger the more mortal danger he felt in the air. But as he briefed his team of shots, his face was impassive. The SFOs were in mufti today, T-shirts and jeans and Asics trainers.

'One last ride to Borodino Street,' Jackson said. 'Another officer and myself will set up on the other side of the road with our colleagues from West End Central, directly across the street from the Khan residence. The rest of you stay in the jump-off van two streets back. And then we wait. Questions?'

Tibbs raised his hand.

'What exactly are we waiting for, Skipper?'

'All hell to break loose — or teatime,' Jackson said, and now he gave them the famous grin. 'Whatever comes first.'

Scarlet Bush stirred in the seat beside me as her phone emitted a discreet ping.

'My piece just went live,' she said.

Her laptop was opened on the home page of the *Daily Post* website. A photograph of Azza Khan leaving her home was displayed.

And Scarlet's story filled the screen.

WORLD EXCLUSIVE:
THE GODMOTHER OF TERROR?
By Scarlet Bush
Crime correspondent

The *Daily Post* has learned of an extraordinary connection that links the mother of the so-called drone terrorists who brought down an Air Ambulance helicopter on Lake Meadows shopping centre to one of the founders of international terror. It is a story that stretches across decades and links the Lake Meadows atrocity with the mujahedeen who fought the Soviet Union in Afghanistan. The *Daily Post* wishes to make clear that Azza Khan has not committed any crime. But her dead sons and the older brother she hero-worshipped have created

untold human misery over the last
forty years — and the connection
places a respectable 65-year-old
British housewife at the centre of a
web of evil.

Phones began to ring, beep and vibrate all around the
briefing room.

'Social media is having hysterics,' Edie murmured.
'How often do you see that happen?'

'Yes!' Scarlet hissed. 'Yes! Yes! Yes!'

'Bad Moses,' Jackson told the room. 'He is the reason
we are going to Borodino Street. Because our colleagues
at West End Central believe the man responsible for killing Ahmed Khan and Ozymandias, as well as crippling
Sir Ludo Mount, may — just may — show his ugly mug
when Mrs Azza Khan is revealed to be possibly something
other than an innocent bystander to all this blood and
mayhem that we have been wading through this summer.'
Jackson nodded curtly. 'Gun up and let's go to work.'

He stopped me as the shots were getting into the
jump-off van.

'You really think Bad Moses will show when the world's
media are going to be camped on that doorstep?'

'I don't know if he can stop himself,' I said.

In the end, Scarlet Bush did not get her ringside seat.

She stayed with Whitestone and Edie and the shots in the jump-off van a block away from Borodino Street. She would have had a closer view of what happened if she had joined the media vans and reporters who thronged Borodino Street, waiting for something to happen, kept back from the front door by a Police Support Unit of uniformed officers. The officers were relaxed. Scarlet's story had pushed the right button with the world's media but the public had not returned to Borodino Street. So the feet on the street were relaxed, anticipating an easy shift.

I was in the front bedroom of the house across the street from the Khan residence with Jackson, Tibbs and Joy Adams. The room had the musty, locked-up smell of a place that had not been lived in for some time. The residents of Borodino Street were moving on, happy to take the developers' money, happy to put this place behind them.

Now only the Khan family remained.

Jackson and Tibbs checked their kit as Joy scanned the street with a compact pair of binoculars.

'So you're not going to nick the old girl?' Jackson said.

'As far as I know, she hasn't done anything,' I said. 'Nothing happening, Joy?'

'It's just reporters,' she said.

And then her body stiffened.

'Wait,' she said.

She turned to look at me, her face falling.

I took the binoculars from her.

'The end of the street, sir.'

I saw him immediately. The tall, powerful black man walking slowly through the throng of reporters. Most of the uniformed officers that were scattered along Borodino Street never gave him a glance. But I saw one young officer give him a respectful nod.

Father Marvin Gane.

'Sir, he's not doing anything, sir!' Adams said.

Jackson and Tibbs were already at the window.

'Big black dude in the dog collar,' Jackson said, shouldering his G36 Heckler & Koch. The short barrel of the weapon poked out of the open window. 'Heading towards the Khan residence.'

'Copy that, skipper,' Tibbs said, already at the adjacent window, nestling his body into the assault rifle.

The pair of them watched Father Gane through the telescopic sights of their weapons, and two red dots from their gun scopes appeared on the big man's torso.

'Sir, that's not our man, sir!' Adams shouted.

'Then what the hell is he doing here?' I said. I called to Jackson and Tibbs as I headed for the door. 'Don't shoot until we know he is a credible threat.'

Tibbs snorted.

'That's sort of what we do,' Jackson said, not taking his eye from the lens of the assault rifle's scope.

I ran down the stairs two at a time, calling in White-stone on the Airwave radio. Nothing. Just the crackle and crack of digital white noise. I pulled out my iPhone and tried again.

'Max,' Whitestone said.

'This could be our man. North end of the street. IC3.'

IC codes – identity codes, also known as Phoenix Codes – are codes used by the British police to denote ethnicity of a suspect. IC3 is black.

'On our way,' Whitestone said.

But when I stepped outside, Father Gane had dropped to his knees. He had made no attempt to approach the Khan house. He had stopped just beyond the scrum of media.

And he was praying.

I stared at him on his knees and then up at the sky, at the helicopter that suddenly hovered just above the rooftops of Borodino Street. And then Whitestone and Edie were there, the SFOs with them, the shots fanning around the praying man, uncertain what to do.

Whitestone and Edie both looked up at the helicopter, the sky full of its metallic roar.

'But we didn't bring a helicopter,' Whitestone said.

And then it was all done very quickly. Another team of shots was piling out of a jump-off van and blowing off the front door of Borodino Street with a Benelli shotgun. Jackson's team stared at each other, and turned their heads towards the radios on their shoulders, seeking instructions from their team leader. Layla appeared at the upper-floor window, pulling a swathe of black cloth across her face as she watched the street.

At the sight of her, the photographers went into a feeding frenzy. Reporters surged towards the shattered front door.

And then two unmarked Jaguars pulled into Borodino Street, blues and twos turned up to ten, arrowing in to the space in front of the Khan house, taking over. Armed Response Vehicles were suddenly waiting at either end of the street.

Everyone had forgotten about Father Gane. I stared down at him. He was still on his knees with his eyes closed, still praying for the redemption of those who have been separated from God.

Then Flashman of Counter Terrorism Command was easing his big rugby player's bulk out of one of the unmarked cars and the woman I had last seen outside the holding cells of West End Central got out of the other unmarked Jag.

She still looked like some kind of schoolteacher or academic, totally out of place on that street full of rabid reporters and armed police, all stoked with adrenaline and unsure what would happen next. But she had the calm authority of someone who knew she was in ultimate command.

She nodded to me politely and Flashman grinned.

'Take the rest of the day off, Wolfe,' he told me. 'Buy yourself a frock. We've got it from here.'

Azza Khan came out of the house flanked by two female officers. Officers emerged behind her carrying desktop computers and laptops, already tagged and bagged. Azza Khan was eased into the back of one of the unmarked cars and driven away, destination the cells of Paddington Green police station, blues and twos turned all the way up.

I walked up to the woman who was running this show.

'Mrs Khan is a person of interest to the intelligence services?' I said.

'She is now,' she said.

'Maybe you should have been watching her from the very start,' I said. 'No, don't tell me – you can't watch them all, right?'

'The truth is far worse than that, DC Wolfe,' the spook said. 'The truth is that we can't even watch most of them.'

My phone vibrated as I watched them drive away.

I Will Make You Crawl Soon

And suddenly a single red dot from an assault rifle's gun scope appeared on my chest.

It hovered by my heart for a long sickening moment and then it was gone. I looked up at the windows of the house across the street. Jackson and Tibbs were no longer there.

'They blew it for us,' Whitestone said. 'CTU and the spooks blew it for us. We might have had Bad Moses tonight.' She cursed bitterly. 'And now we have lost him forever,' she said.

'No,' I said, turning off my phone. 'He'll come again.'

Because I knew that next time he would be coming for me.

34

When there was no more that the vet could do for Stan, and time would heal him or it would not, I carried him back to the loft and made a kind of nest for him in every room of our home out of old, familiar blankets and some favourite well-gnawed toys.

He had one nest in the main area of the loft, and another in the bedroom, and another in the kitchen. A water bowl was placed near every nest, but they remained untouched. Edie and I tried to tempt him with morsels of cheese and chicken but Stan – a true foodie among dogs – was not interested.

He watched me from his bedroom basket as I called Scout for her goodnight poem. I had been putting it off for ages, but tonight I read her 'The Power of the Dog' by Rudyard Kipling.

'There is sorrow enough in the natural way
From men and women to fill our day;
And when we are certain of sorrow in store,

Why do we always arrange for more?
Brothers and sisters, I bid you beware
Of giving your heart to a dog to tear.'

Silence on the other end of the phone.

'What do you think old Kipling's saying there, Scout?'

'Old Kipling?'

'Yes.'

She thought about it.

'Don't get a dog.' A pause. 'Don't ever get a dog because it hurts too much when … '

She swallowed hard and left the rest of it unsaid.

Stan stared at me from his nest in a corner of the bedroom, bright eyes gleaming in the darkness. He was unmoving, unchanging and he was so unlike the dog we had known and lived with and loved for so long.

'I think he's saying the opposite,' I said. 'Old Kipling. I think he is saying that the way we feel now – when Stan is sick, when any dog is really sick – is the price we have to pay for all those good times we had with our beautiful boy. And Kipling is wondering if it's worth it – all the pain you feel – as the price for all the laughs and fun and walks in all kinds of weather. And you know what, Scout? I think that Kipling thinks it is worth it.'

My daughter inhaled, then let it go. It was not quite a sigh. And I could see her face in my mind. A thoughtful, serious little girl, already too familiar with loss.

'I have to brush my teeth,' she said, and my heart ached for her. I wanted to put my arms around her and protect her, or to at least tell her that I understood how she felt tonight, but Scout was out of reach now, living in another family, not the one we shared, and living in another home, not my own.

'Don't forget the back,' I said.

'OK. Here's Mummy.'

And then there was the customary pause while her mother took the phone but did not speak as she waited for Scout to make her way upstairs. When she came on the line, Anne's voice was choked with emotion.

'Did you read my email?' she said.

'What email?'

'This is not a good time, Max. Since Oliver lost his job, it's been so hard for me. I've done my best, I really have. You know I have. Nobody knows how hard it has been for me … '

I found my laptop.

There was an unopened email.

Dear Max,
I am sorry …

It went on for ages. Reams of all the stuff Anne was sorry about. Unbroken paragraphs of regret. She was sorry about everything. Sorry that her husband had lost his job. Sorry that this was a difficult time for Scout to come and live with her. And sorry for herself. That most of all.

I slammed the laptop and the email was gone. I did not need to read every word of it. I got the gist. And I didn't care about her husband or his job or her.

All I cared about was my daughter.

'Don't cry, Anne,' I said. 'Everything's going to be all right.'

As I hung up the phone, Edie came into the bedroom wrapped in a towel and still damp from the shower. I pulled her to the bed. The towel slipped to the floor. I placed a kiss on her wet shoulders.

'What's happening?' she said.

'Scout's coming home,' I said.

We wrapped Stan in a blanket and carried him down to Smiths of Smithfield. A kindly Australian waitress put down a plate for him. He did not even sniff it. He sat on Edie's lap, swathed in his blankets, and all he wanted to do was sleep.

Edie's hair was still wet from the shower. Her hair was the burnished red that looks as though it has a touch of fire in it but the dampness made it darker. She pushed it back from her high forehead.

'I don't understand,' she said. 'You mean your ex-wife has decided she can't look after Scout?'

'Anne — my ex-wife — has problems at home,' I said. 'Problems with her husband. Problems that have come up after he lost his job. And I was wrong — I thought that nothing bad ever happened on the kind of street where they live. But I guess they can happen anywhere.'

'And what about us, Max? I've always been Scout's friend. But I'm never going to be her mother, am I? What will we be? You, Scout and me?'

I felt the endorphins kicking in.

'We'll be a family,' I said.

A family once more, I thought.

Is that really what we would be?

Yes, that is exactly what we would be. Perhaps not the kind of family that any of us was expecting. Perhaps not the kind of family you see in commercials. But a family all the same.

'I almost forgot,' I said. 'I have something for you.'

Edie was looking wary. This was all moving very fast.

I reached into my pocket and took out a set of keys. Two Yale and one Chubb, all of them brand new and gleaming.

I talked her through them.

'This one is for the front door on Charterhouse Street. These two are for the loft.'

She took the keys and held them in the palm of her hand, the lights of the soft summer evening catching the freshly cut metal.

'Who else has keys to the loft?'

'Me. Mrs Murphy. Jackson still has a set. And Scout, although she is too small to reach the lock. I give her another year.'

'That's exalted company.'

'It just makes things easier, Edie. Coming and going. No big deal.'

'I guess you must like me a little bit.'

'You're all right.'

'Thanks.'

Finally we smiled at each other. She exhaled.

'I might take Stan for a walk before we put him down for the night,' she said.

'But Edie – he can't walk.'

'Then I'll carry him.'

She looked out of the big windows of Smiths of Smithfield at the meat market stirring into life.

'You told me once that dogs live in a world of scent. So maybe all the smells of the neighbourhood will do him some good. And if it doesn't make him better, then maybe it will make him happy. Isn't it worth a try if it makes Stan feel happier?'

'Yes,' I smiled. 'It's worth it.'

So Edie took Stan in her arms and she held him close as she carried him off in the direction of West Smithfield, where Charles Dickens' description of our neighbourhood is carved into the stone chairs.

I watched them until they disappeared and then I walked through the market's great arch, past the line of old red telephone boxes and the plaque marking the spot where William 'Braveheart' Wallace was executed, and I kept walking until I came to the small strip of shops on the far side of Smithfield.

Music was drifting from the flat above the one I was heading to. I stopped to listen to it. An old country hit, heartfelt and ironic all at the same time. 'Don't It Make My Brown Eyes Blue' by Crystal Gayle. I looked at the shop but it was closed for the night.

MURPHY & SON
Domestic and Commercial Plumbing
and Heating
'Trustworthy' and 'Reliable'

I went round to the back of the shops and up a flight of stairs.

Mrs Murphy answered the door.

'Guess what?' I said and she stared at me for a moment before throwing her arms around me, and both of us were laughing, and Crystal Gayle was singing in the background.

'My Scout's coming home,' Mrs Murphy said.

*

I stood outside our front door, scanning the street for a slightly built redhead carrying a small red Cavalier King Charles Spaniel in her arms.

I wanted to be home safe and sound with the pair of them.

But there was no sign of Edie and Stan.

Perhaps they had already come back. And now of course Edie had her own set of keys.

I had had a cup of tea with Mrs Murphy – 'You will have a cup of tea,' she had told me, as always making her invitation sound like a prophecy – and it was quite possible that Edie had given up on reviving Stan with the world of scent and the ten-kilo dog had started to feel heavy in her arms.

They're already home, I thought, slipping my key into the lock.

I stepped inside, the building cool and dark after the summer night street.

The figure moved quickly from the shadows of the stairwell.

He raised the stubby yellow Taser and aimed it at my face.

And then he shot me.

35

I was slammed back against the door and collapsed on the welcome mat, writhing with the pain of 50,000 volts of power invading my central nervous system.

There was the immediate loss of motor skills and muscle control. I was writhing on my back and then my entire body stiffened and spasmed with a back-arching agony that made me groan and drool and cry out with pain. Five seconds lasted for a hundred years. A century of pure, incapacitated pain. And then the pain was in my eyes, and I saw a slowly shifting universe of tiny white stars. *Tick-tick-tick* went the thing in the dark figure's right fist and every metallic-sounding tick was like being hit in the head with my guard down.

I gasped for the breath that would not come.

And I looked up and the first thing I saw was the haircut, the brutal Depression-era haircut, shaved at the back and the sides and shorn to a short crop on top, and I did not understand, because George Halfpenny was sitting in a jail cell.

And then my mind or vision cleared, and I was looking up at his brother, Richard Halfpenny, thick and fleshy and built like a small bull, his surly face staring at the Taser X3 in his hand and cursing it. The X3 model fires three shots and I realised with a sinking heart that he was planning to shoot me again. But I saw now that the Taser was wrapped in brown duct tape and that he must have picked it up during the riots rather than buying it from a reputable weapons dealer.

And it would not fire again.

He leaned over me, this strong, stocky man who stank of junk food, and he easily lifted me to my feet with his large calloused hands, and then those hands were inside my leather jacket, searching for the keys to my home. He found them.

And as he bundled me into the lift, half-carrying and half-dragging my limp body, my frazzled muscles still twitching with a damaged life of their own, I could imagine him slipping into the building when one of my neighbours had let themselves in.

And then I felt my stomach fall away.

Perhaps it wasn't one of my neighbours who he came in with. Perhaps it was Edie.

He threw me into the lift and I bounced off the far side, sliding to the floor until he grabbed a fistful of my T-shirt and pulled me up.

I watched him press the button for the top floor.

He knew it was the top floor.

He smiled at me.

'Time to play,' he said.

We got out of the lift. He fumbled with the keys. The door of the loft flew open. And I was shouting as he bundled me inside.

'Go! Get out! Go!'

But the loft was empty.

Thank God. Thank God. Thank God.

Halfpenny left me crumpled on the floor of that vast open space and checked both the bedrooms. They must have been empty because I heard no sound. He saw me slowly trying to get to my feet as he came out of my bedroom. He had been heading for the bathroom but now he made a detour. I swayed uncertainly before him.

That's the problem with any Taser. It disables the victim for just long enough for the arresting officer to apprehend, subdue and dominate. But even 50,000 volts wasn't going to keep me on my back all night long.

So Richard Halfpenny swiped me backhanded across the face with the duct-taped Taser and I felt it make instant mush of my lip and cheek. I sank down on one knee, my nerve ends flaring with pain. I spat out a gob of blood.

'You killed Ahmed Khan,' I said. 'You stuck that old Nazi knife in his neck. Whitestone was always looking at the wrong brother. *Blut und Ehre.*'

'Blood and honour,' he said proudly. 'He deserved to die, raising those murdering bastard sons.'

'And it was you who ran down Ludo Mount,' I said.

'I was aiming at you,' he said. 'But Sir bloody Ludo would have been no great loss. Because he protected them. He took their side against his own people.'

He kicked me in the ribs and I went down on both knees.

'Just like you,' he said.

Keep him talking, I thought. *Buy time. Get stronger.*

'The Ten Commandments was a nice touch,' I gasped. 'I was looking forward to the one about coveting my neighbour's donkey – or is it his ass? I can never remember.'

His face clouded.

'Don't make fun of the Bible,' he said. 'You wouldn't make fun of *their* religion, would you? So don't make fun of ours.'

'You never struck me as the religious kind, Richard. Can I call you Richard?'

His boorish face got an almost wistful look.

'I *want* to believe,' he said. 'I really do. But I think that if God ever existed, then He must have died, or forgotten us, or just walked away disgusted with it all.'

Keep the moron talking, Max.

'But why top the weapons dealer?' I said. 'He's on your side, isn't he? You believe in the same lost cause, don't you? The Thousand-Year Reich and all that.'

But then I saw it.

'Because he sold you the knife that killed Ahmed Khan,' I said, seeing it in my mind. The nickel-plated pommel, the grip of black Bakelite with the gold-etched black swastika on a red-and-white diamond. *Blut und Ehre*. 'You bought the knife from your pal Peter Fenn. Ozymandias. And then he tried to blackmail you, didn't he?'

'He called it a loan. He needed a loan. He wanted to get back to Thailand. There was some girl who he met in a bar there.' He shuddered at the weakness of human flesh. 'Some little whore. And so he needed money to go back and see her.'

Richard Halfpenny sighed, and looked around the loft absent-mindedly as if he was thinking about making me an offer.

I started getting up. He aimed another kick at my ribs but I dug my elbows in and let my arms take the point of his shoe. It still hurt. But not as bad as a broken rib. But I was so tired that I could no longer stand. He watched me as I slid to the floor, his mouth twisting with disgust.

I was on my hands and knees, trying to coax my breath back now, the nerve ends still ringing in every part of my body.

'But what about you, copper?' he said. 'Why do I want to see you crawl before I slot you? Any final thoughts before I cut your face off?'

I looked up at him, rubbing my ribs.

'How did you even get my phone number?'

'Because,' he said, his face clouding with fury, 'you gave it to *my brother.*'

And the mention of his brother George sent him into a frenzy of kicking and stomping and punching, and he beat me until I was crumbled in a heap, curled up and trying to protect my head and my balls and my ribs. He stood there panting for air.

'My brother,' he said, his voice cracking with emotion, 'could have been a great man. And *you* ruined it. *You* spoiled everything. *You* made sure he got put away. Because you always hated him, right from the first night. *I'll be watching you*, you said. How *dare* you talk to a great man like that? How dare you, you stupid copper?'

I looked towards the door, torn between wanting Edie to arrive before the end, and hoping that she came back too late. I held up my hands.

'Nothing to do with me, Your Honour,' I said. 'Your brother George seriously injured a policeman and that's why he will do hard time. And it's not true that I always hated your brother. I liked him. It was you I couldn't stand, you freak.'

He came toward me, planning to kick me to death but I held up my hands higher.

'Wait, wait,' I said. 'Please. Listen, Richard. You need to understand something. Your brother George is a smart guy. But he was never going to be a great man. Wrong parents, wrong schools, wrong accent. Fifty years ago, maybe, he might have had a shot at greatness. But not now. *The fix is in at birth.* The attention your brother got on Borodino Street was going to be the high point of his life. Can't you see, you dumb, ugly bastard? Your brother – and everyone just like him – is beat before they begin. George was going to push that rickshaw until the day it killed him.'

'I told you,' Richard Halfpenny said. 'I told you again and again. *You're going to crawl.*'

'Sorry,' I said, getting unsteadily to my feet. I wasn't going on the floor again unless he killed me. 'I don't crawl for anyone.'

He took a knife from his jacket.

'Waffen-SS dress dagger with *totenkopf* – literally, dead head – on the handle,' he said proudly.

'I'd ask for my money back,' I said, squinting at the knife. 'Looks like a fake.'

I saw the six-inch double-sided blade, with the eagle and the swastika on the hilt, and the skull and bones on the black grip, and I saw the same bleak dreams of world domination that have been ending in the nightmare of tears and misery and ruined cities for a hundred years.

It looked very old. It didn't look like a fake. I was just pulling his leg.

It must have been from his collection.

And I knew he had been saving it for me.

'Crawl for me,' he said. 'Or I will start cutting bits off you that will make you beg to crawl.'

'No.'

'*Crawl.*'

'Just get it done, you fat bastard.'

And then the toilet flushed.

We both stared at the bathroom door.

A slow smile crept across Richard Halfpenny's bloated face.

'Ah,' he said. 'She's home! The lady of the house. That hot little redhead. Hiding in the smallest room. Even better.'

'I am going to kill you,' I said.

He kicked me in the stomach. The air came out of me with a sickening *ooof*! And I doubled up.

'Unlikely,' he said. I watched him move across the loft and try the handle of the bathroom door. It was locked.

He pressed his shoulder to the bathroom door.

He took his stance and braced himself to smash it down.

He grinned back at me and winked.

'She's playing too hard to get,' he said. 'I love that shit. I do hope you are going to enjoy watching me with her.'

I took a step towards him as he turned his face to the door and in that sliver of a second the air tore apart with the sound of a 9 mm handgun being fired from inside a confined space.

A single shot from inside the bathroom.

Richard Halfpenny was thrown backwards and I was watching him die at my feet before the sound of the air being split wide open had faded away.

The gunshot wound was in his chest.

Centre of mass. The way the experts learn to shoot.

Black blood bubbled from the corner of Richard Halfpenny's mouth.

And I saw the shot was perhaps one inch to the left side of the medial line, the midline of a human body where the core of human life is located directly to the left or right – the heart, the lungs, the spine, the liver.

So just off the medial line. But still a bullseye, still the work of a highly skilled operative who was aiming for the middle of his target.

My bathroom door now had a hole in it the size of an espresso saucer at the Bar Italia. I heard the lock slide back.

Jesse Tibbs walked out, not looking at me, standing over the man on the floor, the Glock that Jackson had given me still aimed at his centre of mass.

Because Tibbs had been taught that one shot is not always enough.

But it was enough for Richard Halfpenny. It was enough for Bad Moses.

Tibbs lowered his Glock 19, released the magazine, stuck the gun and the clip in separate pockets.

I sat on the floor, rubbing my ribs, my ears ringing.

'I wanted my gun back,' he said, kneeling by Half-penny's side, checking his pulse. 'Very clever, hiding it in the ceiling. It was the second place I looked. What was wrong with under the mattress of your bed?'

Jackson the thief, I thought.

'Your friend thought he would take my private shooter from my locker and arm you at the same time,' Tibbs said. 'Two birds and one stone, right?

He made no attempt to help me to my feet.

'Once or twice I even thought he was tailing me,' he said. 'But Jackson had me wrong. I always hated you but I was never going to slot you. I'm not that dumb. I thought we could take it to the ring or a car park. Anywhere you wanted it. But I thought we might settle our differences like men.' He looked at the body between us. 'I guess we did.'

'Tibbs,' I said. 'You saved my life.'

'Yes,' he said. 'It's what I do.'

'How did you get in?'

'Well, I didn't need a bloody shotgun.'

'I'm sorry about Ray Vann,' I said. 'I'm sorry about your friend. I know you blame me. And I'm sorry you hate my guts.'

He shrugged as if it was all behind us now.

He stared thoughtfully at the dead man on the floor.

'I just think you get it wrong, Wolfe. You and the rest of the world. You think it's a job.' He looked at me now. 'And it's a war, pal. It's a war.'

He moved towards the big loft windows, pulled wide open for the last of the summer's heat.

'Anyway,' he said. 'My war's over, I guess.'

'Tibbs,' I said. 'We can sort this out. Richard Half-penny was a serial killer. He was going to kill me. You've done nothing wrong.'

'No,' he said. 'I'm done. I might get away with topping Bad Moses here. But it's the Glock with the serial number gone, you see. I can't explain that. I will never be able to explain that. And that's jail time. And I can't be locked up, Wolfe. Maybe Jackson was trying to do me a favour.' Jesse Tibbs smiled at me for the first time. 'Maybe he was trying to save both of us.'

Jesse Tibbs stood at one of the big open windows and looked down on the street four storeys below. I could not understand what he was doing. And then suddenly I got it. Checking for pedestrians, I saw, checking for innocent passers-by. And I felt the panic and sadness rise up in me as I got to my feet and staggered across the loft towards him, seeing him slide his right arm between his belt and his jeans, and then the left arm.

The jumper's insurance policy. Hands and arms locked inside the belt. So the fall cannot be broken. So that the hands can't be held out at the final moment of life.

So that there is no final chance to change your mind.

And then, with his arms pinned to his sides by his belt, Tibbs sat himself on to the window ledge and I was weak from the serious beating that Richard Halfpenny had given me and I knew that I did not have it in me to stop him.

Then we both stared at the door of the loft as it quietly clicked open.

'You all right, Jesse?' Jackson Rose said easily. 'I knew I would find you here.'

As he crossed the great open space of our loft, Jackson took it all in. The dead body of Richard Halfpenny, the good hiding I had taken, and the last plans of Jesse Tibbs.

Without rushing but without breaking step, Jackson walked calmly to the window and gently pulled Jesse's arms out from inside his belt. And then Jackson held him tight, the pair of them sitting on the window ledge as if they had all the time in the world, as if it was still a beautiful night, and Jesse Tibbs buried his face in Jackson's chest so that we could not see him sobbing.

'You're all right,' Jackson told him. 'And we're going to take care of you now.'

36

Anne was looking good.

My ex-wife still carried herself like she was late for a photo-shoot at *Vogue* and was really miffed about it. She still turned heads and kept them turned when she walked – no, she strode – into the small café where we met in the shadow of Southwark Cathedral. She still had the model's strange magic – that alchemy of height, bones and skin – of appearing to be slightly different to the rest of the human race.

An adorable alien, then, running late.

She waved to me from the door and she had checked her phone twice before she reached the corner table. Here was a woman who was moving on, ready for whatever was coming next, fitting me into a very small window.

'Thanks for meeting me,' she said.

'No problem,' I said.

Oh, the excruciating formality of former partners.

'You must be very busy,' she said. 'Are they sure that was Bad Moses? The man who got shot?'

I nodded. She shuddered with theatrical horror.

'But that's all done and dusted,' I said. 'So it's a slow day at the office.'

She nodded briskly, checked her phone again, placed it face down on the table so that she would not be tempted to peek, and signalled for the waiter. A nice young Australian came running.

'Did you order?' she asked me.

'I was waiting for you.'

We both insisted that the other order first.

We got it done eventually and I reflected that we were never this polite to each other when we were living together. We were never this polite when we loved each other madly.

But we were total strangers now.

Those people we had been were gone forever – the young uniformed cop with no living relations craving a family immediately with the most beautiful girl he had ever seen, and the stunning young model whose career was not panning out quite as spectacularly as planned, predicted or expected – for it turned out there were many, many beautiful girls in the world, and some of them were taller, thinner and younger than Anne, even back then.

We were a different man and woman now. I guess we both grew up. It was as simple, as everyday, as that. All we shared now was our past.

And our seven-year-old daughter.

'Scout,' she said. 'She's such a doll. And she's been so good at our place. I have just loved the time we have had together. She's so smart and lovely,' she said.

'Yes,' I said, and I saw Anne meant it, and I felt some ice inside me – the ice that had been frozen so hard and so unforgiving against my ex-wife for so long – begin to melt.

She tapped the table with her elaborate fingernails and I remembered that she had been a smoker. She wanted a cigarette now.

'I'm sorry it hasn't worked out,' I said. 'I know you wanted to make it work. I know that – in your heart – you want to be a good mother to Scout.'

The waiter brought our coffee.

I sipped my triple espresso and waited for him to leave.

Anne blew on her skinny soymilk latte.

'Since Oliver lost his job, things have not been so brilliant at home,' she said. 'There's the mortgage—'

I held up my hand. 'It's none of my business, Anne.'

A flash of defiance.

'I love her just as much as you do,' she said. 'Whatever you may think.'

'I have to believe it,' I said. 'Because I can't stand the thought of Scout not being loved by you. It's unbearable to me, that possibility. And I do know you love her, in your own way. But you love yourself more. Please – let me finish. And I think that when you have a child, you either put that child before everything else in the world – everything – or you don't. Plenty of men don't – can't – put a kid before themselves. They think their happiness comes first. Or their fulfilment or destiny or sex life or whatever they want to call it, and however they want to rationalise it. But it happens with women, too. And the children – these children who get left – they get hurt. Of course they do. But the people who do the leaving – those men and women – they get hurt even more. And you have hurt yourself more than you could ever hurt Scout.'

'Good old Max,' she said, attempting a laugh. 'Never knowingly off the high moral ground.'

She looked towards the door, chewed her bottom lip, and I could see that she was giving serious thought to leaving right now. Then she sighed, and I saw her eyes shining with the emotion that she was holding back.

And when I felt my heart go out to her, I thought it was some kind of sentimental feeling for what we had once shared. But then I saw it was something new.

I felt sorry for her.

'You don't know what's going on in my life,' she said bitterly. 'The sleepless nights. The rows about money. Not knowing where the next six-figure salary is going to come from – or if it is going to come at all. Do you *really* want Scout in the middle of all that?'

I shook my head.

'Scout can come back to me. With pleasure, with joy. Of course she can come back to me. My door is open to her and it will be open to her on the last day of my life. She has the key. Nothing in the world is more important to me than my daughter.'

'Saint Max!'

'Nowhere near it. I'm just trying to be the best father I can be, Anne. I don't even think I'm very good at it. Work gets in the way. I'm not as selfless as I should be. But I'm trying.'

'I tried,' she said. 'Bad time. That's all.'

I felt like touching her hand, just to show her that I got it. She had not seen this coming and those are always the hardest blows.

'I thought that nothing bad ever happened on the street where you live,' I said. 'I thought you had it all worked out. And I thought that you were certain to stay with Oliver forever.'

'Well, probably we will,' she said. 'But things change.'

She glanced at her watch, and I wondered for a moment if there was already someone else, and then I realised that I didn't give a damn any more. It's a thin line between love and total indifference.

All I felt for Anne now was a memory of feelings that had long gone, and the acute awareness of this new feeling. She was a woman with a restless heart, and it was unlikely to make her happy.

There wasn't much more to discuss.

Scout's room in London was exactly how she had left it. Miss Davies, her beloved teacher from New Zealand, had ensured that there was a place reserved for Scout when school resumed in September.

'I'll get her a pet to cheer her up,' Anne said, raising her eyebrows at this brainwave. 'How about a hamster? Hamsters are good because they're low maintenance and they don't live long. I had one when I was a little girl. Squeaky.'

'But why would Scout want a hamster?'

You couldn't take a hamster for a walk on Hampstead Heath. The porters who worked on the night shift at Smithfield meat market would never learn the name of a hamster. Squeaky and his kind were never going to love you like we all want to be loved.

'Scout's dog died, didn't he?' Anne said. 'I know he was very ill. Sam, right? Or was it Sid?'

'Stan,' I said, and then I could not stop grinning.

Because Edie's treatment had worked.

Carrying Stan around a neighbourhood where meat had been sold for five hundred years had revived his spirit. Somewhere in that juicy universe of scent, Stan had recovered his appetite, and then his Cavalier King Charles Spaniel energy, and finally his old food-motivated self, his small heart open to the world, eager for friendship and fun with anyone on four legs or two.

'Stan's going to be fine,' I said, as my ex-wife frowned at her phone.

She bolted her frothy coffee. She was keen to get on.

'So are we finished?' she said.

'Yes,' I said. 'We're done here.'

On the top floor at West End Central, DCI Flashman of Counter Terrorism Command had parked his enormous bulk on my workstation. As I walked into MIR-1 he wiped his fringe of white-blond hair from his forehead and smiled lopsidedly as though he was still bloody gorgeous.

'So you got your man, Wolfe,' he said. 'Congratulations.'

'SFO Jesse Tibbs got Bad Moses. Not me. Richard Halfpenny gave me a kicking until Tibbs took him out with an unregistered firearm that Halfpenny had purchased from the late Peter Fenn, the weapons dealer also known as Ozymandias.'

That was our story. And we – Jackson, Tibbs and me – would all be sticking to it.

'No medal this time then?' Flashman said. 'Shame. But another one bites the dust. And his brother will do hard time for crocking that young uniform, even if the judge is an old softy. How's he doing, by the way?'

'PC Sykes is out of his coma but rehab is going to be long and hard,' Whitestone said. 'Sykes is a tough kid. I think he'll walk again.'

Flashman clapped his large hands once. 'So another couple of scumbags are off the streets and we can all sleep safe and sound tonight, thanks – in part at least – to London's favourite detective, DC Wolfe.'

I stared at Flashman's belligerent grin.

He had not come to 27 Savile Row to offer his congratulations on nailing Bad Moses.

'Courtesy call,' he explained, reading my mind.

The rest of my mob was facing him. Whitestone. Joy Adams. And Edie.

She looked at me and in less than an instant something passed between us with the secret telepathy of lovers.

How did it go with the ex?

Scout's coming home.

Edie smiled.

Whitestone and Joy were still staring at Flashman, their arms crossed, unimpressed.

'CTU are releasing Mrs Azza Khan without charges,' Whitestone said.

'Because – as I was explaining before you joined us, Wolfe – there's not enough evidence to prosecute her under any of the existing terrorism laws,' Flashman said. 'It wasn't Azza Khan who brought down that Air Ambulance helicopter on Lake Meadows and it wasn't her who killed Alice Stone – it was her sons. Listen, I've spent hours with the woman – she's your standard deluded, self-pitying, not-very-bright religious maniac who was allowed to settle in a country when she feels not a shred of love, affection, gratitude or loyalty towards this country. Just the opposite, in fact, between you and me and the garden gate. But then whose fault is that – hers or ours?'

'But she's the poison,' Whitestone said. 'You know she is, Flashman. Scarlet Bush was right. It all comes back to her. Her sons were standard weed-smoking failed DJs on benefits who had their tiny minds turned to jihad. And all the poison comes from her – and all the old bigots just like her who are never the ones to use the knife, or drive the van into pedestrians or detonate the suicide vest.'

'Yes, yes,' he said. 'I know all of that. And I said to her – *If it is so horrible living among all of us drinking, fornicating, freedom-loving kaffirs, then why don't you go and live in a Muslim country, darling?* And do you know what she said to me?'

'Don't call me darling,' guessed Joy.

'After that,' Flashman said. 'She told me – *But why should I go to live in another country when every country belongs to Allah?*' But as far as CTU can tell, she has never invited and encouraged support for a proscribed organisation in violation of the Terrorism Act. I can't prosecute her for believing what she wants to believe. It's a free country.'

Flashman stood up, stretched and yawned.

'So we'll keep an eye on her,' he said. 'Of course we will. Azza Khan will be a person of interest for a little while, until another few thousand new persons of interest come along. We'll do our best, all right? You want me to lock her up when she hasn't broken any laws? When there's been no criminal offence? What about her human rights? I'm shocked, truly shocked.'

He left us.

Whitestone looked at me. 'I always liked the wrong brother for the Bad Moses murders,' she said. 'Sorry, Max.'

'Easy mistake to make,' I said. 'But all they shared was that haircut. The brothers could hardly have been more different. For all the racket on social media, Richard – Bad Moses – was always just a simple-minded, violent thug who had found a cause big enough for all his frustration and hatred. It made him closer to the Khan brothers than he ever realised. But I don't think George Halfpenny hated anyone. I think George loved this country and thought it was worth preserving. He had thought about things when he was pedalling that rickshaw around the city. He had his set of beliefs and, for the first time in his life, people were listening to him.'

'And now he's going down for what he did to PC Sykes,' Whitestone said. 'Which is a tragedy for the Sykes family and for George himself. He might have got out from behind that rickshaw and done something with his life.'

'You never know,' I said.

'And how are you doing?' Whitestone said.

My knee ached when the weather turned cold. My ribs were bruised. My intercostal muscles – the ones that lift the ribcage every time you breathe in and out – felt like they were torn. Some of my nerve ends still rattled and jangled and jumped about with a will of their own, sparking with the afterglow of the 50,000 volts of power that had recently passed through them.

But the last of the summer sunshine was shining on my city. Scout was coming home. Our dog Stan had long, good years to live. And Edie was at her workstation and already packing her bag because it was a slow day at the office. She smiled at me and ran her fingers through her red hair.

'Never been better, boss,' I said.

37

We were in Edie's one-bedroom flat above a junk shop on the cheap side of Highbury Corner. She was all boxed up and ready to go. Today was the day we started living together.

The removal men had just left and we would not see them again until Charterhouse Street, when we met them outside the block of flats directly opposite the main entrance of the old meat market.

Outside our home.

Edie sealed the duct tape on a cardboard box of CDs and books and turned to face me.

'Are you sure about this, Max?'

'Let me think,' I said.

I touched my mouth against her mouth.

The fit was uncanny. I mean, I doubt if there was another pair of mouths in the world that fit together quite so well.

'But we'll be one of those families,' she said, pulling away. 'We'll be blended! I know Scout likes me but maybe not so much when I'm at the breakfast table.'

I pulled her close again. Everything fit. Not just our mouths. Sometimes you just know where you belong. And when you know – really know – where you belong, then you don't need to know anything else.

'We'll be fine,' I said. 'That's what we'll be.' I kissed her one last time. 'Now let's go home, Edie.'

We carried the few remaining boxes down to the old BMW X5.

The street was empty apart from a woman in a full black burka walking down the middle of the road, carrying a pink and purple rucksack in her right hand, an *Angry Princess* bag, the bright splash of childish purple and pink colours standing out starkly against the funereal robes.

The curve her face – or what I could see of it – was familiar.

Because the woman was Layla Khan.

And I had seen that rucksack before.

I had seen it on that first day in Borodino Street.

And I saw it all clearly at last, I saw what had been there all along, staring me in the face, and I knew it was true even before Layla reached into the rucksack.

'Max?' Edie said. 'That's Layla, isn't it?'

She began to walk towards the girl.

And I knew now how the two Croatian hand grenades had left the house on Borodino Street. I knew with complete certainty that Azza Khan had stuffed them into the merchandise of last summer's Hollywood hit animated movie, and that she had carried them out in *The Angry Princess* bag through the armed officers ushering them to safety.

'Get back inside,' I called to Edie.

But she had already left me and now she was walking slowly towards the figure in black.

They drew closer. They stopped. They faced each other, close enough to reach out and touch.

'Layla,' Edie said.

'We destroy your buildings,' she said.

There was something in her hands.

In both of her hands.

They looked like death – black, lattice-faced spheres with a gold-coloured handle and ring pull, identical to a key ring. I was not close enough to read the name of the manufacturer on the side. But I knew what it said. *Cetinka*, it said, on those two grenades that should have been destroyed at the end of someone else's war twenty years ago.

'Edie!' I screamed.

'But you destroy our countries,' Layla said.

'This is your country,' Edie said, and I saw her wrap her arms around Layla Khan with infinite tenderness, hugging her as Layla Khan removed the pins from first one Croatian grenade and then the other.

The sunlight caught the metal pins as they bounced on the sun-baked concrete of the little street.

Edie held her tight and smiled into Layla's face, but I no longer recognised that face, it was someone I had never seen, the poison was in her now, and then I was thrown backwards without hearing the first explosion, or the second explosion, only the muffled sound of the air being forced asunder with astonishing violence, and then the echo of the rendering, like the sound of a door being slammed a thousand miles below the earth.

I was on my back.

I could hear what I first thought was falling rain, and then realised it was the sound of breaking glass dropping from shattered window panes the length of the street.

I looked around.

The broken bodies of the two women lay together in the middle of the road. A patch of red hair fell across the ghost white face of Edie Wren. I called her name, and it was a noise that came from a place inside me that I did not know existed, and it was the cry of something that had been smashed beyond repair.

And at last I began to crawl.

38

The hospital was never silent, never dark, never sleeping.

Even in the small hours, long after they had doled out the medication to get us through until dawn, there was the still yellow twilight of the hospital lights coming from the nurses station and the corridor, and there were still the noises that pulled me from my drugged and feverish sleep, like sounds from the underworld.

The moans and the snoring of the sleeping. The groans and gasps of the distressed who were awake or asleep or somewhere in between. The murmured voices and soft laughter of the nurses at their station and the urgent slap-slap-slap of their rubber soles on the polished floors.

And worst of all was the shattered soundtrack inside my head.

I moved my weight to ease the pain in my legs that kept breaking through the fog of morphine and the only way that I knew for certain that I sometimes slept were the dreams that I glimpsed sliding away from consciousness upon the instant of waking.

Fred was there, inside my head, approaching the bed with his long hair pulled up in a topknot, and his wicked pirate's grin on his face.

'You're so lucky to be training,' he said.

And Mrs Murphy was there at some point in the night, when there was unbroken darkness in the world outside with only the soft gloaming of the hospital lights to guide her.

Mrs Murphy sat in the one seat of my small room and she turned her head towards me, Stan asleep at her feet. 'You'll have a cup of tea with your dinner,' she predicted. And Sergeant John Caine came out of the shadows of the Black Museum, Room 101, New Scotland Yard.

'I'll put the kettle on,' he said.

Then I slept some more and when I came round Jackson was there, the lone chair pulled up to my bedside. He patted my arm and I caught my breath, understanding that my oldest friend was really here and not inside my head.

'You've got a bit of shrapnel in your legs,' he said quietly. 'But they still work. No worries. No problem.' He gave me his grin. 'A bit of shrapnel in the legs? Join the club.'

I cleared my throat of the thick lump that clogged it.

'Edie?' I said.

He patted my arm again.

'Edie's hanging in there, Max. The woman that did it died instantly.'

The woman? He meant Layla Khan.

'But Edie is still fighting,' Jackson said. I watched him hesitate. 'She's not awake yet. But she's a tough kid.'

I nodded.

'Scout?' I said.

He smiled and I saw the gap-toothed grin that I had been looking at all my life.

'I spoke to Scout on the phone,' he said. 'Don't worry. She's good. She's fine. She wants you to get well. Nothing's changed, OK? Scout's coming home.'

I closed my eyes and I was aware of every breath and I felt the tiny fragments of black metal in my lower legs.

Edie was sleeping.

Scout was coming home.

And Layla Khan was dead.

'Stan?' I said.

Jackson grinned.

'Stan's with Mrs Murphy and her family. Having the time of his life. Her grandchildren are spoiling him rotten. He will be waiting for you.'

'Tibbs,' I said. 'Jesse.'

It was not a question.

'Jesse's already back at work,' he said. 'Nobody blames him for topping a murderer with his own gun. How could they?' Jackson shook his head. 'Jesse was my fault. I should have just let the pair of you batter each other. Get it out of your system. The way they settled it in the old school. You'd be best mates by now. He was never going to slot you. The worst that would have happened is he would have given you a good hiding. Or you would have given him a good hiding. And I should have let it happen. Live and learn. Or hope we do, at least.'

The morphine was closing my eyes, dragging me down.

I felt Jackson pat my arm and I tumbled into the darkness.

'Anything you need,' he said. And then, 'Don't forget — you can make new friends but you can't make old friends.'

Or perhaps that last bit was just inside my head.

And the dead also came to me that night.

My parents were there at one point in my morphine sleep. And they were not young and they were not old, my mother and father, but they were exactly as I remembered them, they were totally themselves, the very essence of them, but on the other side of a glass-like wall that separated one world from the other, a wall that was higher than the sky, and conversation was not possible, not a word, even as I felt the love and the loss and the missing of them, the missing of them that I saw was with me every day of my life.

And then George Halfpenny was there, in the one chair, reading his ancient paperback copy of *Origins of the Second World War* by A. J. P Taylor from the prison library, and I thought he must be among the dead, and I looked for the mark around his neck of the men who die in their prison cells, the livid death mark always a diagonal wound, cutting up towards his ear where the sheet or the belt or whatever it had been had angled up towards the knot. But the death mark was not on his neck and I knew that he was among the living, and I knew that George Halfpenny would live because he wanted to return to his brother Edward, the young man in a wheelchair, the brother who loved and needed him, who would always love and need him, and who made it impossible for George to do anything but cling to life.

'Human blunders usually do more to shape history than human wickedness,' he said, and I did not know if that was a quote from A. J. P. Taylor or George Halfpenny.

I slept.

I woke.

It was still dark and more quiet than it had been at any point in the night. I listened for the slap-slap-slap of the rubber soles of the nurses as they went about their labours, and I listened for the sound of their voices, warm and amused and young, as they talked very softly at their station, and I listened too for the other patients tormented in their sleep.

But I heard nothing.

The night was still and silent and at peace with itself at last.

And Edie was sitting at the window in her T-shirt and pants, the legs I loved tucked up under the butt that

I loved and a concerned look on the face that I loved. She brushed back her red hair and fixed me with her green eyes.

And she looked at me with endless sadness and she said not a word.

Then it was morning and the ward was awake and the smell of breakfast in the hospital made me sick and made me think that I would never want food ever again.

Joy Adams sat in the only chair, watching me carefully with her huge dark eyes, and Pat Whitestone stood by my bedside.

My boss. She was holding my hand.

'Edie,' she said.

'She's a tough kid,' I said.

My voice was so hoarse it sounded like someone else but it was full of a grainy hope.

'The bravest and the best,' Whitestone said. 'A very tough kid. But I have to tell you that Edie didn't make it, Max.'

I stared at her for a bit. I looked at Joy. There were tears running down her face. I looked back at Whitestone.

'OK,' I said.

'Edie never recovered consciousness.'

'OK.'

'She slipped away in the night. She wouldn't have felt any pain. Edie died doing the job she loved, Max.'

'OK.'

They went away after a while, because hospital beds always rob you of things to say, there is never anything to say in the end, no banal observation to be made, or sincere condolences to be offered, and there was breakfast and morphine to be taken or declined.

The sky rolled across the sky and it felt for the first time that the night was coming in much faster, the days of our long summer running out at last, and that night no one came to me, not the living nor the dead, because they all leave you alone after a while, and I was wide and fully awake – the drugs no longer working – when I came at last to the dark and silent moment that you find in the still centre of every night, even when you are in a hospital bed.

And that was when I pushed my face into the pillow and I wept for Edie Wren, and for myself, and for the children who would never be born.

39

The leaves were turning the colour of our dog.

Stan and I drove to the street where it looked like nothing bad had ever happened and I parked the old silver BMW X5 outside the house with the FOR SALE sign in the yard.

We were neither early nor late. I had timed our arrival to the minute and as I put on the handbrake the door opened in a blur of adults and small children milling in the hallway, and at the centre of them all there was the face of my daughter.

Scout was saying her goodbyes.

I eased myself from the car, the pain in my lower legs flaring, the muscles still stiff with injury from the jagged black fragments of shrapnel that would be there forever. I reached across Stan to the well of the passenger seat to take my walking stick.

When I straightened up by the side of the car, taking some of my weight on the stick, Scout was watching me, her face clouding over at the sight of her damaged old dad.

We stared at each other and in the look that passed between us there was a glimpse of the distant future, a time that we would know fifty years from today, the time when the child becomes the carer and the parent is the cared for. That time was waiting for my daughter and me around a lifetime from today, and the summers would fly by, one by one, and there was nothing that either of us could do to stop it coming.

Then the moment was gone. I took a faltering step up the garden path and paused, wincing with pain. And then it didn't matter because I called my daughter's name.

And Scout ran to our car, and to her dog, and to my arms.

Wrong place,

Wrong time,

Has the wrong girl been

#TAKEN

When masked men attempt to kidnap the mistress
of the biggest gangster in Europe, they make
two fatal mistakes.

They snatch the wrong woman.

And they cross the wrong detective.

#TAKEN
The new book from TONY PARSONS
Coming April 2019

Turn the page to read an extract...

1

AS PERSONAL AS HELL

It was nothing personal.

She knew that the two men in the car behind her, driving far too close and grinning foolishly beyond the tinted windscreen, could have chosen any woman to bully.

She had been driving out of the West End, crossing the Marylebone Road and starting to pick up speed on Albany Street, the long stretch of straight road that skirts Regent's Park, and their big black 4x4 was suddenly there, filling her rear-view mirror, its diesel engine roaring and so close it was as if they wanted to drive straight through her.

And although it was nothing personal, their behaviour did not feel completely random. They wanted to teach her a lesson.

They wanted to show her. They wanted to show her good.

It was nothing personal, but there was a reason why they were driving that close. She had done something to push their touchy little buttons.

It could have been the car she was driving – the latest 7-series BMW, so new it still had that glorious showroom smell and sheen. And that would have been almost funny because it was not even her car – her battered little Fiat was in the garage, unable to squeeze past its MOT – but of course they did not know that.

And perhaps it wasn't the car. Perhaps she had pulled away too fast at the lights, anxious to be home, the hour late now, that they had felt their insecure manhoods shrinking as she left them dawdling in exhaust fumes.

Or perhaps they had been offended by the jokey sign in her rear window, black words on a yellow background. *Baby, I'm Bored*, it said, a single girl's play on those *Baby on Board* signs you saw everywhere.

Not my sign, she thought. And not my life.

Or perhaps it was nothing to do with the brand-new car or the *Baby, I'm Bored* sign or the way she was driving. Perhaps they were just a pair of macho assholes. That was always a possibility.

And as she skirted Regent's Park, all the beautiful Nash buildings to her right, like castles made of ice cream glowing in the night-time, and the park itself a sea of unbroken blackness to her left, the two vehicles were suddenly alone on that lonely stretch of road.

All that darkness to the left, all that moneyed elegance to the right.

And the car behind so close that if she braked it felt like they would crash into her.

And now she was scared.

Her foot gently brushed the brakes. Barely enough to slow her borrowed vehicle but enough to make its brake lights blaze red.

The driver behind slammed on his own brakes, rubber shrieking, and his face tightened with fury as their vehicle receded.

She put her foot down now. She really needed to be home. She ached for home now.

She was watching them in the rear-view mirror, watching their car get smaller, watching them far too closely, because she almost missed the sharp left turn in the road, she almost kept going, which would have been very bad indeed, but at the last moment she looked forward and cursed and tugged down hard on the left side of the steering wheel.

She took a breath, held it, speeding past London Zoo, accelerating for the junction where she would turn right into St John's Wood and the road for home. She exhaled with relief, seeing the light was green.

'Imagine life is a highway and all the lights are green,' her father had once told her, and she smiled at the thought of him.

She turned right on her green light.

And they followed.

'Oh, what's your problem?' she muttered, already knowing the answer.

She was their problem.

St John's Wood now, the huge houses behind iron gates, and the streets empty.

And the black car filling her rear-view mirror.

The car came closer, so close it must surely touch, so close she had stopped breathing.

And then suddenly they were on the big junction at Swiss Cottage and it was over.

They roared past her, and she glimpsed their faces as they tore away, not even looking at her, their simple minds bored with their vicious little game.

She exhaled. And she glanced over her shoulder to look at her six-month old boy in the rearward-facing baby seat, feeling overwhelmed with relief and love.

'It's okay now,' she said, though she knew he was sleeping.

Cars were the one guarantee of getting him to nod off.

And then there were the big roads that led to the small roads home.

The Finchley Road was clogged with traffic even at this time of night, but still no sign of the black car, and she turned right at the old church, up Frognal Lane, climbing all the while, heading for the rooftop of the city.

Now the big houses of Hampstead on either side, and she was still climbing. She slowly turned onto a tree-lined back road that looked as though it were in the heart of the country.

There was a private security guard in his van across the street. He glanced up at her without expression as she turned onto the private road that led to her home.

And the way home was blocked by the big black car.

They were waiting for her.

She slowed and stopped, reaching for her phone, because this was so wrong, and it was against the law, and then it all happened very quickly.

The two men were out of the car, their faces covered with some kind of mask, those masks that look like skulls, designed to halt the heart with a stab of fear, and they were walking quickly towards her car.

As if it was all planned.

She fumbled with the central locking but her doors opened on both sides, and someone's hands were on her, gripping her by the arms just above the elbow, and the one who was on the passenger's side walked round, his skull mask grinning in her headlights, to help drag her from the car.

She was screaming for help.

They lifted her from the ground, as if she weighed nothing, the one holding her arms not changing his grip and the other one lifting her by the ankles. They carried her towards their car and she screamed and screamed and screamed.

And then the security guard was standing there.

One of the men said one word.

'Don't,' he said.

And the security guard didn't. He stood there, a boy in the presence of two men - unmanned, paralysed, just watching as they loaded her into their car.

And now she felt the violence in them. Not spite, or sadism, or wounded, woman-hating pride. But violence. Violence in the hands of deeply experienced professionals who did this sort of thing for a living.

She saw her baby son, and she called his name, and the child was still sleeping on the back seat, wet-lipped and head lolling under the *Baby, I'm Bored* sign, and she let out a howl like a wounded animal because she knew with total blinding clarity that she would never see him again in this life.

And that was when she understood.

This was personal.

This was as personal as hell.

Wrong place,

Wrong time,

Has the wrong girl been

#TAKEN

Coming April 2019
ORDER NOW

TONY PARSONS

Tony Parsons left school at sixteen and his first job in journalism was at the *New Musical Express*. Since then he has become an award-winning journalist and bestselling novelist whose books have been translated into more than forty languages. His semi-autobiographical novel, *Man and Boy*, won the Book of the Year prize.

He lives in London with his wife, daughter and their dog Stan.

Tony's first journalism after leaving the NME was when he was embedded with the Vice Squad at 27 Savile Row, West End Central. The roots of the DC Max Wolfe series started here.

Exploring the world of the Murder Investigation Room at West End Central and the Black Museum in New Scotland Yard to the home he shares with his daughter and dog in a loft high above Smithfield Meat Market, DC Max Wolfe is never far from trouble.

Keep in touch with

TONY PARSONS

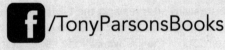 /TonyParsonsBooks

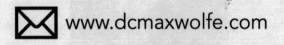 @TonyParsonsUK

Find out more and sign up to receive exclusive news and content at

✉ www.dcmaxwolfe.com